Funny Boys

WARREN
ADLER

Funny Boys

THE OVERLOOK PRESS
Woodstock & New York

This edition first published in the United States in 2008 by
The Overlook Press, Peter Mayer Publishers, Inc.
Woodstock & New York

WOODSTOCK:
One Overlook Drive
Woodstock, NY 12498
www.overlookpress.com
[for individual orders, bulk and special sales, contact our Woodstock office]

NEW YORK:
141 Wooster Street
New York, NY 10012

Cataloging-in-Publication Data is available from the Library of Congress

Book design and type formatting by Bernard Schleifer
Manufactured in the United States of America
ISBN 978-1-59020-034-6
10 9 8 7 6 5 4 3 2 1

Funny Boys

T HE WOMAN OPENED THE DOOR TO GORLICK'S SUITE AND
two men emerged. The shorter one grabbed the
woman's buttocks and squeezed.

"Is that a tush, Pep, or what?"

"World class," the taller man said.

Mickey Fine, who had been waiting in the corridor
puzzled over the men. The shorter one wore a brown pinstripe double-breasted suit with a red rose in its lapel and
a beige fedora. His glance washed over Mickey like a spot-
light in a prison movie, freezing him in its glare like a pinned
insect.

The other was taller, handsomer, dressed to the nines in a
blue serge suit and matching satiny blue tie on a white-on-white
shirt. He wore a pearl gray fedora and his black shoes were spit-
shined, in contrast to his shorter companion's scuffed browns. He
was also handsome in a hard way and his lips wore a thin smile that
was anything but warm.

Mickey watched them both swagger toward the elevators. It
was the tall one who looked back at Mickey, studying him briefly,

as if trying to recall him from some previous occasion. Mickey had the same sensation.

"Mr. Gawlick will see ya now," the woman said, dissolving his effort at remembering. She was tall, with a voluptuous figure and a low-cut dress that showed much fleshy cleavage. He followed her as she pranced into the suite on swivel hips that swung at an exaggerated wide angle. A tush like the Pied Piper, he thought, confirming the earlier comment. Follow it anywhere. Does it come with that swing? he wanted to say, then thought better of it. But the idea did boost his energy level and chase away the edginess that the appearance of the two men had brought on. He came into the suite with a theatrical bounce and a face-aching smile.

Clouds of smoke layered the air in Sol Gorlick's suite. He was a short corpulent man with squinty eyes and thick lips. As Mickey entered, he was just lighting a long expensive-looking cigar. The jacket of his double-breasted suit was open, showing sweat puddles on his blue shirt. His pants were high-belted over a balloon-like stomach and his bald head appeared lacquered, reflecting the slanting rays of late afternoon sunlight.

His complexion was waxy and although his face was round and fat, his skin did not hang in jowls. Greeting Mickey with a nod, he pointed with his cigar to a chair beside the coffee table.

"Sit," he grunted.

Mickey sat in an upholstered chair beside the coffee table, on which were a number of used highball glasses, a half emptied bottle of seltzer and nearly empty bottle of Johnny Walker. Salted peanuts were strewn around the table. There was also a silver pistol cigarette lighter and an ashtray filled with smashed cigarette and cigar butts.

The woman who had shown him in sat opposite Mickey on a

matching chair, crossing her legs, showing an expanse of pink flesh on either side of her black stocking suspenders.

"This is Mickey Fine, Mr. Gawlick," the woman said. Gorlick's big behind sank deeply into the soft cushions of the couch. He sat upright, his back stiff, his belly resting on his thighs. Mickey noted that he had star sapphire rings on the pinkies of both hands.

"Here I'm Fine," Mickey said. "But finer in Caroliner." Keep the one-liners coming, he urged himself. He prayed that his nervousness wouldn't erase his memory.

Gorlick smiled thinly, nodded and picked up a paper from the coffee table. Mickey watched him as he puffed on his cigar, blowing thick smoke rings as he read. Mickey could see it was the letter he had sent outlining his experience. Not earthshaking. He had been a waiter and substitute tumler at Blumenkranz' in Lock Sheldrake for two summers. For three summers before that he had been a bus boy at Grossingers and been in some of the week-night shows.

Off-season he played small club dates, mostly Jewish veterans and women's groups. Days he helped in his father's ladies underwear store on Sutter Avenue in Brownsville. Nights he went to CCNY.

"It's short," Mickey said. "I ran out of lies."

"You're twenty-two?" Gorlick said, inspecting him.

"All year," Mickey replied.

"He looks like a Jewish Tom Mix. Don't he, Gloria?" Gorlick said, tossing his head toward the woman.

"And here I thought I was passing for a goy. I know. You saw my horse, Tony." Mickey turned toward the woman. "He's circumcised. How can you hide it?"

Gloria made a sound like a Bronx cheer.

11

"Sometimes I forget and say 'Oy Oy Gold' instead of 'Hi-Yo Silver.'"

"That's the Lone Ranger," Gloria snickered.

"You think he's not Jewish? Why do you think he travels with his tanta?"

Gorlick, not reacting, puffed a smoke ring into the air, then picked up a stray peanut from the cocktail table and popped it into the smoke cloud belching from his mouth.

"Such a tumler," Gloria said winking. "He's a real cutie pie. The girls would get a kick out of him."

Mickey felt her inspection, distracted by the swell of the upper part of her full breasts. But when he forced himself to shift his glance, he found himself watching that stretch of pink bare thigh.

"What kind of a store your father got?" Mr. Gorlick asked, looking over the paper again.

"Foundation garments," Mickey said, not with a slight twinge of embarrassment. People always reacted with a snicker and Gorlick and Gloria were no exceptions.

There was humor in it, he knew, but mostly to others; less to Mickey or his mother or father or sister. To them the store meant survival and they lived above it. To the Fines foundation garments were serious business, although Mickey had developed a repertoire of jokes about it.

"Corsets, girdles, things like that?" Gorlick asked, smiling.

"We fix flats, too," Mickey said, looking pointedly at Gloria, who needed none of his father's wares. As if to emphasize the obvious, Gloria straightened in her chair and flung out her chest.

"Bet you seen plenty," Gorlick chuckled.

"Plenty is the word for it. It's turned me into a vegetarian."

Gorlick grunted another chuckle, then turned his eyes back to the paper.

"What kind of courses you taking?"

"General," Mickey said. "If things don't work out, maybe, as a last resort, I'll become a shyster." Despite the joke it was a bone of contention between him and his parents. To them becoming a tumler was not a proper career path, although they often laughed at his jokes. "I get a kick out of making people laugh," he told them. You can still be a lawyer and make people laugh, they would say. It was a never ending complaint.

"A shyster." Gorlick nodded. "At Gorlick's a shyster would have a field day." He turned and winked at Gloria, who smiled thinly.

"That's if show business doesn't pan out," Mickey said, reluctant to reveal his secret yearnings for comedy stardom.

"A putz business," Gorlick said.

"Maybe he wants to be a movie star," Gloria interjected. "The Jewish Tom Mix and his faithful horse, Moishey." She laughed heartily, her big tits shaking.

He felt a sudden twinge of resentment, wondering if they were taking his ambition seriously. That part was not a joke.

"What we are seeking here," Gorlick said, "is a special kind of tumler for 'Gorlick's Greenhouse'—a classy boy, a diplomat, an organizer, a social director with "tum," ya know whatimean?"

"Also funny, Solly," Gloria said. "Goes without saying. Sure funny. It also helps if you can sing a little."

Mickey nodded. He had a fair voice.

"And a good dancer. A refined talker. Ya know whatimean, a smart classy funny boy who can keep the guests happy."

"They liked me at Blumenkranz," Mickey said. He was at somewhat of a disadvantage over that. He had been set for the

13

season at Blumenkranz, another Catskill hotel, then Mrs. Blumenkranz hired her brother's son for the job. With ten days until Decoration Day, when the Catskill hotels traditionally opened, he was in no bargaining position. It was Blumenkranz who had recommended him to Gorlick, who had apparently had some disagreement with the tumler he had hired then fired.

"Blumenkranz," Gorlick sneered, "A pigsty cockeninyam operation. We're not like the other hotels. We're special. We got a special clientele." He took a deep drag on his cigar and looked at Gloria. "Small but eleganty. One-fifty guests max on weekends. A showplace. Great coozeen. Kosher but gourmet. We don't even have to advertise. All woid of mouth. In the middle of the week we got the wives, the kids, the girlfriends. Weekends when the boys come up we expect you to put on a show, sometimes we hire a specialty act, and we got a three-piece band all week. I say sometimes, because mostly the boys want action."

"Action?"

"Big time action. Poker. Crap tables. Slots."

"Is that legal?" Mickey asked, instantly regretting his hasty response. Blumenkranz and Grossingers had been straight places. But Sullivan County, which covered the Catskills, was considered wide open for gambling in some of the hotels. He had played slot machines at hotels near Lock Sheldrake.

"Legal shmegal. Not my business."

Mickey shrugged, watching Gorlick use his big cigar as if it were a baton.

". . . it's the weekdays I worry about, especially when it rains. When the boys come, ya know, they inject a happier prospect, if you get my meaning. But on the weekdays the girls get bored with the machines and not all are not into cards. You gotta tumel them, keep them happy. They get bored, moody, start to complain about the coozeen. On the weekends they tell the boys and we got tsouris." Gorlick raised his eyes to the ceiling, as if he needed validation from a higher source.

"Tell him about last year's, Solly," Gloria piped. She extracted a compact from her bag and began to fix her makeup.

"A schmuck. Not bad on a stage. A good dancer. A schmoozer. He could tell a lotta jokes. A genius at Simon Sez. But on the floor, he was not a diplomat. Worse, he was a schmuck with a schmuck, if you get my drift." He looked toward Gloria, who peeked out from behind her compact and giggled.

"I love it, Solly."

"In the right place, at the right time, a young schmuck with a schmuck is a valuable asset. At the wrong place at the wrong time it's tsouris. This schmuck's schmuck gave me tsouris."

"One thing I know is my place, Mr. Gorlick," Mickey said seriously, calculating that the matter was a serious issue with Gorlick.

"It's your schmuck that's got to know its place," Gorlick said, looking down at the paper on the coffee table, "Mickey."

"No question," Mickey said. He was remembering Blumenkranz. On weeknights the women were barracudas. To some, he hadn't been averse, but he knew it was tricky business. "I know how to draw a 'Fine' line." The pun sailed right over Gorlick's head.

"Last year's social director is still in the hospital," Gloria said from behind her compact. "It's a miracle they let him live."

"I won't even tell you what they did to him," Gorlick said. "But you can imagine."

"Jesus," Mickey said, feeling a sudden chill as he envisioned what they might have done.

"We gotta cure, tumler," Gloria said, winking. "Only it costs."

Gorlick looked at Gloria and shook his head.

"Hey, Solly. What about our two minute special?" Gloria giggled.

"Now funny. Show me funny," Gorlick said, flicking an ash into the ashtray on the coffee table.

But the stab of fear had dampened Mickey's enthusiasm. He was also confused. He thought he had been funny, showing them his funny attitude and his ability to integrate funny patter into the conversation.

"Tumler shtick," Gorlick prodded.

"I've got a terrific file. One liners and routines. Lots of black-outs." Mickey said. But when they didn't react, he cleared his throat and stood up.

"Now take my boss. He's the biggest man in who owes who. If he can't take it with him—he'll send his creditors. He gives me plenty of exercise. When he gives me a check I have to race him to the bank."

Gloria giggled.

"Boss jokes are okay," Gorlick said.

"Except for Garlic. He hates to be called Garlic," Gloria interjected. Gorlick nodded.

"That would be in bad taste," Mickey said, searching Gorlick's eyes for a glint of acknowledgement. He found none.

"Jokes on wives are okay. Shvartzers. Pollack jokes. But be careful on smut. There are kids around."

"Stinky little brats," Gloria piped. "Course they think they're all Little Lord Fauntleroys and Shirley Temples."

"And that's the way you treat them. Make nice, nice, nice," Gorlick said. "And be careful with the ladies. They like dirty but not in front of the men. The boys get edgy, think you're try to . . . you know . . . heat up the frying pan. With the men everything goes. They love smut, smuttier the better. But the biggest no-no

of all. Hear my woids." Gorlick put a fat finger in front of
Mickey's nose. "Absolutely no wop jokes. You put that one in
your tuchas." Gorlick tapped his temple. "Get in the habit, just
in case."

"You have wops in a kosher hotel?" Mickey asked inno-
cently.

Gorlick bent forward and glared at him. His cigary breath
was not pleasant.

"Nobody tells a wop joke in front Albert Anastasia."

"Albert who?"

"Mr. Anastasia is a very important man," Gorlick said. He
scratched his head.

"I get it. A celebrity. What is he? A bandleader? An actor?
A ballplayer?"

Gorlick's eyes narrowed and his thick lips seemed to grow
narrower with pressure. He looked toward Gloria, who shrugged.

"Goomba goes crazy when anyone makes fun of wops. Even
Mussolini. In a kosher hotel, a tumler says the word guinea or wop
or makes Italian jokes, Anastasia has a shit conniption." Gloria
explained.

"And who gets the blame?" Gorlick shrugged and pressed a
thumb to his chest. "Yours truly."

"They get real mad, they play with matches, " Gloria said,
lowering her voice.

"Burn me down, like they did to Shechters."

"With the Jewish boys, it's different," Gloria said. "They like
the bad-boy rep cause people think Jews are, you know mollycod-
dles, mama's boys, fraidy cats. Like they been kicked around
because they didn't fight back."

Gorlick glanced toward Gloria and raised his eyes to the
ceiling.

17

"You're from Brownsville and I suppose you never heard of Kid Twist or Pittsburgh Phil?" Gorlick asked.

"An old vaudeville act, right?"

"It's no act, Mickey," Gorlick said ominously. "You just seen 'em come outa here."

"Those ones," Mickey said. "Bad actors both of them."

"Jesus," Gorlick said. "You never heard of Abie "Kid Twist" Reles and Pittburgh Phil Strauss? The guy they call Pep. Where you been? In China? They got reps a mile wide."

"Reles? Strauss? Kid Twist? Pep?"

His memory kicked in and he felt his stomach turn to a block of ice.

"You okay, boychick?" Gorlick said.

"He's like a white sheet," Gloria said.

Reles and Strauss! Kid Twist and Pep. Those two he had just seen come out of here. He wiped a film of icy sweat from his forehead. It took him a moment to recover.

The image of his father's battered face surfaced in his mind. They had come into his father's store one night. Mickey had been upstairs. Luckily his mother was playing cards at a friend's house.

It had all happened so quickly. Mickey had heard muffled sounds and ran downstairs to the store. His father lay on the floor writhing in pain, his face bloody and bruised. Reles, the short one, was standing over his father with what looked like a piece of pipe wrapped in newspaper. The other man, Strauss, started to move to intercept Mickey who was heading for Reles.

"No, please," his father had shouted. "Mickey, please. Leave us alone."

"Leave you alone?" Mickey said dumbfounded, stopped in his tracks. "They're trying to kill you."

"Kill him? Whatayou crazy?" Reles said, shooting Mickey a glance with feverish agate eyes and a twisted grin. "Shmekel knows da score." He looked at his father on the floor.

"Dis is business, kid," Strauss said.

"I owe them money," Mickey's father croaked.

"Nothin poisonal boychick," Reles said. "Ya borrow money from Roth's bank, ya pay on time." He looked down at Mickey's father, then swung the newspaper-coated pipe, hitting him on the shoulder. His father screeched in pain.

"I promise," his father whimpered. "Please go way now."

"Hey, looka dis," Strauss said suddenly, holding up a pair of women's pink satin panties. "Dis is real pretty." He stuffed it in a side pocket. Then he picked up the box from which it had come. "I'll take 'em all. Ya want some faw yaw hooers, Abie?"

Reles looked up and laughed.

"I got no hooers, Pep. Youse da guy wid da hooers. I got my Helen."

"I fawgot, Abie," Pep sneered. "Lucky you."

"Put 'em on my tab," Pep said to the older man.

"You can't take that," Mickey cried. "That's salable merchandise."

"Mickey, please," his father cried. He was trying to shimmy up one of the display counters to stand upright. Mickey ran over to help.

"Dese are not fun times faw us, Fine," Reles said. "Pay up and save yourself da tsouris."

"I promise."

"Not nice, Fine. Passing bum checks. A shanda."

"I thought it was covered," his father said.

His father had finally managed to stand upright, although

unsteadily. Blood was gushing from his nose. His shirt was heavily sprinkled with it.

Reles pointed the end of the pipe to his father's chest. Then he nodded toward Strauss.

Mickey felt himself grabbed in a hammerlock from behind. He struggled but to little avail; Strauss pressed a hard bony knee into his spine, doubling him over.

"Ya got any scratch to pay off Daddy's markers, schmuck?"

"Please. Don't hurt Mickey please. He had nothing to do with this," his father pleaded. Then he heard a cry of pain. Lifting his head, he saw his father sprawled on the floor again. He started to crawl on his belly toward Mickey. Reles stepped on his fingers and his father screamed in pain.

"I asked ya nice," Pep said to the helpless Mickey. "I don like to repeat."

"It's not his fault," his father pleaded weakly.

"Whose talkin to you, putz?" Reles said, kicking his father in the ribs. Then he turned to Mickey. "Pep asked you nice. Even a down payment shows good fate."

"I give him da toilet, right, Abie?" Strauss said.

"Got a can?" Reles asked Mickey's father, who lay on the floor watching Mickey. Blood and tears were running down his cheeks. Reles walked behind a counter to the one dressing room. Beside it was a door. He opened it.

"Fat ladies take a pea heah," Reles said, as Mickey was manhandled and forced to his knees on the floor in front of the toilet.

"Now we goin to play submarine, kid."

"How much?" Mickey gasped.

"Whats da number?" Pep asked.

"I feget, Pep," Reles said. He dipped into a side pocket and brought out a notebook he opened, searching for a name with spatulate fingers.

"We need tree hunert," Reles said. "But we take a down payment. Say fifty."

"I'll go to the bank tomorrow," Mickey said. Actually he had three hundred fifty saved in his account just in case he needed it for law school in the fall. Or to go to Hollywood.

"Ya got nuthin in the house?" Pep asked.

"Please. Leave my boy alone," Mickey's father shouted. He had managed to lift himself off the floor once more and was standing looking into the cubicle using the walls for support.

"Again he don answer, Abie," Strauss said. Mickey felt Strauss grab him by the hair and begin to force his head down.

Mickey's father made an attempt to step forward into the cubicle, but Reles pulled him out by the back of his belt and hit him solidly on the underside of his knees. The man screamed and fell to the floor, writhing in pain.

"Bastards," Mickey screamed. But he could barely get the word out as Strauss forced his head into the toilet and pulled the overhead chain. Water and noise swirled around him as Strauss emersed his entire head in the toilet bowl. Mickey struggled but Strauss held him fast. He felt as if his lungs would burst.

Then, suddenly, Strauss pulled his head out and Mickey, approaching hysteria, took deep gasps of breath. Mickey's father, writhing on the floor, began to sob hysterically.

"I got about forty in the house," Mickey blurted through his gasps.

"See what a nice boy ya got, Fine," Reles laughed. "Fine pays a fine."

"And tomorrow I'll see you get everything."

"Evyting?" Pep asked.

"Whatever my father owes."

"Dis is one fine kid, Fine. Ya oughta be proud."

"I like dis, Fine," Strauss chuckled. "Knows da score."

"Whats ya name, kid?" Reles asked.

"Mickey."

"Mickey. Hey, dats fine," Reles roared.

"Like Mickey Finn," Strauss said giggling. For a moment he relaxed his grip on Mickey's hair. "You tink he needs one more reminda? I kinda like dis shit."

"Maybe one maw fa good luck," Reles said.

"Down da hatch, kid," Mickey heard Strauss say. Then came the pounding water and soon he was gasping for breath. Strauss pulled him up again.

"You get da drift? " Reles said.

Mickey nodded. Pep still held him in a viselike grip.

"Next time we keep ya down dere," Pep said.

Mickey nodded. There was no point in resisting. He saw his father reaching out an arm in his direction. Strauss pulled Mickey to his feet.

"Fawty now, right?" Reles said.

Mickey nodded. Strauss walked him upstairs, to the little chest next to the cot where he slept. Opening a drawer, Mickey took four tens from under his underwear and gave it to Strauss.

"You're lucky, kid. I'm da easy one. That Abie's an animal."

They came downstairs into the store. His father was slumped on a wooden chair, his eyes glazed, his face bloody.

"And tomorra da whole marker, right?" Reles said.

"Ya don play round wid Abie," Strauss said.

"I swear," Mickey said. "I swear. Only go now."

"We tank you faw da hospitality," Reles said.

"And I tank you for the panties." Pep held up the box.

"Dey gonna be more awf dan on," Reles said laughing.

Later that night, after his father's wounds had been attended to, he had confessed what he had done. He had borrowed money from "the bank" in the candy store on Saratoga and Livonia under the El. A man, the son of the owner, got approval for $300 for ten weeks with a payback of $60 a week.

"I gave them post-dated checks. They're "shylocks." I knew it. What could I do? I can't get goods, we can't sell anything."

"Papa, that's double interest."

"I needed it. What bank would give it to me?"

His father started to cry. "You should have told me, Papa."

As promised, Mickey paid off the loan the next day. Odd, he thought, how he couldn't remember the men right away—as if he had blanked out the whole experience.

"Sure," Mickey told Gorlick soberly. "I think I know who you mean."

"You think?" Gorlick said. "They enforce things. But don't ask."

"Like shylocking?"

"Like everything," Gorlick shrugged. "I told you, don't ask. Never. It's not your business. Not mine neither. I run a hotel."

"It bothers you?" Gloria asked Mickey.

Mickey thought about that for a moment.

"Not me," he said, almost choking on the thought. He needed this job. "Live and let live."

Gorlick tapped his temple again.

"So use your tuchas." Gorlick, having made his point, stuck his cigar in his mouth and nodded. "Remember the rules. We got here a very special clientele.

"Explain about the combination, Solly."

Mickey must have looked puzzled.

"You never heard of the combination?" Gorlick asked.

Mickey shrugged and looked helplessly toward Gloria, who shook her head in a kind of flouncy disgust. He knew all he wanted to know about these men.

"Brownsville and Ocean Hill," Gorlick explained. "The sheenies and the wops. These are the boys that run the show."

A hotel for gangsters and their families, Mickey realized at last. A cold chill ran up his spine.

"Combination. Get it. We got Jewish customers and Italian visitors. They come to Gorlicks to meet. So no wop jokes. Never eva."

"Jew jokes are mostly okay," Gloria said. "Jews like to laugh at themselves."

"I got lots of those," Mickey said. "Like 'Don't give up. Moses was also a basket case.'"

"Yeah," Gorlick chuckled.

"How about 'We got a sign over the urinal. Says the future of the Jewish people is in your hands.'"

Gloria giggled.

"Save that for weekdays. The girls love shmekel jokes."

"But talk only, Fine. Talk only."

"Got it. We swat flies at Gorlicks. We don't unbutton them."

"No fly jokes, Fine. We got horseflies in August." Gorlick turned to Gloria.

"You think he understands the emmis."

Gloria looked him over as if he were a prized race horse.

"Believe me, I got it," Mickey said. "Their business is their business and my business is funny."

"It's inspiring, right, Solly? The combination." Gloria said.

"Yeah," Gorlick said through a smoke cloud. "An American

success story, the way these boys do business and love each other. Catolic and Jew. They come to Gorlicks for the relaxation and the action and this is where the Jew boys put their families for the summer. The wops have their own places, but they come here to meet. The wops like the kosher coozeen."

"So no wop jokes," Mickey reiterated, groping to get back into a tumler mood. After all, his father had healed, the money had been paid back. Even his father had agreed, despite the brutal methods used, that this was business. "I went in with open eyes," he told Mickey. "So who is the real criminal? Them or me?"

"It's a respectable Jewish place, strictly kosher. We gotta lot of goyem help." Gorlick went on. "We got shiksa waitresses and maids. You'll hear things, Fine. You know what I mean. Bad Jew stuff."

"Don't listen," Gloria said. "It's expected."

"Mostly they know better," Gorlick said. "If not . . . if the boys hear. . . ." He made a slashing motion across his neck.

Mickey nodded, his stomach fluttering.

"And no gangster jokes," Gloria said. "Especially not in fronta the girls. They are very sensitive about this subject."

"Gangsters consider themselves businessmen and wish to be referred to as such," Gorlick said. "And they must always be called Mister."

"Like Mr. Kid Twist and Mr. Pittsburgh Phil?" Mickey asked. When Gorlick and Gloria didn't laugh, he said, "Just a joke."

"Monickers are for them and the news boys. Not for you," Mr. Gorlick said. "We had an incident with Mr. Buchalter. One of the waiters called him Mr. Lepke."

"Even though he used Mister," Mickey said.

"These are very sensitive men, Mickey," Gorlick said.

"What happened to the waiter?"

"Don't ask," Gorlick muttered.

"They can be very demanding," Gloria said. "Right, Solly?"

Gorlick nodded. "And they are very possessive of their women," he said. "Hence my earlier reference to shtupping."

Gorlick puffed his cigar and watched him.

"Discretion is the better part of value," Mickey said, the pun chasing the pall of gloom.

"Yeah. Yeah," Gorlick said. "Something like that." He turned to Gloria, who had closed her compact and was smoothing her skirt. "So whattaya think, Gloria?" He glanced back at Mickey. "Gloria is a specialist in entertainment." Gorlick winked. "Right, Gloria?"

"Bettah believe. Teddy Katz would have been a mistake to hire," Gloria said. Apparently this was the man they had fired before the season.

"She thought he was too pretty."

"All we needed was a tumler who looked like Clark Gable. In my opinion we saved him from a not-too-good fate. These boys don't play games about things like that."

"This ones so so," Gorlick said.

"At least he's no Gable," Gloria said. "He doesn't look like a chaser."

Mickey faced her and showed his good white teeth. He was picturing her spread-eagled under Gorlick's corpulent body, her smooth white thighs hugging his whale-like middle. In his mind, he saw the porch swing of her hips in double time.

"Not a world beater," Gloria said. He noted that she had lipstick on her teeth. "And his jokes stink."

"I didn't show you everything. I got the whole Jessel routine with the mother down pat." He put one fist to his ear and one to his mouth. "Hey Mother, this is your son Mickey, the one with the checks . . ."

"I'll say this," Gorlick interrupted. "He's a real tumler. He gives me a headache."

"I do imitations, too," Mickey persisted, summoning up his Edward G. Robinson. "Ya ya, you boysh get your gats and come wish me to the Soush Side."

"How many guesses?" Gorlick said.

"Want to see my Eddie Cantor?"

"Not today," Gorlick said.

"Who's this?" Mickey said, summoning up his Joe Penner. "Wanna buy a duck?"

"You're shpritzing me." Gorlick said.

Gloria's continued contemplation was an elaborate routine. She lit a cigarette with the pistol lighter that had been lying on the cocktail table then got up from the chair, brushed down her dress, looked behind her to straighten the seams of her stockings, then walked across the room, hips swinging, her cute ass bobbing.

At the other end of the room, she stopped, took a squinty drag on the cigarette, picked a morsel of tobacco from her tongue, then, throwing out her ample chest, she posed against a doorpost, eyeing Mickey up and down.

"Great audition, kid," Mickey said, imitating Cagney. "You got the job."

Gorlick moved his head from side to side.

"Not bad," he said, barely cracking a smile.

"You a fagele?" Gloria asked suddenly.

"Oh my God," Mickey said mincingly, waving a limp wrist. "You do know."

"A fagele they wouldn't like," Gloria said. "They like a real tease."

Mickey hid his embarrassment. He did not like being judged like horseflesh.

"Considering the others we seen," Gloria said, "and since we need someone in ten days, maybe you should give him a try."

Gorlick turned to Mickey. "I personally am not overly impressed."

"I swear, Mr. Gorlick," Mickey said, raising his right hand. "If I let them down may I drop dead."

"Believe me, boychick, that's no joke."

"They kill people that aren't funny?" Mickey asked with elaborate innocence.

"For less than that," Gloria said as she came back to the chair and sat down.

Again Mickey caught a peek at pink flesh beside her stocking suspenders. The sight, with its resultant twitch of lust, somehow mitigated the sense of the ominous. Their warnings seemed unreal, make-believe, a kind of initiation ritual for a tumler rookie.

"The important thing," Gorlick said, shifting his body on the couch and lowering his voice. "No matter what you see, what you hear, you gotta always make like them three monkeys."

"See no evil, hear no evil, speak no evil," Mickey said acting out the words, walking around the room like a gorilla.

"Enough already," Gorlick said. "You got it."

"You mean BO or the job?" Mickey asked, sniffing under his arms.

Gorlick looked at Gloria.

"There's a fine line between a tumler and a nudnick." Gorlick said.

"Finally you're getting the message, Mr. Gorlick. A 'Fine'

line. That's me. That's what I feed them. Fine's line."

Gorlick took another puff on his cigar and shrugged.

"Step outa line, boychick. It's your funeral," Gorlick said, pausing, as he relit his cigar, which had gone out. "And my hotel."

"You won't be sorry, Mr. Gorlick."

"It's twenty a week with free meals and a room. From Decoration through Labor Day."

"I was hoping for thirty," Mickey said. He knew he was being lowballed because of his weak bargaining position.

"First thing we argue about money," Gorlick said. "For this opportunity, you discuss money. You be a good boychick, you'll get tips—you'll double what I pay you." He took a deep puff on his cigar and displayed a scowl.

"All I'm asking is a fair deal," Mickey said.

"Talk to President Roosevelt then. Gorlick pays twenty. By right, you should pay me for the privilege."

"Twenty-five then."

"Right away with the money. There's a depression, Mickey. Haven't you heard?"

"Blumenkranz mentioned thirty," Mickey said.

"Sure, it's not his money," Gorlick said. "Twenty or nothing."

"All right then, Mr. Gorlick," Mickey said. "This is my last offer. Twenty a week with room and board. I warn you. Not a penny more."

"This Mickey is a mensch," Gorlick said, stuffing the cigar in his mouth and putting out his fat stubby hand.

Mickey Fine took it in his. He wasn't sure whose hand was sweating more, his or Gorlick's.

Then he moved to the door, stopped and turned.

"I leave you with one thought, people."

"Please," Gorlick said. "Enough."

"Anytime someone orders a pastrami sandwich on white bread from a delicatessen, a Jew dies."

"Getoutahere tumler," Gorlick said.

Mickey did a skip and jump movement, saluted, opened the door and left.

2

THE MOVIES AND MOVIE STARS WERE THE CENTRAL FOCUS of Miriam Feder's life. No one called her Miriam. To everyone she was Mutzie, even to herself. She went to the movies three, sometimes four times a week, depending on when they changed the pictures. Since they were all double features she saw between three hundred and four hundred pictures a year. Sometimes she saw them twice, especially if they starred Jean Harlow or Marlene Dietrich or Franchot Tone or Errol Flynn, her favorites.

On weeknights she usually went to the Loews Ambassador, which showed the first run pictures, or the Blue Bird across the street that showed the older pictures. Since they gave away dishes on weeknights, her mother's kitchen was filled with hundreds of movie dishes. The dishes somehow canceled out the guilt she felt about spending the extra money each week for movie admissions, although the time away from her homework had considerable impact on her schoolwork.

On Saturday nights she went to the Loews Pitkin, usually with a date. They showed two pictures and a vaudeville show, which she never liked, but at least the boys she dated couldn't get fresh when the lights were on.

31

Mutzie, who would be eighteen in August, was a senior at Samuel J. Tilden High School, set to graduate in June. She had taken a commercial course and could type and take shorthand and, if worst came to worst, would get herself a job as a secretary. Her mother would have liked her to marry Henry Goldblaum, who was an apprentice cutter in the shmata business and would soon be in the union, which would mean a steady dollar.

To Mutzie's mother a steady dollar was the most important thing in life. Mutzie's father, who had a pushcart on Saratoga Avenue selling sundries, was a loud-mouthed, argumentative radical who considered all authority corrupt and exploiting. He was also, as near as Mutzie could make out, always changing allegiances. Sometimes he claimed he was an anarchist, sometimes a socialist, sometimes a communist.

"Always an argument," Mutzie's mother complained. "You say black, he says white. You say it's morning, he'll say it's night. All my life an argument."

Mutzie agreed that her mother had reason to complain. Harry Feder was impossible. He was always sour, always mad at something or someone, and never smiled. When he was not selling sundries on his pushcart, he spent his time in front of Hoffman's Cafeteria on Pitkin Avenue arguing with others who also hated their current existence and felt exploited and suppressed by the "authorities."

"You watch," her father would say in one of his repetitive monologues whenever he was at home. "All the bastards want is to bleed us dry. I say trust nobody. Hitler uses this Jew business to unite those rotten Jew-hating Krauts. Mussolini has the wops conned. Those Japs are screwing the Chinks and Franco is no worse than the commies in Spain. Stalin's no angel either. Roosevelt's no better. He uses sweet-talk. All they want is to control you, keep you down, suck you dry. Don't believe none of them. You think La Guardia's gonna clean up this city? He's on their payroll. You think this depression wasn't planned? Every few years, they have to do it. Keep people under their thumb."

Mutzie's mother would raise her eyes to the ceiling.

"And he's the only good one," her mother would complain, offering her own repetitive rebuttal. "A good living he should make. That's all I ask. Then he can sit in the toilet all day and make speeches."

"At least I work for myself," her father would counter.

"That's good. But why, when you work for yourself, don't you pay yourself a good salary?"

Mutzie's brother Seymour, who had quit high school as a sophomore, spent most of his time hanging around candy stores and pool rooms. He told his family he did odd jobs and he always seemed to have enough money for fancy clothes and dates. He gave his mother ten dollars a week for room and board, always with a big show at the dinner table on Friday nights.

"Seymour's a good boy," Mutzie's mother would say, kissing her son on the forehead as she put the ten dollars in her apron pocket.

"A Brownsville Bum," her father would mutter.

"A bum is someone who's broke, Papa," Seymour would counter.

"Present company not excepted," Mutzie mother would say with an intensely sarcastic look at her father.

Mutzie, although she had little respect for her older brother, refused to allow herself to be drawn into these arguments. Anything she had to say to Seymour she said privately.

"Notice Mama doesn't ask where the money comes from," Mutzie told him.

"Where do you think? You think I steal it?"

"I don't want to know."

"Bet you think I'm a punk," Seymour snarled, poking a finger in her face. "Well I want you to know I got respect. Respect in the right places. I'm gonna be somebody. You watch."

She hardly wished to watch and didn't much care. She preferred thinking about movies and movie stars. Life was gorgeous on the silver screen, exciting, romantic, adventurous. Life in their cramped three-room walk-up on Amboy Street, where the hallways stunk perpetually of boiling cabbage and worse, was grim and boring.

The best that could be said about Henry Goldbaum was that he was a nice boy who didn't get too fresh. He was also a snappy dresser since he got his clothes wholesale in the garment district. "Actually below wholesale," he boasted.

"When I get into the union I can clear twenty-five, thirty a week," he would explain to Mutzie. "That means if you want we could get married."

"How romantic," Mutzie mused to herself, deliberately leaving the question unanswered. She liked Henry but she didn't love him, one of the rare facts about her life that she confided to her mother.

"Love is for Jean Harlow," her mother told her. "The important thing is you're not an old maid."

Despite herself, the threat had the ring of reality. To be an old maid was a fate terrible to contemplate and her mother was not one to withhold her anxieties. A number of her friends were getting ready to get married after graduation, which increased the pressure on her to consider the joys of a future with Henry Goldbaum.

Not that she didn't cast around with her eyes to observe other possibilities. Often when she went to the Ambassador or the Blue Bird on the corner of Livonia and Saratoga she would see a number of well-dressed men standing in front of the candy store eyeing the women that passed. She was always slightly afraid to pass them, fearful that they might make some remark that would embarrass her, although she wouldn't have minded an admiring remark or two.

One man in particular who seemed to spend a great deal of time standing in front of the candy store caught her eye. He was taller than the others, a very handsome man, always immaculately dressed with his shoes polished and his beautifully shaped pearl gray hat worn at a rakish angle.

On the rare occasions when she did not cross the street, passing in front of the candy store instead, she would sneak peripheral glances at him. When she did this, a thrill of excitement ran through her and she sensed an air of risk and adventure that made her heart race. She imagined that he looked at her with equal longing. Of course, he showed not the slightest sign of such interest, but she attributed that to his innate shyness and his gentlemanly demeanor.

One day she asked her brother who this man might be, describing him with a deliberate air of indifference.

"You mean Pep," Seymour said proudly.

"Pep?"

"Pittsburgh Phil Strauss," Seymour continued. "Real class. The women are crazy for him. You'll just have to stand in line, little sister." He bent over and whispered to her, "He's way up. Real high up in the combination, a very important individual."

Pittsburgh Phil Strauss. Even the name had the ring of excitement and she thought about him often.

One Saturday night during a date, Henry got fresher than usual. They would sit on the stairs of the fourth floor landing and neck, a Saturday night ritual. On this particular night, Henry attempted to put her hand on his penis.

"No," she protested, fighting to release her wrist from his hand. Up to then, she had allowed him some liberties. She had let him kiss her bare breast and nipples and touch her crotch over her dress.

"All I want is for you to touch it over my pants," Henry pleaded. "There is a thing that happens to men from all this frustration."

"Then you had better just control yourself."

"We're keeping company, Mutzie," Henry whined.

"You're taking too much for granted, Henry," Mutzie countered.

"A man can't wait forever. You know a girl doesn't have that many chances. You'll be eighteen in August." Henry warned testily.

"So I'll be an old maid."

"But I love you, Mutzie."

She shut off any further conversation with a long soul kiss and she let him squeeze and fondle her bare breasts.

Mutzie could not deny the pressure on her, especially since her girlfriends bragged loudly about their upcoming marriages. Henry was entitled to an answer. Her mother was entitled to see her "settled," which was the most important thing expected of a daughter. She was, she acknowledged to herself, on the horns of a dilemma.

What Mutzie really wanted was the kind of life depicted in the movies, a life where "true love" was a woman's most important aspiration. Finding "true love" was the most important thing in life, and, as the movies had taught her, when it did come, it came with everything, gorgeous clothes and jewelry, a beautiful apartment with exquisite furniture, chauffeured cars, trips to foreign countries, wonderful friends and hundreds of admirers.

She would often discuss these possibilities with her one-time best friend Rebecca Schwartz. Rebecca, as Mutzie's mother had attested, had "her feet on the ground" and "knew where she was going." Rebecca, who was short and pudgy with a sweet dimply smile, had been Mutzie's friend since first grade.

She was going steady with Brucie Goldstein, whose family owned an appetizer store on Saratoga Avenue and who would one day have an appetizer store of his own. To Mutzie's mother Brucie was a "catch" and she lost little opportunity in telling her so. It was her mother's goading, Mutzie believed, that led to the final argument with Rebecca that ended their friendship.

"You can't just step inside a movie screen, Mutzie. It's not real. That kind of life is not possible."

"That's what you think," Mutzie had replied.

"What I think?" Rebecca had said, visibly troubled by Mutzie's constant refrain about how life was in the movies. Mutzie was certain that her mother had told Rebecca to "talk some sense into Mutzie."

"I'm not saying you can't have dreams. But you can't be out of touch with reality."

They had been walking together on Pitkin Avenue, shopping for a bathing suit that Rebecca needed for her one-week honeymoon at the Nevele hotel in the Catskills. Rebecca was not overjoyed at seeing her chubby body in a bathing suit, which surely had contributed to her irritation. For Mutzie's part, the whole idea of Rebecca's impending marriage had become a flashpoint for Mutzie's mother's constant jibes and was making her nervous and anxious.

"What's reality?" Mutzie had shot back.

"Reality is today, May 6th, 1937. Roosevelt is president. La

Guardia is Mayor. This is Brownsville. We are walking on Pitkin Avenue. I am getting married next month. I'm marrying Brucie Goldstein and we're going to have two children. And some day Brucie is going to have a store of his own. That's reality."

Rebecca's remark had come out as a burst of pique, full of irritation and rebuke.

"There's more to life than herring and potato salad," Mutzie had shot back.

"What's that supposed to mean?"

"All day long in a store with a dirty apron. Is that a life?"

"So Miss Harlow is showing her jealousy."

"Jealous of you? That's a laugh."

"I'm marrying somebody substantial with a future. What's your future?" She pointed to the marquee of the Loews Pitkin which was showing *A Tale of Two Cities* and *The Thin Man.* "For ten cents you can live somebody else's life for three hours, then when you come out again you're still here in Brownsville and everything's the same. Besides, it's not so bad here. If I were you I would marry Henry and settle down to a nice life."

"A boring life," Mutzie shot back.

"Boring to have a husband and children and a business of your own? That's boring? What will you have, Mutzie? Dissatisfaction. Always thinking that the grass is greener. You'll be an old maid and dry up like a prune, like one of those old shiksa secretaries."

The image triggered a burst of anger in Mutzie.

"And you? What will you be? A butter ball with fat arms and swollen ankles, always stinking of herring and onions."

Rebecca flushed deep red and her lips trembled with rage. "Why you rotten little stuck up hooer," she shouted, stopping dead in her tracks, her cheeks scarlet and quivering.

"Look who's calling who a hooer," Mutzie said. Rebecca had told her that she had gone "all the way" with Brucie, describing the experience in vivid detail. Mutzie fished in her mind for something awful to say to Rebecca, something that reflected her true feelings and would demolish Rebecca's smugness about "reality" once and for all. Suddenly she remembered a crude remark that she had heard boys use at school to describe a fat girl. "Won't be long you'll have to pea for Brucie to find the place to put it."

"Oh my God. Oh my God," Rebecca sputtered, flecks of saliva showing on the sides of her mouth. "I don't ever want to speak to you again," Rebecca shouted, stamping her feet. "Never ever as long as I live." Her eyes rose skyward. "May I drop dead."

With that, she turned and waddled off, leaving Mutzie with a sad sense of victory.

Breaking up with her best friend left Mutzie frightened and anxious. "I would go down on my hands and knees to Rebecca," her mother cried when she heard about the fight from Rebecca's mother. Tears rolled down her cheeks. "Now you won't even be invited to the wedding. None of us."

"I'm sorry about that, Mama," Mutzie conceded.

"So you won't apologize?"

"Never. Not as long as I have breath."

"A stubborn mule. That's what I got." Her mother raised her voice in near hysteria. "Why are you doing this to me? Rebecca has a future. What have you got, Mutzie? With this attitude you'll also lose Henry. Then what?"

"So I'll be an old maid," Mutzie muttered.

"What did I do to you to deserve this?" Mutzie's mother shouted. "I'm glad my mother didn't live to see this. What a daughter does to a mother!"

Mutzie knew that after the hysteria had subsided, her mother would engage in long bouts of cranky pouting, screaming invectives at her father and giving Mutzie the silent treatment. As much as she ridiculed such treatment, Mutzie felt its effect. With high school graduation coming up, she felt herself faced with weighty decisions. She was frightened about her future. What if her mother was right? What if she did miss out on her chances? Maybe she should marry Henry Goldbaum. She resolved to consider it very seriously.

On her next date with Henry, she studied him very carefully, trying to picture what a future with him might be like. He was a pleasant young man, handsome in a rugged way with curly brown hair and hazel eyes, and he also smelled nicely of aftershave. He was steady and responsible and would, when he got into the union, be able to support a family. Such considerations could not be ignored.

They went to the movies and saw Marlene Dietrich and Robert Donat in *Knight Without Armor* and another picture called *Married Before Breakfast*. She tried to compare Henry Goldbaum with Robert Donat, but, even discounting the British accent, her imagination simply could not stretch that far.

Even when they began to neck on the landing of her apartment building, she forced herself to imagine what living with Henry on a permanent basis might be like. Like her mother, after a day of shopping and housekeeping, she would have a hot meal on the table when he came home. He would tell her about people in the shop, cutters like him, how the bosses had maltreated him, how he was worth more than what he got, how the unions cheated him. Later would come babies, diapers, formulas, school. Was that it? Normal, respectable, safe, comfortable, steady.

She thought, too, of sex with Henry. Would that be worth the other, the boring drudgery that would make her grouchy, irritated and unhappy like her mother?

That night she even let him go further than he had ever gone before, letting him push her panties aside and get his fingers on her bare thing.

"I love you, Mutzie," he told her as he moved his finger back and forth on her thing. He was a little rough, but she wasn't entirely indifferent to the sensation and she could feel her heart pumping and her breath coming in deeper gasps than usual.

He put her hand on his penis and this time she grasped it over his pants.

"May I take it out?" he whispered. She could feel his face grow hot and he accelerated the action of his fingers on her thing. She did not answer his question, and he probably assumed it meant that he could. Which he did. She had never in her life felt a man's hard-on. It felt hot and velvety.

"Just rub it up and down in your fist," he told her.

She did as he asked, feeling strange as he moved his body to the rhythm of her fist. Although she wanted also to look at it, she was fearful that he would see her doing this and that would embarrass her. Instead she kept her eyes closed.

"Oh, please marry me, Mutzie. I love you so much. Oh God I love you."

The titillation of his finger on her thing was making her feel good. She had done this to herself on occasion and it had also felt good. Sometimes it made her shudder with pleasure which, she knew, meant that she had had a climax, although it did leave her with the feeling that she had done something nasty.

Suddenly, she heard Henry gasp and his hard-on seemed to twitch and jump and she felt warm sticky fluid on her hand. Then he removed his fingers from her thing, which she could not quite understand, since she felt that a little more work on his part would make her reach a climax.

"Oh God, Mutzie," Henry said. "We've got to be married now."

"Because we did this?" Mutzie said. She felt let down, slightly disappointed.

"Partly," Henry said. "It shows how much we need each other. Besides, after awhile you'll want to go all the way. That's nature's way of showing how deeply two people need each other."

"It is?"

She could find some logic in this. And she agreed that sooner or later they would go all the way. She imagined that once they did it in the natural way, she would also climax when he did.

"So are we engaged or not?" Henry pressed.

"I'm not sure," Mutzie said honestly, although she felt the pressure to say yes.

"I can't live with that anymore, Mutzie. I want a yes or a no."

"I don't think I'm ready, Henry," Mutzie said after a long silence. Suddenly she thought of Jean Harlow. What would the beautiful Jean say to this? she wondered. Oddly, by thinking of Jean Harlow, she suddenly confronted the reality of the present. Where was she, after all? On the fourth floor landing of a walk-up apartment house, which smelled vaguely of dust and cabbage. All around her, it looked grimy, dirty and depressing. Henry's shoes were scuffed and unshined and she noted that there were slick oily stains on his dark pants.

"It's either yes or no," Henry pressed. He had stood up and was leaning against the railing. He lit a cigarette and she could see his face light up with the glow of the match. There was Henry Goldbaum. No Errol Flynn, no Clark Gable, no William Powell. Just Henry Goldbaum, who would one day be a cutter and bring home enough money so that she could live in an apartment house just like this one.

"Then no," she said, standing up.

"No? How can you say no?"

"I said it," she said.

"Me?" Henry said, punching a thumb into his chest and blowing out a long stream of smoke. "You turning me down?"

"You asked yes or no. An answer right away. Tonight. So tonight I say no."

He grimaced, his lips curled in a crooked smile.

"I can't believe this," he mumbled, stiffening. He took another deep drag on his cigarette.

"I'm sorry, Henry," Mutzie said. She had taken out her key and pushed it into the lock of her apartment.

"You're sorry? Your mother will be pissed."

"So I'll be an old maid. A dried-up shiksa prune."

"You'll regret this as long as you live," Henry said, raising his voice, as she shut the door. "Goddamned hooer," he shouted. She waited on the other side of the door, anger rising. "That again," she sighed. Then she heard him run noisily down the stairs, banging the walls as he went.

But that night as she lay in bed and the anger began to subside, her feelings were totally different than she had expected. Instead of feelings of anxiety and fear about her future, she felt free, courageous, optimistic. Where was it written that she must settle for less than her expectations? Who said people can't live the lives depicted in the movies? She had been to the city many times, where she observed the glitter and glamour of people living what seemed to be lives that were lived in the movies. She saw them ride in their fancy cars, dine in fine restaurants, attend the opera and the theater. She read about their lives in newspapers and magazines. Who said it was not possible for a poor Jewish girl from Brownsville to reach such aspirations?

That was when she decided to become, to literally *become*, what she dreamed of becoming. Nobody would stop her. Not her complaining mother or crabbing father or her teachers or her schoolmates.

For the past two summers she had worked as a file clerk in an office in downtown Brooklyn and had managed to put nearly one hundred fifty dollars in a savings account. She withdrew one hundred dollars. This, she decided, would finance the first phase of her campaign of transformation.

Thankfully, she went through the week without her mother confronting her with hysterical outbursts of recrimination. Her mother's strategy was to sink deeper into her pouty silent treatment, indulging instead in rhetorical diatribes meant for Mutzie's ears, but not directly addressed to her. This, thankfully, made it easier for Mutzie not to respond, which only increased the decibel level of the diatribes. The fact that her mother's reactions were so predictable and clichéd actually made it easier for Mutzie to cope with it.

"You ain't seen nothin' yet," she told her mother silently.

Not that Mutzie didn't love her mother. But the facts were that Mutzie's mother was old-fashioned, too traditional and uneducated in the ways of the modern world, too isolated, narrow-minded, too bitter and hysterical. To Mutzie's mother, Brownsville was the universe. She never went to the movies, never read newspapers and magazines and never listened to the radio. Mutzie had tried on numerous occasions to "educate" her mother to this new way of looking at life. But it was impossible. It was too bad that being hurt would be the price of her ignorance.

On Saturday morning, Mutzie went to a beauty parlor on Sutter Avenue carrying a movie magazine.

"Make me look like that," she told the operator, showing her a picture of Jean Harlow.

The operator, who was a dyed redhead, inspected her carefully.

"So you wanna be a movie star?" the operator quipped.

"I wanna be a person," Mutzie shot back.

"You prepared for the reaction?" the woman asked. "The men will think you're a loose lady and the women will be jealous and catty and call you a hooer behind your back."

Big deal, Mutzie thought. I've been called that to my face. Mutzie shrugged.

"Let people who don't know me think what they want. I'll still be me."

"Your mother know you're doing this?"

Mutzie shook her head.

"She'll have a shit conniption."

"That's her problem," Mutzie said, steeling herself for what she knew would be forthcoming.

Three hours later, she was, indeed, a different person—a brand new Mutzie. She loved her new look. The operator had even put a beauty mark in the exact same place as Jean Harlow's.

Then she went shopping for new clothes. You couldn't wear the mousy clothes she normally wore if you looked like Jean Harlow. Walking up Pitkin Avenue to Hopkinson Avenue, she felt wonderful. People gave her second looks. Men turned around when she went by. Passing a candy store, she noted that some of the men actually whistled. The attention made her feel lighthearted, glorious, conscious of herself and the power of her sex.

Without trying to, even her walk changed. She felt her hips swing more, her shoulders straighten, which emphasized her breasts. With the remainder of her hundred dollars and some extra credit, she bought clothes more befitting a blonde, including a red dress, a beige shirtwaist, maroon skirt and two tight sweaters.

"Get yourself a pointy bra," the sales clerk told her, winking. "Throw it at 'em, hon. They love it." She took the clerk's advice.

Then she went to a cosmetics store and had the lady make up her face in keeping with her new look: lots of powder, eye shadow and the right color lipstick. It was more makeup than she ever wore in her life, but she was quite satisfied with the results.

"There you go," the woman at the cosmetics counter said. "The Jean Harlow of Brownsville."

"Really," Mutzie said. She felt herself the happiest woman alive.

Her mother was not home when she got back to the apartment, which gave her time to try on her new clothes and admire herself in the bathroom mirror. She had to stand on a stool to see herself full view, but she liked what she saw.

All in all, she decided, she had a pretty good figure, maybe a little too curvy in the rear and bigger thighs than she would have liked, but her legs were well turned and slender. Now that eyeshadow emphasized her brown eyes, they looked bigger than before, more mysterious. Her nose, which had seemed to her longer than necessary, now looked softer and her full angel lips looked lusciously kissable in their shiny coating of cherry red lipstick.

She had always been happy with her breasts, which were upturned and full with nipples that stood out from pink areolas, not the brown kind that many woman had. Of course, her tight jet black bush of curly pubic hair was a dead giveaway as to her true coloring, but then that was a private place reserved, from now on, only for the man she loved. She actually regretted that Henry had touched her there, as if somehow it was a defilement.

Her mother's reaction was actually worse than she had expected. She fumed and sputtered.

"Your father will drop dead on the spot."

"Isn't that what you always hoped would happen?" Mutzie said. She had already decided to take a more aggressive stance with her mother to defend her actions.

"On top of everything, a filthy mouth," her mother said. "Now you look like a real hooer."

"How original. I'm still a virgin, Mama," Mutzie said coolly.

"Not looking like that you aren't."

"You want a doctor's certificate?"

"Bad enough for me," her mother said, waving a finger in Mutzie's face. "Everywhere I show my face, people will say: Oh she's the one with that hooer for a daughter. All right. so you'll make us a laughing stock, disgrace our good name."

"What good name, Mama? Papa runs a pushcart."

"I will admit he is no world beater, but he is a man of intellect and dignity. One look at you and he'll plotz and order you out of the house."

"Order me? What is this, the Marines?"

Mutzie did not come to the dinner table until her father had sat down and her mother had served the soup. As usual, her father had grunted his arrival, gone to the bathroom, and stripped down to his undershirt, his normal dinner attire.

Mutzie wasn't hungry and would have been happy to stay in her bedroom, but she had vowed not to be intimidated. However, she came to the kitchen table dressed in her ordinary clothes, not those that she had just bought. No sense in aggravating the situation further, she decided.

Mutzie's mother had just sat down to her soup, waiting for the fireworks to begin. Mutzie's father looked up. He had a glazed, preoccupied look on his face.

"You think they'll get the veterans' pensions through Congress? Never. Not those hypocritical bastards."

"You got eyes, Harry," Mutzie's mother said, startled by his indifference.

"Eyes? Sure. And I can see what's coming. We fought their war for them, now what do you think we'll get."

Mutzie's father was in the Army in the World War, but he had never gotten further than Fort Dix before the Armistice. Congress was apparently considering giving a permanent pension to all who had been in the war.

"Take a look at the hooer we got in the house, Harry," Mutzie's mother said.

"We're entitled. But will the bosses allow it? Never in a million years."

"Nothing is different about her?" Mutzie's mother asked trying to get his attention.

"What difference? Always the same. The rich get richer. The poor get poorer. We're cattle down here at the bottom. Sheep. Animals." Mutzie's father pointed his spoon. "And if they do give us the pension, the real reason will be to lull us into gratitude so that when they call us again for the next war we'll go like happy little lambs to the slaughter."

Mutzie's mother got up from the table and stepped behind Mutzie. She grabbed a handful of her hair and jerked her head forward.

"This. Putzvatig. This."

Mutzie extricated herself from her mother's grasp and pulled away.

"A bleach blonde hooer. Shmekel. That's what we got living here."

"So?" Mutzie's father asked, a look of puzzlement on his face.

"You can't see this disgrace coming down on her head? Look at her. A courva we brought up. An old maid courva. She turns down Henry Goldbaum, then she does this."

Mutzie's mother was building up a strong head of anger. But her father just looked at her in confusion. He was used to her constant harangues, but this was more serious than most. Mutzie's mother moved back to her place at the table, but she did not sit down.

Mutzie's father inspected his daughter with growing interest. His eyes narrowed. When she was little he hugged and kissed her a great deal, but his interest in her had waned once she became a teenager. Not that he didn't love her. She was sure he did. He had never been mean to her or unkind in any way, nor had he ever beaten her or, for that matter, ever given her any advice, pro or con about life, except in the broadest political terms.

Suddenly her father looked at her and smiled. Mutzie could not remember the last time she had seen him smile.

"You know who she looks like," her father said. "That actress."

Mutzie saw her mother rear up like a bucking horse.

"Communist mamzer," she screamed, picking up the soup plate in front of her and dumping it on her father's head. The soup, a thick concoction of leeks and barley, ran down her father's face. Then she stormed out of the room, into their bedroom and slammed the door.

"This woman is meshuga," her father said, looking at Mutzie, the soup plate still on his head, looking very much the World War doughboy.

Mutzie was not surprised about the effect her transformation had on other people. There appeared to be no middle ground, no neutrality. Other girls in the school bleached their hair, but none were truly platinum, as platinum as Jean Harlow and cut in exactly the same fashion. None used makeup in such a blatant contrasting fashion and not one had a drawn beauty mark in the exact place on her face as Jean Harlow.

With her tight sweater and pointy brassiere and her new way of walking, she did admittedly attract lots of attention in school and on the street. Of course, she heard remarks, but they were mostly behind her back and she pretended not to hear them. Generally, those girls who were not jealous were polite in their assessment of her new look. Some thought it was gorgeous and said so. A few of her teachers thought it was trashy. They also said so.

Miss Russo, her homeroom teacher was the most outspoken in her criticism.

"I am shocked by this, Miriam," she told her. "This is not the girl I used to know. You look like a scarlet woman."

"Would you like me to wear an "A" on my sweater?" Mutzie asked, surprised at her own defensive belligerence, but confident that she had done the right thing.

"At least you remember your Hawthorne, Miriam, but this is not the sweet girl that I used to know," Miss Russo said.

"Did you really know me, Miss Russo?" Mutzie asked, turning away. There was no point in dealing with such bigotry.

Of course, the boys treated her very differently. She got both whistles and catcalls, admiring glances and nasty remarks. Some were very forward and tried to get friendly, but she gave them short shrift. In a few weeks high school would be over and she would probably never see any of them again. Or care.

Mutzie noticed, too, that the transformation had also made her think differently about herself. She felt more certain about herself, more self-confident, more aggressive in the way she talked and observed others. She felt like "somebody," as if this new look reflected the real Mutzie, the real person who had emerged from her cocoon of anonymity.

It gave her the courage to parade in front of the candy store on the corner of Saratoga and Livonia where Pittsburgh Phil and his cronies hung out. With her tight sweater, pointy brassiere, Jean Harlow hairdo and dark eyeshadow, she felt his eyes wash over her admiringly when she passed. More than anything, it was that look that she had hoped for and dreamed about.

It was her brother Seymour who brought her the news that Pep wanted to meet her.

"How come all of a sudden?" she asked, suspecting the answer, but wanting to hear it said nevertheless.

"He tinks yore a looka," Seymour said. "For Pep to say dat is somethin."

"Suppose I say no?" Mutzie teased.

She watched Seymour's bony face grow longer, enjoying his visible loss of arrogance.

"Nobody says no ta Pep. Nobody. He says he wans to meetcha that's an awda." Seymour looked into Mutzie's eyes and he could see the fear in them. "I'm ona spot now, Mutzie. I don deliver, I'm up shit's creek widout a paddle."

"Well then," Mutzie said, enjoying her imperial attitude. "I wouldn't want to do that to my big brother."

The next evening, just after dinner, Seymour accompanied her to the corner. She had fussed with her face and hair for hours, then put on a tight sweater over her pointy brassiere and her new skirt and truly felt she looked her best. In fact, after she put on her beauty mark she actually winked at herself in the bathroom mirror.

Well now, aren't you something, she told herself standing in profile and throwing out her chest, while Seymour banged on the door impatiently.

"Ya don make Pep mad, Mutzie. Get outa der."

She deliberately delayed her exit, letting Seymour punch out the door until Mrs. Krauss in the next apartment began to scream.

"Jeez," Seymour said when she came out, his anger quickly dissipated. "You look a million, Mutzie."

Feeling like a million, she walked with him to the candy store.

"Memba now. You put in a good woid faw yaw big brudda. Right?"

"If the subject comes up," Mutzie said haughtily.

"You make it come up, Mutzie. Ya unnerstand?"

Mutzie looked at him and shrugged.

"Do my best, big brother."

That settled, Seymour began to move faster.

"Not so fast, Seymour," Mutzie said as they began to approach the corner. She could see the towering figure of Pep standing among a group of men. As she came forward, they all turned to look at her. She loved that, and her eyes met those of Pep, whose seemed to actually sparkle under the brim of his immaculate pearl gray fedora.

He stiffened as she came forward, his lips curled in a smile, his teeth sparkling.

"I brung ya my sister, Mutzie," Seymour said. The men surrounding Pep ogled her appreciatively. Pep nodded. "This is Pep, Mutz. Pittsburgh Phil Strauss."

Mutzie put out her hand and Pep took it in his. His hand was smooth and soft and she noticed that his nails were manicured. He wore a neatly pressed blue suit, a striped tie and a white-on-white shirt. There was a starched white handkerchief in his jacket pocket with three points showing. Obviously he took great care with his grooming and his clothes. Most important, his shoes were highly polished and glistened with the reflection of the streetlights.

He held her hand in his for a long moment, looking into her eyes. Her knees felt wobbly.

"I seen ya aroun, Mutzie," Pep said.

"Ain't she sumpin, Pep," Seymour said.

Pep shot him a look of dismissal.

"See ya aroun, Seymour," Pep said.

"She's a looka, right, Pep?" Seymour persisted.

"A real looka, Seymour." He winked at Mutzie. "An we gotta job for ya tomorrow. Right, Bug?" He turned to the squat man beside him. The man nodded.

"Yeah. A liddle wheel work," Bug said sourly. He seemed dirty and unpleasant-looking, more like the others who stood around on the corner. Some of them had mean, unsmiling faces and little fish eyes that ogled her suspiciously. Pep stood out, head and shoulders above them, handsome and princely. Seymour nodded gratefully and backed away, waving to Mutzie before he walked off.

"Ya bruddas a good kid," Pep said. "We got idears faw him, don't we, Bug?"

"Yeah," Bug said grimacing.

"Ya wanna take a drive?" Pep asked. "I gotta Caddy."

"Oh yes," Mutzie said, perhaps a bit too enthusiastically.

"You gonna see Albert, Pep?" the man called Bug said.

"Yeah," Pep said. "And the Kid."

"Lemmee know," Bug said. "I gotta make plans."

"Yeah, sure. See you guys lata," Pep said, taking Mutzie's arm in his and starting to walk down Livonia, which was under the El. They walked toward Douglas, past the open pickle store, the cleaners and the grocer. As she walked away, arm in arm with Pep, she saw the eyes of the men on the corner watching them. Also, people that passed looked at them with admiration. Aren't we a handsome couple? she thought, stiffening her posture, feeling the pressure of her pointy brassiere against the tight sweater.

Being the girlfriend of a man like this, she would be somebody. People would look up to her. She would have respect, prestige. Okay, she had heard rumors that some of the things he did weren't exactly kosher, but what did that matter. He was somebody, admired, important. He wore classy clothes and drove a fancy car. People would envy her. Life with him would be an adventure, exciting, like in the movies, a long way from the drab future she could contemplate with Henry Goldbaum.

Pep's Cadillac looked brand new. It was black and shiny with beautiful leather seats. Pep opened the door like a real gentleman and waited until she was comfortably seated before he closed it. She felt his eyes watching her body as she bent and seated herself primly.

"This is gorgeous," she said when Pep had gotten in beside her. He leaned over and bent toward her, putting his face close to hers.

"So is this," he said, his hand caressing her cheek. His touch felt electric and she felt a flush rush to her face. Then he bent lower and kissed her neck. She was too startled to move.

"You're a fast worker, Pep," she said.

"You ascareda me, Mutzie?" Pep asked. She had pulled away from him, more out of reflex and propriety than desire.

"Why should I be scared?"

"Evabody's ascareda me," Pep said. He put his keys in the

ignition, started the car and pulled away from the curb in a burst of speed. The car moved through the Brownsville streets, then headed toward Ocean Hill.

"I'm not," she said.

"I gotta see these people," Pep said, turning toward Mutzie. Pep patted her on the thigh. "Then I'm gonna show ya a good time."

Mutzie looked toward him and smiled.

"Sounds good to me." She was ecstatic. Here she was in the car with Pittsburgh Phil Strauss, *the* Pittsburgh Phil Strauss. He was obviously engaged in important business. She felt honored to be with him.

The car moved smoothly through the streets. As he drove Pep turned to Mutzie and winked, but said little. For her part, she wanted to know more about him, what he did, what his life was like. But that, she decided, would make her appear nosy, and she didn't want anything to spoil things. Besides, he might not want to talk about what he did. Should it matter, she wondered? The effect of being with him was what really mattered and she felt great.

He stopped the car in front of an Italian restaurant with a big striped awning over the entrance and they went inside. Pep nodded to a group of men sitting at a round table in the rear and led her to a seat at a table for two on the other side of the restaurant.

"Give da lady anyting she wants," Pep said to the fat Italian waiter with a stained apron that went from his chest to his ankles.

"A chianti, lady?" the waiter asked when Pep had gone. She nodded, not sure what it was, and watched the men peripherally. They talked in low voices. There were five of them, tough-looking characters, so different in looks from Pep. It struck her as incongruous that he should pick such hard-looking business associates.

She waited, sipped her chianti and occasionally looked their way. Although she was growing restless, she did not want to show any sign of impatience. From the intense expressions on the men's faces, this was obviously an important business conference and, she assured herself, that came first. She was actually flattered that he would be taking time out of his business activities for this date.

As she sat there by herself waiting for Pep, a couple of men came into the restaurant. They were big, crude-looking, swarthy men in dark suits. One of them jabbed the other in the ribs, laughed and came over to where she was sitting.

"Well, I'm here, cutes," one of them said. She could smell alcohol on his breath. "What say me and you blow this joint an have a party?"

At first she ignored him, busying herself with her hand mirror and looking closely at her teeth.

"Me and Louie here we gonna have one big party, right, Louie?" the first man said. He shoved his bulk on the seat facing Mutzie.

Still she ignored him, turning toward Pep who was in deep conversation with the men at the table.

"Aw come on, baby. We is nice guys. Right, Louie?"

"We gonna treat you just like a chocolate bar," Louie said, "Lick ya 'til ya scream fa mercy."

"What a pair a knockers," the other man said, leering. He put his hand out for a squeeze.

She moved quickly from his touch, the chair squeaking as she moved back. She could see Pep look up, scowl and quickly come over to the table.

He got behind the man who was sitting down and without saying a single word, grabbed the man by the throat with one hand and lifted him out of the seat. Mutzie was surprised at his enormous strength.

"He diden mean nothin," Louie said, glancing at the men at the table from which Pep had come. He made no move to help his hapless friend.

There was no scene, which surprised Mutzie. The man who had sat down simply rose obediently from the chair and, with Pep holding him by the windpipe, moved docilely toward the restaurant door. Pep opened it and brought the man to the street.

"He's loint his lesson," she heard Louie say, but then through the open door, she saw the man fall to his knees, then to the ground. When the man's head reached the curb, Pep swung out with the point of his shoe and kicked the man directly in the face.

He started to come back inside, stopped, looked over at the prostrate man then kicked him in the groin. Then he turned and came back into the restaurant.

Although Mutzie was certainly surprised by Pep's sudden action, she felt strangely exhilarated by the scene. Pep had stood up for her, protected her. That was something. She was also surprised that she could summon little compassion for the man who had accosted her. They had it coming, she decided. She hated being pawed and insulted by strange men.

"He won't bodder ya any more, Mutzie."

"Thanks, Pep," Mutzie said. She felt genuinely grateful.

"Gonna be soon, kid," he told her patting her arm. "Coupla minutes more."

"Okay with me, Pep," she said pleasantly.

It was nearly an hour before the men finished their meeting and Pep came over and sat down. Later, while they were eating their spaghetti, two of the men passed their table as they left the restaurant.

"This Pep got taste in skirts," one of the men said. He was thick and squat with eyes that glowed like burning agates. He wore a broad smile but it didn't seemed to radiate much joy.

"This is a very pretty goil, Pep," the other said. He seemed more benign, Italian-looking with a crop of curly black hair.

"Thank you, Albert," Pep said.

"How come you don't tank me, Pep?" the squat one said.

"This Reles always embarrasses me in front of ladies. That's cause he's jealous."

The man called Reles laughed.

"He's got more notches on his shlong than Buck Jones has on his six-gun."

"These boys," the man called Albert said to Mutzie. "They play like this alla time. Pay no attention."

"The short one is very crude," Mutzie said when they had left.

"Kid Twist?"

"That his name?"

"Monicka. Nickname."

"Like you're Pittsburgh Phil, right?"

"You don't like that one? They call me Pep for short. Better than Harry. Harry Strauss."

"Much better."

They were silent for a while as Pep studied her closely with his confident lovely brown eyes.

Pep was, as she had hoped, very polite and attentive. He tied a napkin around his neck to keep his shirt spotless and she noted how carefully he moved in his clothes to keep the creases neat. She liked that. When they left the restaurant, they held hands while they walked to the car. In the car, he put on soft music and she nestled in the crook of his arm as he drove, caressing her shoulder.

"You look like a movie star, Mutzie."

"Really?" Mutzie said, feigning surprise, loving the comparison.

"I like movies. Gangster stuff. You see Jimmy Cagney in *Public Enemy*?"

"I loved it."

"Edward G. Robinson in *Little Caesar*." He held his hands as if he were working a machine gun. "Rattatatata."

"I'm more partial to love stories and musicals, Pep," Mutzie said. She didn't mind gangster movies if they had love stories in them. "Gangster movies have too much killing."

"Yeah," Pep said. "That's the fun part."

They talked about the movies for a while, then turned to other subjects like what she wanted out of life.

"I want the best of everything," Mutzie said.

"Takes dough," Pep said.

"You seem to be doing great, Pep," Mutzie said.

"I got no complaints."

"What, actually, do you do?" Mutzie asked cautiously, suddenly fearful.

There was a long silence. Pep's tongue darted from his mouth and he licked his lips.

"I'm sort of a contractor," he said with a smile.

"Oh," Mutzie said.

"Anyway. I do real good." He observed her, patted her hand and they looked into each other's eyes.

"I could really go faw you, Mutzie. Maybe make ya my one and only."

His one and only. The reference was magical. It was exactly what she wanted. The suggestion validated her new makeover. She had made the right decision, indeed. She felt like somebody now.

"Really, Pep?"

"Really," he said, whispering in her ear.

She was ecstatic and she didn't want the evening to end. It was nearly midnight when he drove her to the front of her apartment building, and when he found a parking space, he shut off the ignition and the car lights.

Then he bent over and gave her a deep soul kiss while his hand gently squeezed her right breast, tight in its pointy brassiere cup. She wanted to unstrap her brassiere and let him kiss her bare breasts, but she didn't want to seem too forward, afraid she might appear like one of those easy girls. It was obvious that Pep had a great deal of experience with women. She liked that. It meant she was in safe hands.

After a few minutes of kissing, he sat up.

"I gotta go," he announced, turning on the ignition.

"Me too," Mutzie lied. It was Friday night and there was no school on Saturday.

"We see each other tomorrow, right?" Pep asked.

"Tomorrow?"

"Late though. I gotta do sumpin first. You meet me on the corner, say, about ten."

"That late?"

"Sure. We'll take a drive."

He bent over and gave her one more deep soul kiss and a squeeze before she left.

Seymour woke her up the next morning and sat on the edge of her bed, eager to hear how the evening had gone.

"Great, Seymour," she said. "Pep is a prince of a guy."

She told him about going to the restaurant and about the two men who had gotten fresh and what Pep had done to one of them. Seymour grinned.

"Bet they not walkin good no more," Seymour said. "Go aftra Pep's girl an ya could say goodbye to ya immies for a long time."

"He was wonderful. I feel good with Pep. You know. Secure."

"Ya put in a good woid faw me?"

"Of course," she lied. In the excitement of the evening, she had forgotten.

"Good goil, Mutzie."

She told him that she had met some of Pep's business associates in the restaurant.

"Like who?" Seymour asked.

She searched her memory.

"A shortish guy named Reles. He called him Kid something."

"You met the Kid? Kid Twist?" Seymour's eyes expressed how awed he was by such an event.

"And an Albert."

"Cheez. Albert Anastasia. Cheez. I can't believe it. I wish I was a goil. Cheez. Albert Anastasia. He's way up in the combination. Along with Pep and the Bug. Cheez. I can't believe it."

"What's the combination?"

"You don know?"

She shook her head.

"Aw, it's just a business name," Seymour said, suddenly cautious and hesitant. "Nothin faw you to know about."

"I'm gonna go out with him again tonight," Mutzie bragged.

"Tonight? Pep's gotta job. I know cause I'm gonna be wid him."

"Then it must be after the job."

"Cheez. You and Pep." He waved a finger in her face. "Remember who put you guys in touch, so now you keep puttin in good woids for yours truly."

Seymour got up. He patted his sister affectionately on the head.

"Who knew what kind of a sister I got," he said. "I always thought you were a dumb brat."

When she got to the corner at a little after ten, Pep wasn't there yet, although the fellow he called the Bug stood there in a group of other men. The candy store had a fountain counter that opened to the outside and she ordered a small egg cream, nursing it while she waited. Occasionally the men looked at her with what seemed like genuine admiration. Already, she imagined, she was being treated as Pep's girl. She loved being branded in that way. Pep's girl. It was like a song.

At ten twenty, one of the pay telephones rang in the candy store and the man behind the counter yelled "Bugsy" and the man called Bugsy came in and answered the phone. He came back outside a few moments later and gave a thumbs up sign to one of the men who was standing around, then he walked over to Mutzie.

"Pep'll be here in about twenty minutes."

"Thank you," Mutzie said, noting how considerate Pep had been to call ahead to let her know that he would be late.

She saw his Caddy pull up to the curb, and when he got out he straightened his clothes. But before he came forward to the corner she watched him buff up his shoes with a piece of cloth that he had taken out of the glove compartment. Then he looked into the Caddy's side mirror and adjusted his hat, then, smoothing his jacket and straightening the handkerchief in his pocket, he moved toward the corner.

"Be a minute, doll," he told her as he moved into the candy store followed by the man called Bugsy. They went into the back room behind the cigar displays and he was out fifteen minutes later standing beside her, looking resplendent, showing a broad,

sparkling smile as he put a hand around her waist and led her to
the Caddy.

He opened the door on the passenger side for her like a true
gentleman then got in on the driver's side. Once in the car, he put
the key into the ignition but before he turned it, he leaned over
and gave her a deep soul kiss, squeezing her breasts. She reached
out and caressed his tongue with her own and she could not deny
the thrill that swept through her.

"You my baby, Mutzie?" he asked when he lifted his mouth
from hers. She felt his breath in her ear, then his tongue as he
tickled her there.

"Yes, Pep," she whispered, meaning it. She had never been
happier.

He held her for a few moments, then with one hand turned
the ignition and moved the car out from the curb. He drove for a
couple of blocks then parked the car on a deserted street near
Betsy Head Park. It was dark and quiet but she could see his
handsome face, looking mysterious and shadowy in the play of
light from the nearest street lamp.

He put his hat carefully on the back seat, then bent over
and soul kissed her again then put his hand under her dress and
caressed her thighs. She had set limits in her own mind on exactly
how far she would let him go and was certain that a perfect gentleman like Pep would obey the limits and be respectful of her.
She would, she decided, go beyond necking to petting, and
would let him play with her thing and touch him on his if he
wanted that.

He seemed very gentle, very caring. After he soul kissed her,
he kissed her face and she felt his fingers playing with her thing. She
felt wonderful, like something warm and pleasant was tickling her.

"I'm real hot baby," he whispered, his breath coming in

heavy gasps. Sitting up suddenly, he took off his jacket, carefully folded it and put it in the back seat. Then he unbuttoned his pants and, rising, exposed himself.

"Pep," she said, stiffening suddenly, slightly confused by his action.

"Got ya a lollipop baby. Ya know what you gotta do."

She looked at it, but then turned her eyes away, feeling his hands caressing her face, then her hair, then the back of her neck.

"Gobble," he said.

She resisted as he tried to pull her head down over his thing.

"I can't do this," she said. "I never thought . . ."

He pulled her head down until her cheek was actually touching his thing.

"You just grab and lick it like a lolly, Mutzie. Come on. Show me how much you love me."

"Pep, please . . . I . . ."

With his fingers he forced open her mouth and it was suddenly filled with his thing and she was unable to talk and barely able to breathe. Then she felt a painful pull on her scalp. He had taken a handful of hair and was pulling her head back and forth. Her mouth was still filled with his thing.

"Open wide, baby. And watch the teeth."

She was genuinely frightened now, not knowing what to do, unable to scream, her head moving painfully back and forth, his thing in her mouth, trying as hard as she could to keep her teeth separated enough for it to go in and out.

After awhile, he pulled her head back and his thing went out of her mouth. He looked at her face.

"You hurt me, Pep." She started to cry.

"Aw, baby," he said, holding her. "I didn't know ya nevah did this. I'm sorry, Mutzie. Really I am."

"I tried to tell you, Pep," Mutzie said. He had grown gentle again.

"No problem, baby. I'm gonna teach ya how to do it right. Okay?"

She wanted to feel indignance and humiliation, but in his arms again, she felt oddly protected and inadequate. He had taken her to some place that she had never been before and she had no idea how to react.

"You forgive me?" he whispered.

She couldn't quite decide what to say, but before she could make up her mind, he had put his hand under her dress. When she tried to push his hand away by grabbing his wrist, he put his other hand in the band of her panties and ripped them away.

"See, ole Pep is not hurting his baby," he said, reaching out with his arms and pinning her against the seat with his body. "Besides, I got plenty of panty extras."

"I'm afraid, Pep. Please. I'm still a virgin," she whimpered. Frightened, she tried to push him away, but she was no match for his strength.

"Yaw gonna get it, Mutzie. Now you gonna be Pep's numba one or ya gonna be Pep's enemy."

Given the options, she had no choice. Someday she knew it would happen. It might as well be with Pep, a person of experience.

"Will you respect me after, Pep?"

It was, she knew instinctively, the bedrock female paranoia, along with the terror of pregnancy. Soiled goods and disgrace, the litany went, passed from mother to daughter over the generations. At this point, the decision was out of her hands.

"I'll respeck you better, Mutzie," he whispered.

He had insinuated his body between her legs, which were

stretched out under him. She felt something move between her legs, something touching her thing, moving up and down her thing.

"Just promise not to hurt me, Pep," she whimpered. There was no point in protesting. He was stronger, and insistent.

"Would I hurt you, Mutzie? Yaw my girl."

"I swear I never did this, Pep."

She felt the pressure of his body on her. He put both hands on the cheeks of her buttocks and thrust.

He put all his weight against her and she felt a searing pain tear into the middle of her. She heard herself screaming inside of her head, but no sound came out of her tightly pressed lips. Above her his body moved without pity, hard and relentless, pounding through her, splitting her.

"One tough cherry," she heard him say hoarsely, like the grumble of distant thunder. For a brief moment, fully penetrated, he did not move and she felt his hand feeling around as if to validate what he had done.

Thankfully, the initial pain receded. She searched her mind for a way to react, reaching into her senses for some quiver of pleasure. It was there, vaguely felt through the rawness of her body. She had become a woman, she told herself. She had been fucked. In her mind, she had always thought of it as a violent, invasive act. So she had been forced to do what was inevitable. I'm Pep's girl now, she told herself. She felt pride in that. Her life had entered another dimension.

Then he started to move inside of her. She felt a searing pain and was on the verge of screaming. Sensing that, he put his hand over her mouth.

"No," he ordered, watching her eyes above his hand. She shook her head and he slowly lifted his hand, ready to pounce at the slightest hint of a scream. She knew better than to do that, just laying there now, waiting for something to happen that might mollify the pain, listening to his grunting sounds as he increased the rhythm of his thrusts.

Then suddenly she felt this mordant curiosity, wondering if Jean Harlow had to submit to this ritual in such a crude and brutal way. Certainly she had never seen a hint of it in her movie life, although she supposed in real life Jean Harlow would be no exception in this regard. Every woman, except maybe old maids or nuns, had to get through this one way or another.

"You like it, baby?" Pep asked between gasps.

Actually, she was trying to like it, hoping that the pain would disappear completely.

"I'm gonna come, Mutzie. Here."

He moved her hand to his thing and closed her fingers around it while he quickly moved out of her. Then she felt a series of jumpy spasms happening to his thing, then she felt warm sticky stuff on her arm. After a while, his thing became soft and he untangled himself from her, then got out of the car and straightened his clothes.

She got out of the car on her side feeling sore, her legs shaking as she straightend her skirt. She knew she was bleeding and she put her torn panties between her legs to keep the blood from ruining her skirt. Then she got back into the car and combed her hair.

Pep reached into the backseat and put on his jacket and hat, then got in beside her.

"You came through like a champ," Pep said, bending over and kissing her forehead. "Not easy the first time. Sorry I had to be a little rough. Next time it'll be nice and easy."

Yet, despite the terror and degradation of it, she felt oddly elated, as if she had made it through an initiation of some sort, a ritual that had to be suffered through. "I'd die if you made me pregnant."

"Hey, Mutzie, I pulled out. You got the evidence."

Pep started the car and drove toward Pitkin Avenue.

"You wanna grab a bite?" he asked.

"Please, Pep," Mutzie pleaded. "I'm a mess. Take me home."

Pep laughed and put his arm around Mutzie as he drove.

"Always get hot and hungry after a job," he said.

She wondered about this, wondered about the kind of job that could cause such a reaction. She wanted to ask, but she supposed he would think it was intruding on his private business, men's private business. This was all so new to her, so strange. Looking at Pep in profile as he drove, she felt that she had somehow grown closer to him through this violent act. She supposed that most women were penetrated in such a way the first time. There was just no possibility of avoiding it. He might have seemed ruthless, but wasn't a certain measure of brutality required? After all, it was like breaking a seal and you couldn't do that except by a good hard push. There was, she decided, no way it could happen the first time without hurting. No way. Every woman ever born had to go through it. God made them that way.

She cuddled against him as he drove. The very fact that he was still interested in her after her resistance proved that he really cared about her. He stopped the car in front her apartment house. Then he leaned over and gave her another big soul kiss which she responded to with equal fervor.

"You were great, baby," he said, when they had released each other.

"Am I still going to be your girl, Pep?"

"From here on in you're my numba one, baby," Pep said.

"And you still respect me, Pep?"

"You betcha."

"And from here on in we'll see each other a lot?"

"A lot, Mutz," Pep agreed. "Only I ain't gonna be around next week. I gotta do a job in Buffalo."

"They keep you pretty busy, Pep," Mutzie said.

"Yeah," Pep said chuckling. "I'm in demand cause I'm good. The best." He shook his head. "Tonight was a doozy."

Before tonight, she had felt that it would be too nosy of her to ask any further questions about what he did. He had said he was a contractor, but she wasn't really sure what he meant. Apparently, he was in some sort of business with the men on the corner and with those men she had seen him with in the restaurant. Considering what had happened between them tonight, she decided to ask him to explain it a bit more. After all, if she was his number one girl, surely he would be willing to share these other aspects of his life with her.

"Pep," she said hesitantly. "What sort of jobs do you do? I mean the kind of work. I know you're a contractor and I know that Seymour was on the job with you tonight and I . . ."

He turned toward her and, even in the dark, she could see the sudden fire of anger in his eyes.

"I got a deal faw you, Mutzie," Pep said. "Simple deal. Nevah, nevah, I mean *nevah* evah ask me what I do. In udder woids, no questions asked. Yaw job now is to be Pep's goil. Nothin else. Pep's goil. Got it? Anybody asks you what you know about Pep's business, all you say is: I'm jes Pep's goil. No more than that. Got it, Mutzie? You sit quietly and be Pep's goil. You don listen to nothin and if you listen you don heah. And you don see nothin. Like a filly with blinders runnin around the track. Got it? You wanna use yaw tongue . . ." he grabbed his crotch, "you save it for this, capish?"

69

His sudden vehemence frightened her. She had over-stepped. What he did away from her was not her business. No way.

"I promise, Pep," she said. "Cross my heart. I will never, never ask that question again."

"That's my numba one," Pep said, patting her thigh. He was quiet for a long time, but she could tell he was thinking about some-thing. Suddenly, he stirred and sat upright, startling her. Pushing her an arm's length from him, he grabbed at the front of her sweater, bunching it in his hand, and put his face close to hers. "Seymour told you sumpin?" Pep snarled. He seemed even angrier than he had been just moments earlier, even angrier than he had appeared at the restaurant when the two men had accosted her.

"Pep. I promised. What did I say?"

"You jes answer. What did that putz brudda ayours say?"

"Nothing. Nothing. He just said he was going on a job with Pep. Is that something terrible?"

"He evah says anyting, you tell me Mutzie. You tell me. You heah?"

Again she was confused. What had she said? Besides, what could Seymour ever say that would warrant such importance. Pep released her and she looked at her sweater.

"You sure fly off the handle fast, Pep."

"Certain tings make me crazy. Like sweet liddle canaries who can't keep der lips clamped shut."

Above all, she didn't want Seymour to come between them. Not Seymour. She hadn't much respect for Seymour anyway, and she certainly didn't want her relationship with Pep to depend on Seymour in any way.

She let Pep cool in silence while she slowly sidled close to him again, then began to caress his face with her hands.

"My pretty boy," she whispered. She brushed his lips with hers. "If I'm your number one you got to tell me what makes you mad."

"That's one thing," he nodded, but the anger had dissipated and he put an arm around her shoulder.

"You and me is gonna make music, Mutzie," Pep whispered. "And I got plans for ya."

"You do?" Mutzie said, assuming the teasing air of the coquette. She tucked her arm through Pep's.

"You evah been to the mountains, Mutzie?" Pep asked.

"Never," Mutzie said, trying to keep herself from being overly eager. Her family could never afford the mountains, not even a room at Rockaway for the summer. Of course, she had heard all about those glamorous places in the Catskills, like Grossinger's, the Concord, the Nevele and Shawanga Lodge, which she had seen advertised in the papers.

"Ever heard of Gorlick's Greenhouse?"

"Oh yes," she lied.

"Best in da Catskills. We gotta connection dere. All da boys goes, wives, kids, goilfrens. Real family. It's a gas. Lotsa action."

He turned toward her and chucked her lightly on the chin with his fist.

"You be good to Pep and I'll show you one helluva time this summer. One helluva time."

"I can't wait, Pep," Mutzie said, her heart beating a tattoo of expectation. She squeezed Pep's muscle and brought his manicured fingers to her lips.

Maybe life could be like the movies, after all, she told herself.

3

FROM A DISTANCE GORLICK'S GREENHOUSE LOOKED LIKE a stretched-out Victorian mansion, complete with porch, cupolas, dormers, and architectural dental work. Most of the Catskills hotels had started as houses, which had been added to as increasing business dictated.

It was situated on a hill about ten miles from Fallsburg surrounded by a wide expanse of grass lawn, which dropped down to a lake with a roped off area for swimming and a dock with a boathouse painted in peppermint stripes. Tied to the dock were rowboats, sailboats and a spit-polished speedboat.

Beyond the hotel were the higher wooded ridges of the Catskills, which were not monumental, but with just enough height to qualify as mountains. The setting was beautiful, tranquil and pristine, hardly a place one would associate with the clientele that Gorlick had trumpeted with such pride.

The hotel was a beehive of activity. Painters were busy putting finishing touches on the white façade and carpenters were repairing the long porch with its line of rocking chairs and lounges. Inside, the lobby was undergoing the last stages of a face-lift. People scurried around frenetically. It was two days before Decoration Day, the official opening of the season.

Gorlick, cigar in hand, wearing paint-stained slacks and an undershirt, was supervising the hanging of a picture on the staircase landing. It depicted a huge expanse of landscape with high mountains in the background and a herd of cows in the foreground.

"To the left," Gorlick shouted to the three men on the ladder working the picture, guiding them with his cigar. "No, now to the right. No, left. Shmekels, I'm talking plain English. Right." He nodded. "Now. Good." Then he turned and saw Mickey, who had just entered the hotel.

"So the tumler has arrived," he said, waving his cigar in Mickey's direction.

"Ketskills before the Yidden?" Mickey said thrusting his chin in the direction of the painting. "Looks more like Switzerland."

"Who asked you?" Gorlick said. "Montens are montens."

Gorlick motioned with the crook of his finger to one of the men who had helped hang the picture, a young man with a square face, green eyes and rust colored tight curly hair. He was short with a bantam swagger and lips frozen into a cocky sneer. When he talked, it was from only one side of his mouth as if the other was paralyzed, which wasn't so, as when he smiled both ends of his mouth rose in unison.

"Hey, Irish. This is Mickey, the tumler. Show him where, okay?"

Irish saluted, turning toward Mickey and lifting his belted pants with his elbows in what, Mickey supposed, was a gesture of toughness. He said nothing and motioned with his head for Mickey to follow him.

Without a word, Irish led the way through the lobby and up four flights of carpeted stairs, a hardship to Mickey who had to carry his suitcase.

"No elevator in this joint?" Mickey asked.

"Only for guests," Irish sneered.

"There are no guests yet."

"Garlic wants us to get used to it."

On the fourth floor, Irish led him through a series of narrow corridors, stopping finally in front of a closed door. He waited for Mickey, who was puffing with the burden of his suitcase, to catch up, then motioned with his head to the door, leaving it for Mickey to open.

The room was no bigger than an oversized closet, with one dormer window that faced the sky and walls that slanted in such a way that one could only stand up straight in its center. Against the wall was a single cot with a stained rolled up mattress. Next to it was an ancient chest of drawers. It was dismal and depressing.

"Cans down the hall," Irish said, flipping a cigarette one-handed out of a pack of Luckies, then lighting it by scratching the head of a wooden match. "Get the bed stuff from housekeeping."

Mickey put his suitcase down on the exposed springs of the cot and inspected the room. It didn't have a closet, although there were two wooden hangers hanging lopsided on a hook. It also smelled of feces.

"Stinks like a toilet here." Mickey said. As if to counterpoint the observation, a toilet flushed on the other side of a paper-thin partition.

"This was one part of the shithouse," Irish said.

"I'm gonna talk to Gorlick," Mickey said, anger beginning to boil inside of him.

"Him? To him you're free room and board. He'll say you're a complainer, ride you like hell. Who needs that?"

"How can I live here?" Mickey said. Another flush sounded in the room. "This is the toilet annex."

Not that living above the store was the Ritz. He slept on a cot in the living room in their one-bedroom apartment above the store and his parents shared a room with his sister, separated by a curtain. But his mother kept everything neat as a pin and the only untoward smell was on Friday morning when she made gefilte fish and even that wasn't half bad.

"Don blame me, tumler. Garlic said show you where. So I showed."

"One night here and I'll jump," Mickey said. "Get blood on his nice lawn."

"So what else is new?"

"The one thing you never do is depress the tumler."

"I gotta better idear," Irish said, offering a surly grin. "I think I can get you a better spot." He lifted his hand. "Not a promise. I said I think."

"You're going to talk to Gorlick?"

Irish blew smoke out of his nose and shook his head.

"Cost you a fin."

"Are you saying I gotta pay?" Mickey said, looking at Irish. "I smell a hustle here?"

"Better to smell a hustle than a toilet," Irish sneered. He started to swagger out of the room.

"You gotta point," Mickey called after him.

Irish stopped, turned, and pointed his fingers as if they were a gun. The image of holdup seemed complete.

"Five is steep," Mickey said. "Will you take three?"

Irish's contemplation consisted of sucking air through his teeth.

"Four is better," Irish said holding out his palm. Mickey counted out four bucks.

"One smart tumler," Irish said, putting the money in his

pocket, then putting his arm on Mickey's shoulder. "You and me is gonna get along."

As if to show his camaraderie, he picked up Mickey's suitcase and carried it down the corridor. He came to another door and opened it abruptly.

A chubby young woman was lying on a bed wearing nothing but panties. She jumped up, her huge breasts swinging, tearing the blanket off the bed and covering herself. Her face showed more anger than embarrassment.

"You getoutahere Irish," she screeched, as Irish lifted a fisted hand and waved it in her face.

"Shut ya hole, Marsha, or I shut it for you."

The threat calmed her.

"This is not what I bargained for," Mickey muttered. Irish threw him a glance of contempt.

"I give it to her as a fava," Irish said. He turned back to Marsha. "You pack up and getoutahere."

"You get no more freebees from me, Irish," Marsha said, miraculously calmed. "It's ovah between you and me."

"This is your room in the foist place, tumler," Irish said.

"Ya lied ta me, Irish," Marsha said, still snarling. She looked at Mickey. "He give me this room hisself."

Irish pulled the blanket out of her hands. She made a valiant attempt to cover her big tits with her arms, but to little avail. Irish laughed and grabbed a handful of breast.

"I give it to her cause a these. Aint them knockers sumpin?"

"Gettaway from me you bastard."

"Just showin off my goods, Marsha."

The girl was docile now, as of she were cowed into accepting the humiliation.

Mickey was embarrassed and uncomfortable. He felt sorry

for the girl. Their eyes met. She shrugged and turned away.

"This is wrong," he said. "I don't want to put her out."

"Hey tumler, you want the room or not?"

"Not if someone else has to be punished for my comfort."

"Look at this, Marsha, a real softie."

"He's got class," Marsha mumbled. "Not a slob like you, Irish." She looked at Mickey and nodded. "I appreciate this kid. I ain't just a piece of meat. "

"It's okay. I'll find another place," Mickey said.

"This one's gotta heart," Marsha said, pointing with her thumb. Her subtle change of attitude seemed puzzling.

"Stop the hearts and flowers and get the hell outa here," Irish said to the girl.

The girl moved to the bed and bent to get her battered suitcase from under it.

"You should see that big ass move, tumler," Irish said. The girl, paying little attention, put on a robe.

"You don't have to go," Mickey said.

"It's not my room anyway," the girl said. "It's his racket. It's a scam, kiddo."

"For that you don't get your cut," Irish said, pushing a finger in the girl's face.

"Does Gorlick know?" Mickey snapped. ·

"Won't do no good. He don want no trouble with the help," Marsha said, her gaze flitting between him and Irish. "Better don rock the boat. Right, Irish?"

When she turned to face Irish again, she looked at him with squinty eyes, her lips tight with anger.

"When the big shots come up this one will be just a little shit," she said. Irish lifted a fisted hand.

"Ya lookin for it, Marsha," Irish said.

"Yeah. Like your dick. Tough to find."

"Fa that I ain't pimping ya with the help this yeah," Irish said, sticking a finger in front of her nose. "And if ya try on yaw own I give yaw face an acid bath, you unnerstand?"

"Big talker," Marsha said, turning to Mickey. "Thanks, tumler." She winked. "At least someone around here has feelings."

She scowled at Irish and left the room with her suitcase.

"Lousy little hooer," Irish said, hitching up his pants with his elbows. "No gratitude. Was me that got her the waitress job in the foist place, was me that woiked out the side action for the help." Again he flipped up his pants with his elbows. "You like this room, tumler?"

It was, indeed, larger and airier with a window that overlooked the lake.

"This really was my room, Irish?" Mickey asked. "You owe me four bucks."

"Dues, pal," Irish muttered. "For that I put ya under my care. Now I give ya the tour. Ya tell the boss, it's your word against mine. I been here five seasons."

Mickey decided not to press the point. No sense starting trouble during his very first day.

Irish took him down by the back stairs. On the second floor, he led him through rooms filled with green felt craps tables, card tables with lights hanging overhead and one roulette table.

"They ever been raided here?" Mickey asked.

"Raided? You crazy? In Sullivan County? Cops are on da take here like everywhere, schmuck. Doncha know that da combination runs da city and da whole state? Whereyabeen? They got New Yawk in the palm a dere hands. Nothin happens dey give da goahead. Anyways, Big Al's troop runs these games."

"Anastasia?" Mickey said. He had remembered that name

from Gorlick's explanation and his own research. Irish stopped suddenly and inspected his face. He seemed impressed.

"You know Big Al?" Irish asked.

Mickey held up two fingers close together.

"You shittin me?"

Mickey deliberately did not answer, staring instead into Irish's green eyes.

"Kid Twist and Pittsburgh Phil?"

"You think they'd hire a strange tumler?" Mickey said, his stomach churning with the memory of his father's beating.

"Jesus. You shoulda said."

"You think Gorlick wants a problem like last year's tumler?"

"Jesus. You know about dat?"

"Speaks with a squeak now," Mickey said.

"Ya don fuck with the troop's ladies. This shmekel he pops somebody's quiff. Ya know how that goes down."

"Believe me, I've been warned."

"You need some pussy?" He tapped his chest with his thumb. "I put Marsha to work." Irish chuckled. "I suppose you also knows the wops, too. The Dasher? Louis the Wop, Happy Maione?"

"You gotta know the scorecard, kid," Mickey winked, playing the charade to the hilt.

Irish reeled out the names with a sense of unbridled awe. These were obviously his heroes, whoever they were. Mickey assumed that they were people in the "combination." Since being hired, he had, of course, done some inquiring, but his neighborhood network was limited.

Most of his friends had been the good boys, the smart boy sissies who had a particular ambition or went to college. They were at the top level of the three-level pyramid. The lowest were boys who hung around the poolrooms, Brownsville bums, many of whom were sure to end up as gangsters. At mid-range were the boys who hung around the corner candy store, of which there was one on almost every Brownsville corner. They were idlers but not bums, not officially, and not pushy or ruthless enough to be gangsters.

Through further research he had embellished upon Gorlick's explanation. The so-called combination was an alliance of Jewish gangsters from Brownsville and Italian gangsters from Ocean Hill a few blocks away. This was surprising, since he knew that as a Jewish boy he was not welcome in any Italian neighborhood.

Because he went to night school, worked in the store and had a particular ambition, Mickey had little time to mix with the neighborhood boys. He had gone to public school with many of them, but they had inevitably drifted apart. Up until he had confronted those gangsters beating up his father, he had had no connection with nor did he realize the extent of the criminality of Brownsville gangsters.

He had discovered that the Brownsville combination were into loan-sharking, labor union extortion, gambling and prostitution and that many of them hung out around a candy store on Livonia and Saratoga that they called "The Corner," and that the candy store never closed. The owner was called Midnight Rose and it was here that his father had borrowed the money from the shylocks in the combination.

But the real business of the Brownsville gang was murder. You hired them as hit men. Mostly they did piece work. If someone from the combination needed someone wacked for business reasons, they contracted with the boys who hung around Midnight Rose's candy store. It was no secret, but so far the so-called reformers like La Guardia, who was now the mayor, and Dewey, who had been picked to clean up the racketeers and was soon to run for New York district attorney, hadn't been able to lay a glove on them.

But the strangest information he had garnered during the period between being hired by Gorlick and arrival was that most of those who had gone to school with him and stayed in the neighborhood were in awe of these gangsters. In fact, they worshipped them. They were heroes, even role models, defying the law, courageous and, above all, tough. You messed with them at your peril.

Proximity to them was everything for these sycophants. It did not take a genius to know that Irish was one of these and Mickey acted accordingly, larding it on.

"I was just saying to Lepke the other day," Mickey said, remembering Gorlick having mentioned a man named Lepke. He had remembered later that he had read about a racketeer named Lepke in the newspapers.

"Ya know Lepke good enough to tawk with?"

Mickey looked at Irish and deliberately said nothing.

"And Joey A. Ya know him? And Frank Costello?"

"You know what happens to nosy punks?" Mickey said, with an Edward G. Robinson inflection.

"I ain't lookin for no trouble," Irish muttered. He squinted at Mickey and continued the tour. Beyond the gambling casino was another room with a long table.

"For serious troop business," Irish said.

"Bet your ass," Mickey replied.

Irish seemed to become reflective as he accompanied Mickey downstairs and through the dining room with large windows overlooking the lake. He pointed to a small stage at one end of the dining room.

"This is where ya do your shtick, tumler. And ya bettah be funny."

"Maybe I'll tie a chain around your neck, Irish, and play the organ."

"Ha ha, tumler." He grabbed his crotch. "The only organ I play wid is dis one."

"I'm sure it earns a clap or two from every performance."

Irish, missing the humor, shrugged and went on with the tour.

"Ya evah know anybody from the Purple Mob in Detroit?"

"You got a long nose for an Irish," Mickey grunted.

"I'm Benny Markowitz for chrisakes. Irish is only my monicker. Cause I look Irish. People say there was a Mick in the woodpile."

"No shit," Mickey said, forcing a chuckle. Along with the rats, he thought.

When they came out into the lobby again, Irish moved closer to Mickey and held him under the arm.

"I hang out at 'the corner.' I never seen you there."

"You testin me, punk?"

"Bet you nevah been on a job?"

"Not my cup a tea. I'm around for laughs mostly." Mickey had deliberately fallen into Irish's speech rhythms.

"Yeah, yeah," Irish said. "You killem wid laughs."

"Sorta."

"I been a wheelman on a couple," Irish said, lowering his voice. "You ask Reles."

"You got a tongue, Irish," Mickey said, watching Irish flush red.

"Whatayathink, Dewey's gonna hear me all a way from Manhattan?"

"A canary's voice travels far," Mickey said, remembering an odd line from a gangster movie. He watched Irish squirm.

"You tink dat?" Irish said menacingly. He looked around him furtively, his head swiveling like a bird. Then he moved it in a quick, jerky way, a sign that something momentous and confidential was about to come out of his mouth.

"I been on two contracts," he whispered. "I seen Pep slice a guy with a pick, a bad number from the baker's union. Never knew his name. Takes da pick like dis." Irish demonstrated with an imaginary ice pick, touching Mickey lightly on the chest and neck. "Bing, bing, bing. Ten, twenty times. Pep got pissed cause some blood spurts on his white-on-white shoit. Den we bury da fucker over in Canarsie. Me an Red Alpert. Ya wanna hear da udder?"

"If I gotta," Mickey mumbled. Irish looked at him for a moment, not certain whether to continue, then probably deciding that it was just the tumler's way of expressing himself. The fact was that Mickey Fine's stomach was curdling with fear. Pep's appearance belied his curiosity. He could have done it to his father without batting an eye. In fact, with a smile.

"A quick hit right in Borough Park in da middle of da day. Brawd daylight. I got da wheel, see, and dis guy Pipkin or Popkin or sumpin comes walkin cross the street. I pull up to da coib and Bugsy gets out with his gat wrapped in newspaper. Pop. Pop. Right in da heart. Back in da car and off befaw da bum hits the ground."

"Nobody saw?" Mickey asked, repelled and fascinated by the matter of factness of Irish's rendition. He searched Irish's face for the slightest sign of regret or remorse or compassion. None were visible.

"Hot car, see. And da gat got no serials. We threw dat down da sewer and dumped da car in Canarsie."

"Canarsie again?"

"Who goes to Canarsie? That's shit country."

"You are something, Irish," Mickey said, searching his mind for a reaction. "And I hear good things about you."

"No shit."

"I hear the boys talkin. 'This Irish got a future.'"

"I told ya."

"A good boy this Irish, they all say," Mickey embellished.

"Someday they gonna give me jobs like Pep and da Bug. I'm damned good wid da rope, too. And I also know dem gats."

A tremor of fear shot through Mickey. Some ambition, he thought. My son, the killer.

"People know a good man when they see one," Mickey muttered.

Irish jabbed a thumb into his chest. "I ain't stupid neither. Day trust Irish cause Irish knows da score." He bent his lips close to Mickey's ear. Mickey felt the breeze of his breath and the smell of it, something faintly sour and milky. "Section tree nine nine, Criminal Code, City of New York. Ya know what dat is?"

Mickey contemplated an answer. No, he decided. This was too esoteric to feign knowledge.

Irish studied Mickey with his bird-alert green eyes. Then he smiled.

"In this State, ya can't convict on a crime by testimony from an accomplice." Irish paused, proud of his rendition. "Got it."

"Oh that," Mickey said, not willing to surrender completely to Irish's street knowledge of the law.

"Gotta have what dey call corrobo . . . corrobor . . ."

"Corroboration," Mickey said, glad to have this tiny crust of redemption.

"To connect da guy wid da act." Irish nodded his head. "See I knows dose tings, dats why dey trust me. Dey know I cut out my tongue first befaw I snitch."

"Me," Mickey said. "I'm partial to old age. That's why a clam lives nearly forever."

"No shit?"

"One thing a tumler knows in life, it's human nature."

Irish studied Mickey again, probably wondering if his remarks should enter his logic system, which was strictly gleaned from the streets, not from books. Irish again raised up his pants with his elbows.

"Wese can help each udder good here. I'm like a jack a all trades. Sometimes I bus tables. Sometimes I wait. Sometimes I drive. I know everting dat goes on here. I know who's shafting who, who's shtupping who, who shtups easy, who you keep your hands off. Anyting you want to know, I got."

Mickey searched his mind for a specific question, seeking to validate the commitment. In this atmosphere, Irish could be quite useful.

"All right, Irish. I got one," Mickey said. It had been on his mind since the interview with Gorlick. "Who is this Gloria?" He did, after all, partially owe his job to her.

"Gloria with the good gams and bazooms?"

"Sounds like the lady."

Irish smiled broadly, showing a mouthful of reddish gums over bad, crooked teeth.

"Gloria runs da quiff. Got this part a Sullivan County sewed up. Got maybe ten hooer houses within thirty miles. Also sends out. Case the boys wants some. Dis here is da mob's turf, all da action, gambling, hooers, the bank, the book, the weed, the whole shmear. Ya know, all the rackets."

"That part I know," Mickey lied again. "I just thought Gloria was Gorlick's girl," Mickey said.

"Garlic? That lard ass wife a his wouldn't let him dip the wick

in a pickle barrel without her permission." Irish winked. "If ya
sweet on Gloria, cost you five oh and that's only for an hour."

"Sounds like you were there, Irish."

Irish winked and hitched up his pants again.

"I been evywhere."

The general routine of the tumler was the same in all of the
hotels in the Catskills. An essential part of a tumler's job was to
know the guest list in advance so that those designated VIPs were
given the kind of treatment accorded to their rank.

Irish was particularly helpful on that score, and on that
Friday when the guests began to check in for Decoration Day
weekend, Irish ran a bragging commentary on the guests, their
wives and girlfriends. He assumed, of course, that Mickey knew
them as well and that this display of his knowledge was merely to
impress Mickey.

"There's Charlie Workman and Allie Tannebaum and Plug
Shulman, and Bugsy Goldstein and Kid Twist Reles and Pretty
Levine and Gangy Cohen and Jack Drucker and Irv Ashkenaz.
Thems da important ones. I know da dames, too."

The names went on and on. Mickey had difficulty remembering, especially the women who, for the most part, were nondescript, especially the wives. There were exceptions, though,
flashier types, who Irish usually designated as girl friends under
the general heading of coorvas. Occasionally Mickey would inter-
ject an "I know" merely to validate his own pretended knowledge,
but Irish was an encyclopedia, too concentrated, focused and
excited by seeing these "celebrities" file into Gorlick's
Greenhouse.

"Pep ain't come yet," Irish said, his eyes darting over the
crowd. "Pep's my Rabbi."

Mickey shrugged and said nothing.

"He be here. He tole me. Usually stashes a coorva heah for da summer. He's got 'em evywhere. Dat Pep's a card. He, Bugsy Goldstein and Kid Twist are da top a da heap."

"So I hear," Mickey said, remembering Pep's brutality. His stomach knotted at the memory.

Gorlick and his fat wife stood by the desk dressed to the nines, hugging and kissing each guest and ordering the help to take the baggage to the guests' designated rooms. It was a madhouse, noisy and confused, looking more like a staging area for refugees than the lobby of a Catskill hotel.

Considering the reputation of these men for killing and general mayhem, Mickey was surprised by their ordinariness. Collectively, they had the look of a very nondescript tribe, resembling working men and women, more like mechanics and waiters and store clerks on a family outing than the kind of gangsters portrayed in the movies.

The hotel became more frenetic and hectic as the day wore on. Kids began to run wildly through the lobby. Many of the men embraced in the abrazo fashion and peeled off into smaller groups, happy in one another's company, leaving the details of the check-in to the women.

Then Mickey spotted the other man who had brutalized him and his father in the store and who he had seen again with that Pep monster in the corridor outside of Gorlick's suite at the Park Central. Mickey moved slightly, trying to make Irish a buffer between him and Reles's field of vision.

"There's Reles," Irish said, poking Mickey in the ribs. "That Kid Twist is one tough bastard."

"A bastard, that's for sure," Mickey said. It was a mistake. Irish shot him a suspicious glance.

"Ain't ya gonna say hello?" Irish said with a touch of sarcasm. "Ya said ya knowed him."

"Maybe he should get set first," Mickey said.

"Ya said ya knowed him good," Irish pressed. He put his arm on Mickey's back and pushed him forward. "Anyway you're the tumler. Go tumel him."

"Bad to tumel them when they come right off the road," Mickey told him, trying to be reasonable. "They're too edgy. They don't want to be kibbitzed around with."

"Ya shittin me, tumler?"

"Get off my back, Irish."

"Now I get it. Ya full of it. Ya been braggin. Ya don know any of dese guys. Right? Ya been shittin me."

"Go screw yourself, Irish."

"Ya said you knowed 'em good." Irish squeezed Mickey's upper arm. It hurt but Mickey would not give him the satisfaction of knowing this. Then Irish hitched up his pants with his elbows.

"Tell you what, tumler. I'm gonna need like two bucks a week from you for . . ." Irish scratched his head ". . . special services. Yeah, that's rich. Special services. A good deal, too. Hell, I give ya back the for. Ain't I generous, tumler?"

It wouldn't end there, Mickey thought. Irish would find ways of abusing him all summer. It was a direct, unabashed challenge. The man had no conscience and, as he had seen with Marsha, could be cruel and quite ruthless.

"You're a card," Mickey said. "A real jack off."

"I ain't laughin. Ya been trowin me da bullshit, tumler," Irish said. "We got ways to take care a bullshitters." Red blotches had erupted on his face. Mickey looked over at Reles.

He was dressed in a brown suit, which looked like the same suit he had worn at the Park Central, scuffed brown shoes and a hat pulled low over his eyes. He wore a shirt buttoned at the collar but with no tie and he needed a shave. He was talking animatedly to his wife who was holding the hand of a small dirty-faced boy.

Despite the domestic scene, the man was as he remembered on that night, eyes glowing agates of hate and the sausage-squat body a container of meanness and cruelty.

"Dey don like punks usin dere name in vain," Irish said.

Mickey calculated the odds carefully. Chances were that Reles might not even remember him. Besides, he would be out of Irish's earshot.

"You want me to put in a good word for you, Irish?" Mickey said, trying to build up some measure of the old arrogance.

"Yeah. You an La Guardia." Irish punched a finger in Mickey's chest. "Dis summer tumler, ya watch yaw ass, cause Irish is gonna be on it."

Irish's words triggered the action. Mickey turned and strode over to Reles. Suspend all fear, he begged himself, but they were hollow words.

"Hi, Mr. Reles. I'm Mickey Fine, the social director."

"Whadayaknow. The new tumler," Reles grunted, eyeing him with laser intensity. Mickey thought he saw a level of indifference and he was relieved. So far, so good, he thought, forcing himself not to look back at Irish, although he felt the man staring at his back. "Meet the wife and Heshy."

Mickey forced a smile and gave the boy a kitcheykoo.

"We're gonna have fun this summer, Hesh," Mickey said to the boy, who looked back at him with the same cold, menacing eyes as his father. "Chip off the old block," Mickey said, forcing his cheerfulness.

"You gonna make it fun ain't ya, Mick?" Reles said.

"I'm here to make your stay a bowl of cherries," Mickey said, watching Irish from the corner of his eye. He looked worried, less swagger in his posture.

"Ain't that the pits," Reles said, followed by a burst of guttural laughter.

"Maybe you should be the tumler," Mickey said with good-natured aplomb.

"I tumel on my own turf, right, Helen?"

"My Abie's a scream," the woman said. She was squat, over-stuffed, with dyed red hair.

"I got anudder one faw him," Reles said, looking at Helen. "You know da one." He tapped an ear.

"Oh no, not that one."

"Why do farts thmell?" Reles asked.

Mickey threw up his arms. "Ya got me," he said.

Reles bent over and talked directly into Mickey's ear.

"Tho deaf people can enjoy them, too."

Mickey doubled up in faked laughter. He looked at Irish peripherally and gave him a chilly look. Irish seemed further deflated. Still bent over Mickey shot him an Italian "fuck you" gesture, hand slapped over biceps.

At that point, the bellhop came with his cart and began to load up the Releses' luggage.

"Make sure these people have rooms with adjoining towels," Mickey said. He put a hand at the side of his mouth and addressed Reles. "There's a couple of good rooms in this joint. On a clear day you can even see the dresser."

Both Helen and Abie Reles laughed, then Mrs. Reles and the boy went off with the bellhop while Reles lingered behind. He bent over and whispered in Mickey's ear.

"You ain't sore about da udder time, are ya, Mick?"

Mickey felt a sour, cold backwash deep inside of him. He looked toward Irish who seemed forlorn and totally defused. At least he had settled that score.

"Neva feget a face," Reles said.

"Business is business, Mr. Reles," Mickey said.

"Pep's toilet drink diden hurt ya," Reles said patting Mickey on the back. "Ya look a million."

"I kept my promise, remember," Mickey said, trying to keep his knees from trembling. "Next day cash on the barrelhead."

"Yaw a good kid, Mickey. I don feget nothin like dat." He bent over and whispered. "Ya take care a Helen and Hesh this summer. Take care good and I take care a ya."

He put his arm around Mickey and squeezed his shoulder. Notwithstanding the ugly memory of that night in his father's store, Mickey felt good, somehow vindicated. Stiffening his posture, he strode back to Irish and moved his face close enough to see his pores.

"You ever pull that shit on me again, Irish, I tell them that Mr. Shmekel Irish got too big a mouth. You fashstay?"

Irish flushed a deep reddish purple and his lips trembled.

"I was only kiddin aroun, tumler. Fact is I only been on one job and I nevah seed nothin."

"Think I don't know that, asshole?"

Irish fished in his pocket and brought out the four dollars he had taken from Mickey. Grabbing Mickey's arm, he lifted it and tried to put the four dollars into his hand. Mickey pushed him away.

"Call it a loan, Irish," Mickey said. "Five for four. You pay a deuce a week all summer then pay me back the rest on the last day."

"Come on, Mick," Irish pleaded, forcing a smile, showing large red gums. "That's even above shylock rates."

"You got it, Irish," Mickey said, returning Irish's smile and putting his arm around his shoulders. "Penalty charges. You and me, Irish. We're business associates now. Aren't we?"

"Sure, Mick, anyting you say," Irish nodded, shrugging his acceptance.

"Get out of line and I'll tell the boys that they got a canary loose outside the cage." Mickey chuckled menacingly.

Not bad, he thought. He was getting the hang of the environment.

4

"IT'S LIKE A BEAUTIFUL DREAM," MUTZIE THOUGHT, AS SHE looked out of the window at the wide expanse of green lawn that slanted gently to the lake. She could see children flashing down the slide, hitting the water and stirring up a splash that in the sunlight looked like crystal bubbles bursting out of the slate gray lake.

Their mothers sat lounging on chairs or playing cards under gaily striped umbrellas. Some of the older children swam in the cordoned off swimming area while a few tiny sailboats, like paper toys, skirted beyond the painted buoys, sails flapping in the light breeze.

She marveled at the way in which her life changed so dramatically. She had become a woman and won the heart of a powerful man who protected her and showed her a new and exciting world, a long way from the drab, colorless, boring life she had been leading.

"Just look at this gorgeous sight," she whispered aloud. She had turned away from the window and looked into the full-length mirror at the new dress Pep had bought her. What men do, men do, she assured herself. They had their reasons. She concluded that Pep was like a soldier in an army that was at war, and in a war sometimes people got hurt, or worse. Like in those war movies about the World War. If you thought of it that way, you knew you had to stop thinking about what happened on the battlefield and act more like the women who stayed at home.

She turned away from the mirror to look outside again. The beauty of the view soothed the nagging irritation of these dark thoughts. Of course, she had gotten good at pretending that she was walking around with blinders on, with ears stuffed with cotton and a mouth that uttered hardly anything except when she alone was with Pep.

So far, being Pep's girl, his numba one as he called her, was like being a celebrity. People said, "That's Pep's girl" and looked at her with what she thought was awesome respect. Besides, if anyone, including his associates in the combination, did not show her respect, that person would have hell to pay. She was very careful not to be overly friendly with anyone and to keep to herself. Besides, she had the sensation that the women were keeping her under extra-special surveillance. Pep had a real jealous streak. Actually, she liked that. It made her feel really special, valuable, worth protecting. And he had taught her all those moves to show her gratitude.

She was, of course, true to her promise. She never again asked him what he did to make his living. She found that she could separate it in her mind. Not that she had to lie to herself. All she had to do was to imagine herself as a thoroughbred horse with blinders running around the track. Over and over again. Round and round. It was nice to be pampered, noticed, admired and showered with perks and presents.

As her father had said countless times, the world belongs to them that have the gelt and the objective was to get it and not be pushed around. Wasn't that the real American dream? Wasn't that what being a go-getter meant? Hadn't she been a go-getter by transforming herself to look like a Hollywood star?

Her role was to be Pep's girl. She was not stupid enough to believe that everything they did was legitimate. Legitimacy, she knew, had lots of gray areas. Prohibition was the law, but drinking went on anyway because people liked to drink; they needed to drink and have fun. In the movies there were lots of people shown drinking and having fun in speakeasies. So what was wrong with that?

Okay, so there was bookmaking. People loved to play the horses and the numbers. They derived pleasure from that. Somebody had to run these things. Sometimes laws were silly. She had seen with her own eyes cops in uniform getting paid off by the boys on the corner. Everybody knew that the law was a joke.

And borrowing money when a bank was too stuffy to lend it was okay, too. The people that lent money to people of high risk deserved to be paid high interest rates for that risk. There were other things, too, that made sense if one thought about it carefully. Businesses did need protection against unscrupulous competitors, and sometimes businesses and unions did need middlemen to negotiate things away from public scrutiny. It wasn't her job to be judge and jury. Besides, she had learned life had trade-offs.

She could put two and two together. She knew Pep and his friends were what people generally referred to as gangsters. She had seen enough gangster movies to know what that was. But she was able to separate what he did, which she didn't know for sure, from what he really was, which was the most important thing. Okay, there were rumors and things said. As she had learned early in life if you are afraid of the dark, don't go into dark places.

Pep's work, she told herself, was certainly adventurous and filled with excitement, and probably courage, too, because what

Pep and his associates did was, she assumed, dangerous work. Maybe there were killings connected to it, but they were most certainly righteous killings, necessary to protect themselves and probably society from extremely evil and greedy people. Like Robin Hood perhaps. She could live with that idea. Still better, she forced herself to put any contrary thoughts completely out of her mind.

The important thing for her just as for the wives and girlfriends of the other fellows in the combination, was that their men were good husbands or boyfriends or fathers or sons and, of course, good providers. Pep was a wonderful son who treated his parents with great respect and was generous in his support. He was also a good uncle and brother. These were the real criteria by which to judge a man's true character as far as she was concerned. Weren't they?

Often she heard people say things behind her back that were not exactly complimentary. Even here at Gorlick's, some of the other women were snooty to her or looked down on her. She attributed that to jealousy. She had the best and handsomest man of all of them.

She heard rumors, of course, that Pep might have other girls. She didn't exactly like it, but she never ever confronted him with such suspicions. That was none of her business, either. After all, she was the one he had chosen to put up in Gorlick's for the summer. She was his number one. If there was a number two or three she never asked.

He was also very sweet and generous to her. He bought her dresses and shoes and gave her presents. He also gave her fancy underwear and he liked her to dress up with garter belts and high heels and brassieres that pushed her breasts into high mounds. He taught her about sex, and especially about those things he liked her to do to him.

In doing those things, she felt like an actress in a movie, and he was the director. Her role was to perform and please him, which she did with obedience and enthusiasm. Once or twice she even had an orgasm, but for her, the most important thing was to give Pep pleasure. Soon she began to believe that her mother's ideas about purity and marriage and being an old maid were laughable. Where would marriage get her?

The game plan at Gorlick's was for the men to come up on weekends and the women to stay on during the week. Some men stayed all week, but mostly they kept to themselves all day, playing cards or taking walks together, meeting with their women or children only at mealtimes.

Pep wanted Abie Reles's wife, Helen, to keep an eye on her, but that didn't work out very well since Helen Reles played cards most of the day and night, which meant that Mutzie was stuck being a babysitter for their son, who was a brat. When she complained to Pep, he put an end to it. The Reles kid was a pain in the ass.

The fact that Mutzie wasn't a card player was a definite social handicap. She was younger than most of the others, too. Not to mention the obvious, which was that she attracted a good deal of attention from the men. This didn't sit too well with the women and probably inspired a great deal of jealousy toward her. Of course, she understood that. Also, there was a certain status in being Pep's girlfriend, which meant she couldn't be friendly with just anyone. Besides, she wasn't the gregarious type. The result was that during the week, she kept to herself mostly, waiting for Pep to come up for the weekend. She sensed that people got used to her being alone and soon accepted it.

At meal times she ate at the same table with Helen and Harriet, Bugsy's wife, and some of the others, but she was rarely part of the main conversation, although she listened to what was being said. Rarely did the women discuss anything about their husband's business, which apparently was the rules of the game. Mutzie was certain that they were watching her to be sure that she was sticking to the letter of the rules.

Being with these women did, however, make her realize that being the wife or girlfriend of a gangster was no bed of roses. Kid Twist had spent three years in Elmira, a state prison, and was always being hauled in by the police on suspicion of something or other. The same was true of Pep and Bugsy Goldstein.

But the women led her to believe that what the police were doing were harassing their men largely because they were not the ones in on the "take."

"They're always picking on the boys because they want a piece of the action," Helen told her. "Simple as that. It's true that sometimes my Abie loses his temper and does things maybe he shouldn't, but as far as I'm concerned he's a good husband and father and provider and those things matter the most to me."

During the first week of her stay at Gorlick's, Mutzie was subject to words of advice from both Reles's and Goldstein's wife. They added up to what she already knew, which was never ever to double-cross Pep or even look at another man while she was Pep's girl.

Although she didn't complain to Pep that she was lonely during the week, he must have gotten differing reports from the other women.

"You bored up here, Mutzie?" he asked her one Friday night after they had made love. Pep was always pretty hot when he came in from the city on Friday afternoons. The first time was always over with quick.

"I'll bet you heard that from the other girls. They probably think I'm stuck-up when all I want to be is alone. I'm happy here, Pep. Especially when you come up."

Above all, she didn't want him to think that she was unhappy, ungrateful or troublesome to him. It was certainly better being at Gorlick's than in the hot city and her parent's stinking apartment for the summer. And she had Pep on weekends and all the prestige that went with being his girl.

"Those cunts are all jealous, ya know," Pep said as they lay naked in bed. "Yaw a looker and they all got them fat Jewish tushes."

"Maybe, but they don't really bother me."

"They bother ya, I'll give 'em a headache they don't feget. Maybe I gotta talk to them."

"I wouldn't like that, Pep. And I'm not bored. Mickey Fine . . . he's the tumler, puts on some really good shows. And there's movies twice a week. You know how I like movies."

"He can be funny sometimes, that Mickey," Pep said.

"He treats me very nice. A perfect gentleman."

"Putz better be." Pep suddenly became reflective. "He's a good kid. We did business wid his fada. They got a staw sells foundation garments. I'm gonna talk to him to keep an eye out."

"You don't have to do that, Pep."

"Maybe ya keep away from dem cunts, ya be better awf. Mickey's job is to make ya happy heah, make ya laugh. I don want no long face when I come heah. I want happy. Women don make love so good when dere not happy. I come up here I want no aggravation."

"Believe me, Pep, I don't want any aggravation for you. No way. All I want is to make you happy."

"You make him happy," he said after a pause, pointing to his growing hard-on. "He's happy, I'm happy."

"What a beauty, Pep," she cried, touching its velvety head with her lips. "It's the most beautiful thing I ever saw." She had learned all about the special compliments he liked to hear.

"It's just faw you baby. Just faw you."

She would spend the weekend as close to him as he would let her get. She would stand right behind him when he played cards with the boys or blackjack at the tables and he called her his good-luck charm. She would even be close by when he just sat around and schmoozed with the boys, most times being the only woman in the group.

She wasn't ever part of the conversation and it wasn't long before she knew she was considered more like an ornament, Pep's ornament, like a tie clasp or diamond cufflinks, a thing to admire then ignore.

She was always fearful that they would send her away, and because of that maintained a kind of indifferent expression, as if she wasn't listening to what the men said to each other. The fact was that it was impossible not to hear, although she tried her best to quickly forget what was said.

They told some weird stories and sometimes it wasn't easy to pretend that she was not listening.

Like Kid Twist's story about some man named Ernie.

"We brung him to my place. My mudder-in-law was in da next room. So I get the rope and Pep gets da pick and so fa da guy knows from nothin, but somehow he sees da rope in my hand and he gets antsy. Den he sees da pick and he goes crazy and he bites Pep's fingah." Reles started to howl with laughter. "And Pep gets real mad and he asks me fa a Band-Aid. I say, 'Now in da middle a dis? Can't you wait till we finish?' But Pep says, 'He's gonna give me goims, maybe hydrophobia or sumpin.' So I said we better hurry so we can get the iodine. 'Iodine' he

102

cries out. 'That hoits. Ain't ya got mercurochrome?'" Again he doubled up with laughter.

"So what happened?" one of the men asked.

"We hurried," Kid Twist said. "My mudder-in-law yells from her room. 'What's happenin down dere, Abie' and I calls back and says, 'Nothin, Ma, Pep just got his fingah bit.' 'You want I should get him a Band-Aid' the old lady calls back. So I tell her ta shud-dup and go back ta sleep and I'll take care of Pep's fuckin fingah."

He bent double with laughter. Naturally, Mutzie pretended not to hear, taking out her compact and fixing her face. She wasn't sure what they meant when they talked of hurrying something, but she was certain that Pep didn't do anything really bad. At least she hoped not.

Sometimes one of the men might mention keeping it down in Mutzie's presence.

"Never mind Mutzie," Pep would say. "She don know nothin, right, baby?"

Mutzie would shrug and nod and bend down and kiss Pep on the lips and he would pat her on the ass.

"You got a great lookin whatamacallit," Kid Twist would say to Pep winking in her direction.

"My protégée," Pep would say, giving the men around the table a big grin. "Best of all, she's good to Peppy, ain't you, baby?"

Her response was always to kiss him or sometimes to sit on his lap. Occasionally Pep would squeeze her breasts in front of the men, but it was playful and not mean and didn't embarrass her, although she would push his hand away as a show of dignity.

Once, Bugsy Goldstein baited him as they played cards. He had, she noted, lost a great deal that night and was probably feeling sore and nasty. Mutzie, as always, stood right behind Pep with her hand on his shoulder. He caressed her arm as he played. It was between hands and she had bent down to get a kiss and while he kissed her he squeezed her breasts.

"Five bucks says dey ain't real," Bugsy said suddenly.

"Ain't real?" Pep squeezed and she pushed his hand away. "Any udder takers on dat?"

"I got five," Kid Twist said.

"Me, too," Charlie Workman said.

"Na," Pep said. "Double maybe." He looked up at Mutzie. "Right, doll?"

She wasn't quite sure what was going on so she nodded.

"Okay, doubles," Bugsy said and the other men at the table agreed. The money was put in the center of the table as if it was a poker pot. Mutzie was wearing a dress that wasn't very low cut and, as usual, she had on a pointy brassiere.

"C'mere sweets," Pep said. He guided her to his lap and put his arms around her. Then she realized that he was undoing the back of her dress. She tried to get away but he held her fast. The men laughed.

"Hey, Mutzie. Money's on da table. Yaw gonna win it for us, right, doll?"

"Pep, don't," she squirmed. Yet, although she was embarrassed, she did not feel frightened. Pep was just having fun, kidding around. It was just a joke. Wasn't it? He wasn't going to really let it happen. Then suddenly Pep grabbed her hard by the shoulders.

"Ya gonna make me tear this shmata?" he said. "Jes a bet, baby, for old Pep."

"Please, Pep," she begged.

"Jes a free show, baby. No harm in it. Dese are my buddies."

She tried to wiggle free and he slapped her hard on her upper arm. Her response was to stop wiggling and hide her face in his neck. Pep unhooked her bra and she felt her breasts fall free. Then he pushed her to a position that gave the men a good look. She kept her eyes tight shut. She felt sick to her stomach.

"Them's as real as your balls, Bugsy," Pep said proudly.

"I don know, Pep, if I can believe my eyes," Bugsy said. "Some things ya can only tell by feel." He put out his hand and squeezed Mutzie's breasts. His touch filled her with self-disgust.

"Real, I tink," Bugsy said.

"Lemmee make sure," Kid Twist said. He moved to where she was sitting on Pep's lap and also felt them. Then Charlie Workman did the same. A sob began to grow inside of her. She tried to imagine this was happening to someone else. It was the most shamful moment in her whole life.

"We win," Pep said, kissing Mutzie's cheek. Then he pushed her off his lap and let her straighten herself. She felt herself about to burst into tears, but she held back. She would not give them the satisfaction. Besides, she was completely confused. How could Pep have let this happen?

"She's a real good sport," Bugsy said.

"Real good," Kid Twist agreed.

Pep stuck out a finger and winked.

"And dat's all ya gonna get," Pep said, laughing.

That night when they got back to the room, she told him. "How could you?" she snapped. "I really felt like a hooer."

"Aw, baby. It was only fun. Da boys got a kick outa it. Dey know you ain't no hooer."

"You wouldn't do it with Helen Reles."

"Who wants to see Helen's tits? Besides, we all seen them. They hang down to her pupik. We're all like bruddas, Mutzie."

"You promised to respect me," she said.

"Jeez, Mutz. I didn't mean no harm. Hell, I'm real proud of those bazooms."

"They are for your eyes only, Pep. And nobody but you touches."

She felt her temper rise. For the first time with Pep, she felt abject fear and the full extent of his control over her.

"Yeah. Yeah. I was just kiddin aroun. And if you show 'em to anyone else I squeeze his nuts off."

"No more, Pep. Promise."

"Cross my heart, Mutz."

By then he was already undressing her and touching her everywhere. He pushed her down on the bed and took off her panties, then he pulled her legs apart.

"They ain't never gonna see this," he said. "Ain't that a sight." He bent down and started to kiss her there. Then he stopped. "Not for forty lousy bucks." He giggled and went back to what he was doing. She felt no sensation. Only fear.

One Sunday in late June she was accompanying Pep to his Caddy, parked in the front driveway ready for the trip back to the city. They bumped into Mickey Fine, who was just hopping out of the Gorlick bus, which had taken people to the bus station in town.

"Hey, tumler," Pep shouted, calling him over. Pep was a hard one to please when it came to humor, but somehow Mickey managed to make him laugh whether on the stage or just offering a passing remark. Pep and Mutzie did not spend much time at the various weekend shows. Pep either played cards, schmoozed with the boys or made love to her. That was his typical weekend.

"Yes, Mr. Strauss," Mickey said. Mutzie could tell that Mickey was afraid of Pep, but then most people were, except his closest friends like Reles and Goldstein and some of the Italian

boys that came up on weekends, like Louis Capone and Dasher
Abbandando.

This particular weekend had not been a good one for Pep
and Mutzie. In the first place she had her period. Pep was too fas-
tidious to make love to her when she had her period, although she
did manage to satisfy him in other ways. But it was not the same,
not for him.

"Ya shoulda called and tole me ya was wearin da rag," he
rebuked her when he discovered that she was having her period.

"I was afraid you wouldn't come up," she said.

"I wouldna," Pep said. "I hate when women got da rag on. It's
a mess and dey stink."

"It's not like it is my fault," she told him in a muted rebuke.

"I'm not saying that wearin da rag was yaw fault, I'm saying
that you shoulda tole me is all."

"I suppose I should have," she admitted, feeling oddly guilty.
"Next time."

He was edgy the entire weekend and spent more time with
the boys and less time with her, which made her depressed. She
tried to hide it, pretending to be happy and giggling a lot. It only
made things worse, as Pep could see right through her ploy.

"I'm sorry, Pep, for making it such a lousy weekend," she
told him. She wasn't sure why exactly she was apologizing, but
she was sure that he was in bad mood and, she reasoned, it had
to be her fault.

"No ragtime next week, right?" he asked, studying her face
to make sure. She shook her head and sniffled, holding back tears.

"And stop blubbering," he told her, but he drew her into his
arms and kissed her head. "Yaw still my numba one."

It was right after that that Pep saw Mickey Fine step out of
Gorlick's bus.

"I got sumpin special for ya to do fa me, tumler," Pep said.

Mutzie liked Mickey Fine, although she didn't always laugh at his jokes. He was always very polite to her, even when he got off one of his so-called funny ones. She did notice that he sometimes seemed to stare at her, although he quickly averted his eyes when she faced him. Of course, she knew she attracted attention, but there was something different in the way he looked at her. Perhaps it was her imagination.

He was a tall man, a boy really, closer to her own age. He had dark curly hair, clear blue eyes and a sparkling smile that seemed to light up his whole face. He was a little on the skinny side and he often told jokes about himself being so thin.

"I'm thin so I can crawl under the door when the husband comes in too early," he said often.

"Yaw gonna make this lady happy, tumler," Pep said.

"I am happy, Pep," Mutzie protested. Aren't I? she asked herself. She was no longer as sure as she had been. In fact, she was afflicted with lots of second thoughts.

"I mean *happy* happy," Pep said, turning to Mickey. "Yaw job is ta see dis lady is in a good mood when I come back here. Got it? Yaw gonna make her laugh all week, tumler." He put his hand in his pocket and peeled off a five dollar bill. He looked at Mutzie and quickly turned his glance away.

Mickey took the bill, looked at it intensely and held it up to his eyes.

"Oy Abie, you should never have gone to that show. Maybe if you stuck around you coulda got your punim on the hundred."

"Is dat a hint?" Pep said, grinning. "Maybe ya keep her in a good mood, I give ya da hunnert."

Mutzie exchanged glances with Micky and raised her eyes in

embarrassment. She hated the idea of his paying someone to make her happy.

"You hear about the Pollack who went to get his eyes tested for a driver's license?" Mickey asked.

"You tell me, tumler," Pep said.

"He puts his hand over one eye and reads. 'CZYTROSKI.' 'Terrific,' the guy who was testing says. 'No big deal,' the Pollack says. 'I know the guy.'"

Pep made a Bronx cheer that sprayed on Mickey.

"Very funny," Mutzie said, with a touch of sarcasm.

"Happy, tumler," Pep said. "I want dis lady happy." He pounded a fist in Mickey's upper arm. At that moment Reles came up to them. Behind him was Workman and a kid named Red Alpert.

"Ya beatin him up again, Pep?"

"I jes hoid one of his jokes," Pep said.

"Hear the one about the alligator at Grand Central?" Mickey began. "A redcap comes over. 'Carry your bags, sir?' 'Yeah,' the alligator says . . ."

"But be careful . . . that's my wife," Reles interrupted, slapping Mickey on the back.

"You heard it?" Mickey asked.

"Ya know how ya find out who gives da best blow jobs," Reles said.

"Jeez, Abie, not in fronta Mutzie," Pep said.

"Woid a mouth," Reles said, jutting a thumb in Pep's chest. "Gettin bashful, baby?" He turned toward Mutzie. "Sorry, Mutz. It was on da tip a my tongue." Reles roared with laughter.

Pep got into the Caddy shaking his head. Reles got in beside him and the other two men got in the back. When he was seated, Pep opened the window on his side.

"Come plant one on old Pep, Mutz."

She came over and stuck her head in the window. She gave him a long soul kiss. When they were finished, he turned toward Mickey, who had averted his eyes.

"Happy," Pep said. "Real happy."

"And you keep that shlong in your fist," Reles said, laughing. The men in the backseat also laughed. Mutzie felt herself flush, but she didn't let on that she had heard. She stood watching as the car pulled away, feeling depressed and sick with a growing sense of shame.

"Sunday must be tough," Mickey said, after the Caddy was out of sight. "I get a little sad myself seeing some of the guests leave."

Under the tumler's veneer, she saw a vulnerable sincerity that she liked, although she did feel uncomfortable with Pep's ordering him to make her happy. She could tell he was also uncomfortable. He called out suddenly to a couple of incoming guests.

"Don't worry, folks, the hotel is fireproof during the season. It's off-season that Gorlick makes his money. He has so much he doesn't know what to burn next."

"That's not funny," one of the women said grimly. "Who is this schmuck?" she asked her girlfriend, a dyed redhead with a painted mask for a face.

"Don't pay any attention to him, he's not an eligible guy. He's only the tumler."

"Reminds me of a girl I went out with once," Mickey whispered to Mutzie. "You heard of nose drops? So does hers."

"You don't have to try so hard, Mickey," Mutzie said.

"Oh yes, I do," Mickey said. Although he was smiling, a sad grimace seemed to pass beneath the smile.

"Pep's a lot of talk. He's not like people say," Mutzie said.

"I think he's great," Mickey said. She caught the note of sarcasm, but let it pass. In her presence, she had learned, no one said a bad word about Pep. Not ever.

"People say so," Mutzie said.

Mickey followed her through the lobby toward one of the back porches, where she then sat on a rocking chair. He sat beside her. Beyond the porch rail the incredibly green lawn undulated downward to a stand of pine trees that screened the road below. It was a tranquil setting, quite beautiful, and they both stared out at it for a while.

"You know you don't have to stick to me like glue," Mutzie said suddenly. "I don't need a babysitter."

"I was just enjoying the view."

"Not afraid that people will talk? You spending time with Pep's girl?"

"Hell, Pep hired me," Mickey said. "I got a sawbuck to prove it."

She felt a flash of anger rise in her chest, but she calmed herself. Looking at him, she again saw his vulnerability and realized he hadn't really meant it to be insulting. She said nothing in response and continued to look out at the landscape. They were silent for a long time until she realized he was staring at her.

"You wanna be an actress or something?" Mickey asked suddenly.

For a moment, she was wary. Above all, she wasn't looking for intimacy, but she was flattered. She shrugged an answer, not wishing to ignore him completely.

"You got charisma, Mutzie," he said. "I've seen the way people look at you."

She felt more than flattery now, as if he were tapping into something very deep inside of her.

"Sure it's not the hairdo?" She fluffed her hair. "It's the Jean Harlow look."

"I'd never know," he laughed.

"Some people think it looks cheap," she said. "But I don't care. Pep likes it and that's all that counts for me."

This is what she had been telling herself, had convinced herself was the truth. In her thoughts, she would never allow herself to think beyond Pep, as if she might have ambitions of her own. And yet, it tantalized her to think that maybe she might be an actress, get to live all those wonderful lives that actresses lived in the movies. All right, it was only make believe. But what was wrong with that? She knew from the fan magazines that when they weren't living these exotic and interesting lives in the movies they were offstage somewhere in sunny California living glamorous lives in lovely houses with swimming pools and going to nightclubs and racetracks.

"Maybe someday I'll go to California," she mused aloud.

"Me, too, maybe," Mickey said. "Be a movie funny guy. Like a Ritz brother, only I have no brothers."

The truth of it was that she had expected Gorlick's to be something like that and in her heart of hearts she was becoming more and more disappointed, although it was better than spending the summer in the hot city. Wasn't it?

There were moments when she wanted to ask Pep if there was a future between them. But she was afraid. Afraid there might be, or afraid there might not be? She wasn't sure. Seymour had told her mother that she was going out with Pep, who he portrayed as a very important businessman which, of course, delighted her mother and filled her with hopeful ideas. Of course, she didn't know how intimate Mutzie and Pep had really become. Nor did she know how Mutzie was really spending her summer. She had told her mother that she was working at Gorlick's as a waitress.

"What about Mr. Strauss?" her mother asked when she called home once a week.

"Oh he visits on weekends," she explained, adding, "He has an investment in Gorlick's." This elated her mother.

"Maybe the country air will put wedding bells in his head," her mother suggested. Mutzie doubted that. Not a hint of such a thought had crossed Pep's lips. Besides, it was a decision with which she did not wish to be confronted.

These were the thoughts going through her mind as she felt Mickey continue to study her. "I just thought, you know. If you wanted to be an actress, or just for kicks, you might want to be in my little skits. No kidding. It would beef things up a bit to have an attractive girl like you in some of my routines."

She felt oddly tempted.

"You think Pep would mind?"

"Mind? He'd be real proud." He paused and she felt his eyes boring into her. "Besides, you really don't look none too happy during the week. Don't think it's not noticeable that you're always off by yourself somewhere." He cleared his throat, somewhat embarrassed. When she stole a quick glance at him, she noticed that he was blushing.

"Maybe some Hollywood scout will discover you."

"Don't be silly," she snickered, feeling secretly excited.

"Really. It would be fun. Dress up the act."

"Maybe I should check first," she said. Pep had given her the number of Midnight Rose's candy store on Saratoga and Livonia. If she ever needed him she was to call.

"Whatever you say. Anyway, the offer stands."

At that moment she was conscious of a short redheaded young man watching them from the lawn. She had seen him

113

around as one of the help. He seemed to be looking at them intently.

"That's Irish. One of the truly dumb. When I want to spend the day not thinking I read his mind."

"That dumb?"

Mickey got up.

"Anyway, think about my offer. Mr. Strauss would be proud." He looked at her and their eyes met. "And you'd be happy." He paused. "I know I would be."

Why not? she asked herself. She could tell Pep that it would make her real happy. Mickey started to leave, but before he moved away she held out her hand. He took it. She noted that it was moist, not clammy, but warm moist.

"As the one-legged hitchhiker told the guy who gave him the lift. Got to hop off now."

"It never stops, does it?" she asked. She liked Mickey, felt a sense of sincerity about him. Yes, she told herself, she would tell Pep that she wanted to do this. She was sure Pep wouldn't mind.

That night she called Pep at the candy store.

"Who is this?" the man who answered said. She recognized the voice as that of the young man behind the fountain at the candy store, Moe, the son of Midnight Rose.

"It's Mutzie," she said. "Pep's girl."

"The one at Gorlick's?"

"Yes," she said. The Number One, she thought. She was beginning to hate the reference and what it implied.

"Pep's gone away for a coupla days," Moe said.

"Where?" she asked. It was a reflex. She had not meant to ask the question, but she had been surprised.

"On a fishing trip," Moe said laughing.

"Oh, yes," she said, trying to take the sting out of the inquiry, hoping he wouldn't tell Pep. "Just tell him Mutzie called. Nothing important. And tell him I'll see him Friday night at Gorlick's."

Pep's business was his business and her business was her business, she told herself. Besides, she didn't think he would mind. Hadn't he told the tumler to keep her happy? This was all part of it.

The next day after lunch she and Mickey began to rehearse in one of the private card rooms that were deserted on sunny days. At first she was nervous and mumbled the lines he had given her.

"You look like you're suffering," Mickey told her.

"I am." The paper on which her lines were written shook in her hand.

He tried to relax her by telling jokes. "Hear about the lady who saw her name in the obituary and called her friend in hysterics?"

Mutzie shook her head.

"She says, 'Did you see my name in the obituaries this morning?' The woman replies, 'So where are you calling from?'"

Mutzie giggled, but mostly out of nervousness.

"Feel better?" Mickey asked. She nodded. "Now read."

"Hello, Sam."

"Who is this?"

"This is Sadie."

"With which Sadie am I having the pleasure?"

"This is the Sadie with which you had the pleasure."

"Oh that Sadie? I remember you and that weekend we spent together. What a weekend. I'll never forget you. And I forgot to tell you, you're a good sport."

"That's why I'm calling you, Sam. I'm having a baby. I'm gonna kill myself."

"Say, you *are* a good sport."

She started to giggle.

"There you go. Get into the spirit. You can't make people laugh unless you're having a good time yourself."

"Yes. I see that." She agreed. In the next hour he handed her script after script of funny lines. She felt herself getting better and better.

"Later we'll do song parodies. The guests love that."

Mickey decided that the show would be put on Thursday night and, maybe if it went over well, they would do it again for Pep when he came up. They worked for three days in the afternoons getting the lines right. She spent every evening in her room memorizing them.

"They're all talking," Helen told her at breakfast Thursday morning.

"About what?"

"You and the tumler," Helen said. "It doesn't look too good. You step out on Pep and you've got a problem."

"Pep?" She felt insulted and confused. "Pep asked Mickey to look after me." She could not say, To make me happy.

"I'm not saying it's true," Helen said. "I'm only saying how it looks."

"I'm merely helping him out with some skits. And they're real funny. You'll see tonight."

"Look, I'm not accusing. It's how it looks. Ya know what I mean. Yeah, business is business. The boys don't hurt nobody cept when it comes to business. One exception, lady. You don't step out on Pep. No way. Pep can be very hard on his girls if they step out on him. I seen it. Ya lucky if your face don't look the same or . . . ya know." She made a throat cutting gesture with her hand. Mutzie felt her stomach lurch.

"Well, I'm not stepping out on him. I wouldn't do that to Pep. I'm Pep's girl and you know it. Don't make trouble, Helen."

Helen put her mouth to Mutzie's ear.

"And the boy will be singing soprano," she whispered.

For a moment, she felt as if her heart had stopped. Helen persisted.

"Word to the wise, kid. I been around these punks a long time. This Pep follows his shmekel. You give that magic wand your undivided attention. Save yourself a lot of grief. Get my drift."

"I would never . . ." Mutzie began, swallowing hard.

The two women exchanged glances.

"Glue them legs together, girlie. One thing more. Sometimes. . . ." Helen's voice dropped to a whisper again. "Sometimes . . . I'm not saying for sure. But sometimes you gotta help him out. Ya know. Like doin a fava for an important friend. Ya know what I mean."

Mutzie froze, recalling her previous humiliation. Not Pep, she thought. He promised. This Reles woman, she concluded, could make real trouble. She had better not push her luck.

At that point little Heshy arrived, his face and knees covered with mud.

"Look at you, little putz," she shouted twisting his ear. "Schmutz everywhere."

After lunch she went to the card room, but she no longer felt comfortable about working with Mickey. As much as she resented the idea, she was not a fool. These women could be very vicious and hurtful. Nevertheless, Helen's warning had found its mark.

"I don't think I can do this," she told Mickey.

His jaw fell, a nerve in his cheek began to palpitate and his expressive blue eyes told her of his disappointment.

117

"But Pep said . . ." he began.

She put a finger over his lips.

"People see things differently," she said. "The women are saying things."

"Hey, Mutzie. Gossip are the spies of life. They've got nothing else to do."

"I don't want to make trouble, Mickey." For you either, she thought.

"What's the harm in making people laugh?" Mickey said. "It's one of the best things you can do for yourself, too. Besides, you got Pep's go ahead."

"Well, I . . ." She paused. "I didn't. I thought I should make my own decision."

"Do you think he'll mind?"

"About the show, I don't think so."

"So where's the problem?"

"I told you, Mickey, people can be cruel."

Mickey studied her with what seemed like great intensity, looking into her eyes. She turned away, hiding them from him. Maybe she was overreacting, she thought, allowing herself to be intimidated. Pep was never intimidated. Pep was afraid of nothing and no one. And Helen Reles was jealous. And it was Pep who made the suggestion. She felt as if she was winning the argument with herself, although she still held back.

"Maybe if we just rehearsed," Mickey pleaded. "You'll feel better and you'll still have time to change your mind."

"I'm not sure, Mickey."

"Don't you want to?"

"Very much." Their eyes locked again.

"Then do it. Be you."

He sang the last line, getting down on one knee.

Getting up, his eyes fixed on hers, he moved toward a table and made a make-believe telephone out of his hands. He made a ringing sound.

"Is Mr. Berkowitz in?" he said.

Mutzie smiled.

"I said, 'Is Mr. Berkowitz in?'"

Mutzie giggled, feeling as if a weight had been lifted. "No. This is Yom Kippur," she replied, as if it were a reflex.

"Well, when do you expect him, Miss Kippur?"

She laughed and Mickey made another ringing sound.

"Hello, is Mr. Berger in?" Mickey said.

"No. He's off to the United Kingdom," Mutzie replied.

"Oh my God. I'm sorry to hear that. Is it too late to send flowers?"

"See. See," Mickey said. "You're a natural. A trooper." Without missing a beat, Mickey said, "You want to hear a song I just composed?"

"What's the name of it?"

"Irving the Fork."

"Irving the Fork. What kind of a name is that for a song?"

"Mack the Knife did bad?"

Before she knew it, she was responding with perfect timing. They did the Sadie routine flawlessly. Then they did a parody of "Making Whoopee" and "Sam You Made the Pants Too Long."

"You'll knock 'em dead," Mickey said.

"Oh, Mickey, I do hope so," Mutzie said embracing Mickey in a friendly hug from which she quickly retreated.

They worked at rehearsing for two hours. It helped Mutzie finally to dispel her anxiety. It was silly to be upset. Pep will love her doing this, she decided, and she'd show him exactly what feeling happy can do.

"What'll I wear?" she asked.

"What've ya got?"

She described the various dresses that she had in her closet. Pep had bought her clothes that showed off her curvy figure. Low-cut dresses, spiked heels, some slacks outfits.

Mickey debated the various costumes she described.

"Come and look," she said, moving to the corridor.

"Maybe I shouldn't," Mickey said.

By then she was feeling stronger, less worried. Her heart and body were absolutely faithful to Pep. Surely Pep knew that. "Don't let 'em pushya around," Pep had told her countless times.

"Won't bother me."

She started up the stairs, eschewing the elevator, knowing that the help was not supposed to use the elevator. Mickey, obviously still frightened, followed a few feet behind. Mutzie and Pep's room was on the second floor overlooking the lake. She opened it and went in, leaving the door open. When he came in he didn't close it.

"There." she said, leading him to her closet. "You pick."

He studied her wardrobe carefully, then pulled out a white silk pantsuit with a flowing neckerchief under a large sailor collar with a blue ribbon trim.

"I saw Ruby Keeler wear one like that once in the movies," she said. "Too bad I dance like a klutz."

Mickey did a jumping heel click. "When do ships grow affectionate?" he asked.

"Give up," she said, having picked up his riddle timing.

"When they hug the shore."

She held her nose then held the pants outfit in front of her.

"Looks great," Mickey said. He smiled, winked and kissed her forehead. "Break a leg," he said.

At that moment, her eyes wandered to the open door of the room. In the doorway was the redheaded young man that she had seen working around the hotel. He lifted his hand in a mock salute and moved away. Seeing her eyes engaged, Mickey looked behind him.

But by then Irish was gone.

5

THEN IT WAS MICKEY FINE WHO WAS HAVING SECOND thoughts. Maybe he had gone too far with Mutzie. After all, she was Pep's girl. He must never forget that. But wasn't it Pep who suggested it?

He explored the logic in his own mind. Pep had commanded him to do a job. Make Mutzie happy. But the women's gossip was not making her happy. Therefore, Pep would blame him, and maybe because Mutzie was not being made happy, he might lose his job —which was to make people happy. Especially Mutzie.

The truth was that his being with Mutzie made him the happiest he had ever been in his life. But sirens sounded in his head. When Mutzie offered to back out, he should have accepted the offer.

Accept the reality, schmuck, he begged himself. Mutzie was nothing more than a bird in a gilded cage and he would forever be a spectator. From the moment he saw her, he had felt something break inside of him. Naturally, he resisted it. She was the girlfriend of Pittsburgh Phil Strauss, a ruthlesss gangster, a man with no conscience. He had seen him at work, seen his mean, sadistic streak. Thinking about it recalled the sensation of near-drowning he had had when he got the "toilet" treatment from Pep.

He believed all of the stories he had heard about Pep and his buddies, Kid Twist, Bugsy, Albert, Lepke, Costello and the others in the so-called combination. Gorlick's hotel was a goldmine of "inside" gossip. He heard it from the waiters, waitresses, chambermaids, busboys, even those guests who were not part of the extended family of these gangsters but enjoyed their proximity. To them, the gangsters were celebrities, invincible, even heroic, people whose influence on cops, judges and polticians prevented them from incurring any punishment for their actions.

It was in the air, an open secret, their exploits more than just whispered gossip. These boys from Brownsville and Ocean Hill didn't play around. Get in their way, they rubbed you out. In fact, that was their business. Murder Incorporated. You wanted someone wacked you got Bugsy Goldstein or Pep or Kid Twist or Dasher Abbandano or Tony Pro and they did the job with efficiency and dispatch. Pep, they said, was the best. He had a natural talent for killing. A quick job. Never left a clue. According to the whispers, the orders came from Albert Anastasia. He passed them down from guys like Lepke Buchalter or Frank Costello, who they called the Prime Minister, or leaders of other gangs in Detroit, Chicago or New Orleans.

As much as Mickey didn't want to listen, he heard. These gangsters had banded together after prohibition and had divided up the country. If someone that had not the approval of the bosses tried to muscle into territory, they called on the Brownsville boys and their Ocean Hill cohorts to do the job of getting rid of them.

It was no secret that they owned cops and judges and politicians. Judging from the clientele coming to Gorlick's, that seemed to be absolutely true. The sheriff of Sullivan County, where the Catskills were located, was a regular guest, as were cops and politicians from the city and the state. The Italians came, too.

They gambled on the slots or blackjack tables while their wives and girlfriends enjoyed the facilities. Gloria's girls were on call to do whatever guests required.

From his own observation of Kid Twist and Pep in the beating of his father and his own toilet ordeal, it was not hard to make the leap in his mind that these men were also vicious killers. Worse, they were killers for hire, which meant that they would kill without emotion, in cold blood. Like doing a show business gig, he thought. You do your act, walk off and collect your check.

Until Mickey first laid eyes on Mutzie, he was prepared to ignore whatever he heard about these people. It was none of his business. He was here to make people laugh, not pass judgment on anybody. But her association with Pep, the alleged cruelest killer of them all, made indifference impossible. How could such a beautiful dream girl consort with such a killer? The disconnect disturbed him deeply. He knew why it did, and it scared him.

Up until Pep made his offer to Mickey, he had barely uttered more than five words to Mutzie. Secretly, he watched her—studied her, in fact. He was always conscious of her presence. She had, he thought, a mysterious air about her, something exotic. She moved with such grace and elegance, just like Jean Harlow. There was no escaping the comparison. Everything about her called attention to the image. He had no illusions. She was far, far beyond his reach.

At first, he thought, he was being very clever in his secret observations. He knew the importance of not appearing the least bit interested. But she drew his gaze like a magnet. Unfortunately, his pose of indifference was not a clever enough ploy for the likes of Irish. Irish was a man with a score to settle.

"Stay off the grass, tumler," Irish had whispered to him one day when he was caught off guard staring at Mutzie as she sat near the lake reading a book. That was before Pep had asked him to make Mutzie happy.

"What the hell are you talking about, Irish?" he had muttered.

"You know," Irish had said, puckering his lips to kiss the air. "Put your eyes back in your head."

Often, when he was alone in his bed, he thought about Mutzie, inventing fantasy conversations with her.

"How can you possibly be involved with that killer?" he would ask her in his imagination.

"He'll kill me if I try to escape."

That satisfied him for a time, but what he suspected was that Mutzie was blindly in love with this killer.

"He's cruel and mean and has no heart. When he is finished with you, he will toss you in the garbage," he told her in his mind. This was a repetitive theme.

"I can't help myself," was her imaginary response.

"But I'll help you."

"I know."

"How can you go to bed with him? His hands are covered in blood and he has had many women. In fact, he probably has girl-friends everywhere. You are just one of a pack."

"I know, but I don't care."

"I'm someone who loves you," he would beg her in these conversations. He would burn inside and he felt the entire center of him yearning for her. It was an awful burden to bear, this strange feeling of both jealousy and devotion.

Which is why, when Pep confronted him that day when he was leaving, he felt that God had reached down and patted him on the tush. Go, my son, God might have said. Here's that little knish you're longing for. Surprise!

As he walked across the lobby the afternoon Irish saw him

with Mutzie, Gorlick, who had been talking to the desk clerk on duty, summoned him with a wave of his hand to follow him into his office. Gorlick waddled around his desk and sat down on his chair. Behind him were photographs of Gorlick's Greenhouse in various stages of remodeling. There were also photographs of Gorlick with famous celebrities. He spotted Gorlick and George Raft. Gorlick and Edward G. Robinson. Gorlick with Mayor Walker.

"What is rule one for a tumler?" Mr. Gorlick asked.

Mickey was puzzled, although he searched his mind for an answer. But before he could come up with one Gorlick answered his own question.

"To exercise extreme caution with one's schmuck," Gorlick said, his eyes staring in the general direction of the offending anatomy.

"Exactly what are you trying to say?" Mickey said, putting a great deal of energy into his sense of outrage. The so-called "word" about him and Mutzie had finally reached Gorlick. This was an irony since, above all, he had heeded Gorlick's advice in the face of great pressure and, in some cases, genuine temptation.

Helen Reles herself had broadly hinted her availability one day on the lake where he had taken her and her little boy for a sailboat ride. She sat close to him as he worked the rudder and the little boy in his life jacket sat on the prow of the little boat.

"You got a chippy, Mickey?" she asked, her hand resting lightly on his knee as if to support her from the gently heeling boat.

"Sometimes a shiksa. Never a chippy," he joked as Helen's hand began caressing his knee taking a detour toward his thigh.

"You should try a real Yiddish mama sometime," she told him, her hand roaming.

"I got one," he said. She snuggled closer and brought her lips up to his ear. He was certain she put her tongue in it.

"I can give you something you'll never forget."

Suddenly he moved the rudder abruptly as if it were an accident. Little Reles fell into the water and Helen screamed. But the boy remained afloat on the calm surface and Mickey jumped in to save him. He had also saved himself.

Similar situations had arisen in other cases as well. He had had experiences at Blumenkranz but here he was doubly careful. The fact was that he had taken Mr. Gorlick's admonition to heart and had no illusions about the consequences.

Of all people it was Marsha who made the situation crystal clear. One night he had seen her come out of the room of one of the male help, one of the sous-chefs, an ugly fat guy. Their eyes met and he must have shaken his head in some gesture of negative judgment. She followed him into his room.

"Ya tink I'm a dirty hooer, doncha, Mickey?"

"Not my business," he replied. He had always been polite with Marsha.

"I think of myself as a business person," she said hoarsely. "I gotta sick kid. I need the dough. What else have I got to sell? I need the extra. In this place, the help needs pussy. I'm the supply. You fuck with the guests, you get canned. Call me a safety valve."

Suddenly and inexplicably her eyes filled with tears and her shoulders shook. Mickey rose from the bed and embraced her.

"I hate myself, Mickey. I feel like dirt."

"I'm a tumler, Marsha. Not a rabbi. Everyone does what they have to do."

She pressed against him and he felt her hard, massive, unfettered breasts, but he felt no desire.

"I got feelings like evabody," she whispered finally as she

calmed down. He released her and she rubbed her eyes with the back of her hand.

"Yaw a good boy, Mickey. Ya treat me nice. That Irish, he got it in for you."

"Does Carter make liver pills?" Mickey said. "I cleaned his clock."

"Irish, he's like a watchdog." She tapped her nose. "It don matter. He wants to make trouble, he makes it."

"Dog, you said?" Mickey retorted, determined to lift the mood. "Man says to a psychiatrist, 'I just can't stop believing I'm a dog.' 'When did that start,' the doctor asks. 'When I was a puppy,' the man says."

Marsha giggled, her mood brightening. He felt good too. Always for the underdog, he thought, shrugging.

"I got some good ones too, Mickey," she said.

"Like what?"

"Man says, 'I'm having an affair.' 'Yeah?' the other man says. 'Who's catering it?'"

"Old, but still funny," Mickey said. "Know this one? You know why a Jewish American Princess closes her eyes when she makes love?"

Marsha laughed, her tits shaking. "Cause she don want to see him having a good time."

"You give me an idea, Marsha. Sometimes I need a shill. You know, when I do a routine in the dining room, I throw you a joke. You throw back an answer." He looked at her, watched her smile happily. "I throw you a buck or two for the gig."

She studied him from head to toe.

"I like ya, Mickey," throwing him a kiss. "Anytime ya want a freebee." Then she smiled coquetiishly, lifted her dress, showed her behind, then shimmied out of the room.

Not his cup of tea, he decided. What she did with Irish was

a turnoff. Still, he was only human. But he was too embarrassed to go to any of Gloria's whorehouses in the area. At times, he did take extraordinary measures, tumeling with himself.

"Stand up one more time and I'll beat you again," he often told his erection. And did. Laughing helped. But nothing helped his fantasizing about Mutzie. Nothing could assuage his yearning. For him, it was a new kind of suffering, and just a glimpse of her in person was enough to satisfy him for a time, calm his insistent heart. Forbidden love. He tried to joke that one away as well, but couldn't.

"You want me to draw you a picture?" Gorlick asked. He was, Mickey could see, dead serious.

"If you're talking about me and Strauss's lady friend, you're wrong. Mr. Strauss wants me to amuse her during the week." He did not say make her happy. "In fact, it was an order and, considering his reputation, I would not think it wise to disobey Mr. Strauss's orders."

Mickey's aggressive defense seemed to take Gorlick by surprise.

"He told you to come up to her room?" Gorlick asked.

"Irish," Mickey mumbled bitterly. "He just wants to make trouble."

"Not only Irish," Gorlick said. Virtue apparently had no rewards, he sighed. He saw the fine hand also of Helen Reles and the others he had rejected. He wanted to tell Gorlick this, but he decided against it.

"We're only doing a show together," Mickey said, determined not to be convicted for a crime uncommitted. He searched his mind for a joke to lighten the moment, but none came. Mr. Gorlick shook his head sadly.

"For your own sake, I gotta fire you."

A hot flush passed over Mickey's face. His throat constricted and his voice rose an octave.

"You can't do that. It's a lie. I wouldn't touch that girl. Not Mr. Strauss' girl. Never."

Mickey felt a surge of hysteria run through him. His heart pounded and he felt helpless.

"I'm sorry, kiddo," Gorlick said. "You were a good tumler. I'll have to find another one in a hurry."

"You can't do this. I'm completely innocent," Mickey protested, growing desperate for an idea to save the situation. "I'm gonna call Strauss," he said.

"Are you crazy?" Gorlick exploded. "You don't know those people."

"I'll tell him that what you're doing will upset his girlfriend."

"You think he'll care. All he needs is one hint that you're doing his girl and you've got big troubles. It's for your own good I'm doing this."

"My own good?" Mickey cried. When was the last time you did anything for anyone else's good, Mickey thought, but his mind was turning over quickly, figuring angles. He was determined not to be driven out by lies and innuendo. "I got a proposition, Mr. Gorlick."

"I need this," Gorlick said looking at the ceiling.

"Give me until the weekend," Mickey said.

"Sonny, you'll never last through the weekend," Gorlick said.

"We'll let Mr. Strauss be the judge," Mickey said, but he was already considering his fallback position. He was going to fight this. And Mutzie would stand by him. Surely, Mr. Strauss would believe Mutzie.

"You want to keep her in your show, too?" Gorlick asked.

"Absolutely," Mickey said. "She's rehearsed. The guests will love it. And it's only one night."

Gorlick tapped his desk and studied Mickey, then he shook his head in despair.

"You're a nut, Fine," Gorlick said. Mickey was relieved.

"And you're a wonderful humanitarian, Mr. Gorlick," Mickey said, back now in his tumler mode. Jokes started to resurface again in his mind. He started to leave Gorlick's office, then came back. "What do you get when you cross a penis, a potato and an ocean liner?"

"I'm not in the mood, tumler."

"A dictatorship," Mickey said. Gorlick's nostrils quivered. A brief spasm of a laugh erupted lightly in his mouth.

"See, Mr. Gorlick," Mickey said. "Funny makes people brothers."

"That was funny?" Gorlick grumbled, studying Mickey, who felt his scrutiny. "Write your will, putz."

Mickey did not tell Mutzie about his near-firing by Gorlick, nor anything of their conversation. During the dinner hour, he made his usual joking rounds with the guests, cajoling the older women, many of them aunts or mothers of men connected with the Brownsville boys.

"I see you left your grandchildren in the city," he told them.

The response was invariably an effusive showing of pictures by the guests.

"So what do you do for aggravation?" he asked.

They laughed. They liked Mickey Fine. He felt it. They loved the games he organized, especially Simon Sez by lakeside every morning, his stand-up routines, even his funny announcements of the day's activities during every meal.

During the week, he was certain he had found the rhythm of the place. He knew what jokes to tell to whom. He had to be extremely careful not to cross the line, although he knew the women truly loved a dirty joke. And teasing sexuality was essential. Away from their men, they were barracudas, and he had become expert in, as Gorlick had warned, keeping his schmuck out of harm's way.

"Tonight I've got a song that spans the generations," he would tell the girls. "It's dedicated to Mae West. I've got the son in the morning and the father at night."

The men liked cruder, often scatological, humor, especially the roughest of the Brownsville boys. These jokes he told only privately. They would be very upset if he told them in front of their women.

"What's the best thing comes out of shmekel when you stroke it?"

"Awright, what?"

"The wrinkles."

Howls of laughter.

"Hear about the waitress scratching her ass when the intern was about to order?"

No comment.

"'You got hemorrhoids,' the intern asked. 'Hey,' the waitress said. 'No special orders.'"

Howls of laughter.

"You hear about the three old ladies sitting on a park bench? A man sits down and exposes himself. 'Oy,' two of the women said. 'I'm having a stroke.' The third woman couldn't. It was too far to reach."

Sometimes he would whisper the jokes in the guests' ears. They loved that, their own private tumler.

Behind the jokes, his heart and mind were filled with feelings and thoughts of Mutzie. It was a private agony and proved the saying about clowns being sad under their painted smiles.

6

MUTZIE LAY ON A RECLINED BEACH CHAIR BY THE LAKE-side sunning herself. Her eyes were closed. Beside her Pep played pinnocle with Bugsy Goldstein and Kid Twist. In the distance, she could hear the voices of the children splashing in the water and the hum of distant conversation.

They were off to one side, away from the bulk of the weekend crowd. She realized that she must have looked asleep, but she was very much awake, recalling events, relieved that Pep had seemed to be so understanding.

He had been in upstate New York all week.

"On a job," he told her. She could, of course, tell he had been on a job by the way he acted sexually. It proved to her that he had been faithful. He was obviously starved and demanding and she did her best to provide him what he needed, tried extra hard. She wanted him to know how happy she was, how happy the tumler had made her.

Between their furious sexual bouts, when he was still and satiated, she had told him about the show and the applause. She even told him some of the jokes from the show. He laughed, but she could tell that his thoughts were elsewhere.

She tried to find out if anyone had whispered those rumors about her and Mickey to him. Apparently they hadn't and she didn't think it wise to bring up the subject. After a job was always a delicate time for Pep. He needed lots of sex, in lots of different ways, and she had learned what gave him the most pleasure.

"Good?" she asked him after each time he had an orgasm.

"Yaw gettin real good at this stuff, Mutzie," he told her.

"Just like you taught me, Pep."

"Pep's the Professor, right, baby?"

Nodding, she snuggled her body against his and kissed his chest and played with his hair.

She knew that no matter how enthusiastic she appeared, she was now acting mechanically, fighting away a tide of disgust. How did it come to this? The only way to cope was to imagine herself as disembodied, someone else, not Miriam Feder from Brownsville. Not the real Mutzie Feder.

By Saturday morning Pep had calmed down and they got up and put on their bathing suits and bathrobes. The waiters brought their lunch to the lakeside and she lay on the lounge to sun herself.

"Sumbitch wouldn't quit," she heard Pep say in a low voice.

"Tough case, eh, Pep." It was Kid Twist's voice.

"I swear he had his heart on da wrong side. Musta picked him ten, twenty times and he was still squirming."

"Happens," Bugsy said. "Memba Porgy Schwartz? Finally had ta rope him 'till his eyes bugged."

"Anyway, I got him," Pep said. "And Tony D in Albany. One pop through the temple and he was down."

"And Marty Katz?"

"He shit his pants. I tink he died befaw I roped him." Pep laughed. "On his knees, he begged. I hadda listen ta all dat crap."

"Tree in a row, Pep," Kid Twist said. "I wish I been with ya."

"Some ya do by yaw lonesome. Some ya need help."

"We're gonna need help with yaknowwho if we getta go," Kid Twist said. "Two ana wheelman ta help. Dumb bastard. Skimmin is da woist. Greediness. Will do it all da time. Albert's comin in tomorrow, along with Frank. We have a meet, we get da woid."

"Shit, you guys get all da fun."

They paused for a moment, apparently continuing their card game. Mutzie found herself listening, although she feigned sleep. She tried to tune out the words, but couldn't. Was this about killing? she wondered, dismissed the thought, then wondered again.

"Feget the chippy," Kid Twist said.

"Ya sleepin, Mutzie?" Pep asked. When she didn't answer he said, "Snow wonder. Fucked huh brains out last night. Musta come six, seven times."

"Me an Helen did triples," Reles said. "One in da mout, one in da ass, one in da same old." He suddenly roared with laughter.

"Shut up, ya wake the knish, Kid."

Such talk was nauseating. It was an abomination. Not that she hadn't heard it before, but now it caused her to approach a new level of disgust and self-loathing. Above all, she hated for Pep to count the times. Six, seven times was downright bragging. Besides, she felt no pleasure in it any more. None at all.

"Evything ready faw da big sitdown tonight?" Pep asked. "Gonna be a real shindig."

"Helen made all da arrangements. Gorlick promised a real fancy dinner." Reles paused. "And a real surprise for a show."

"Surprise?" Pep said.

Mutzie tensed.

"Yeah, sumpin real special, Helen says. Right, Mutz?"

Mutzie froze, showing no reaction. Her heart jumped to her throat.

"Needs huh rest," Pep said. "Aftah last night."

She heard the men's laughter, then Pep said, "We gotta get some quiff faw Albert," Reles said. "He's always horny. Not Frank. He don eat out."

"I'll call Gloria," Bugsy said.

"I gotta betta idear," Pep said.

"What?" Bugsy asked.

"My call," Pep said. "Nothin but the best for Albert. Hell, he's done the best for us, ain't he?"

There was a long silence after that and she heard only the flapping and shuffling of the cards and the alien talk of the game of pinochle, which she didn't understand, and finally she did go to sleep.

Dinner was special, very fancy, and Gorlick hovered around them as if they were celebrities—which to him they were. The table was set with gleaming silver and shiny plates and situated in a spot opposite French doors, through which they could see the lights from the structures on the edge of the lake and the over-head lights of the pier.

Two waiters and waitresses were assigned to them, so the service was lightning fast. Around the table were silver buckets filled with ice and champagne, which was poured into long trumpet glasses. Not everybody drank champagne, however— Mr. Buchalter and his wife drank red wine. Pep, Mr. Anastasia and Mr. Costello drank scotch. Although both of the Italians had families, they never brought their wives to social occasions that were outside the family. Their bodyguards, steely-eyed goombas, stood around trying, unsuccessfully, to be unobtrusive. Some waited outside.

Walter Gage, who they called Gagie, drank nothing but water. Mutzie had met him at the corner in Brownsville and Pep had mentioned that he had been sent up to Sullivan County to run the rackets.

"Nobody more honest than Gagie," Pep had said. Reles and he were particularly close, as Pep had explained.

"Dey been kids togedda. Been in da can in Elmira togedda."

"Asshole buddies, huh, Pep," Bugsy had commented.

Gagie was a chubby, teddy bear kind of guy who said little. When he did speak, his words came in the form of a twinkly wise crack, and when he looked at Mutzie he would always give her a smile and a wink.

She felt every guest's eyes on their table and, despite her growing misgivings, she felt proud that she was with the handsomest one of them all. Pep wore a brand new suit that he had brought up with him for the weekend, a crisp white shirt and a beautiful silk tie. She held his hand under the table and felt the glow of being part of such important company.

On her right was Mr. Anastasia, a dark complexioned man with a cute smile and eyes that were dark and searching. He was very polite and seemed to hang on her every word, which surprised her since she didn't think what she had to say was very interesting at all.

Mostly everybody talked about the heat in the city, which had hit the high nineties, and whether the Chicago White Sox would ever catch the New York Yankees for the pennant. Pep said he was disgusted that the Dodgers played such lousy ball, but Reles, who was a Giants fan, wanted to bet anyone that the Giants would win although they were six games behind and it was unlikely they could catch the Cubs for the pennant.

"I'll take that ten to one," Gagie said.

"That's a putz bet," Reles said. Gagie looked at Mutzie and winked.

She didn't know much about baseball, but when they got to the movies she was an expert and she was surprised to find that even Mr. Anastasia had seen *Wee Willie Winkie*.

"I like da way da kid dances and sings. Cute as a button."

"A Shirley Temple fan," Mutzie exclaimed, looking at Pep. "Mr. Anastasia likes Shirley Temple."

"Please," Albert said. "Call me Albert."

"And I'm Miriam. But my friends call me Mutzie."

"Albert also likes Jean Harlow, don't you Albert?" Pep said winking. "Looks like dis little knish heah, don ya tink?"

"I lika dis one, Pep," Albert said.

"What Albert likes Albert gets," Pep said. "Don he, Mutzie?"

She was confused by his remark, but nodded. Sometimes the men talked in a kind of code known only to themselves and she had gotten used to merely smiling or nodding her head in acknowledgement. Abie Reles, who sat between Mr. and Mrs. Buchalter, spoke in low tones and it was difficult to hear what was being said, although Mrs. Buchalter told everyone that she was leaving "to take the waters" in Europe, which sounded very worldly and exciting.

"Ya come back a new poison," Mr. Buchalter said. "Youse should all do it someday."

They were served chopped liver, sweet and sour stuffed cabbage and mushroom and barley soup. Then came stuffed roast turkey, carved right there at the table by the chef himself, candied yams, peas, asparagus and delicious biscuits.

"No butter, Albert. Strictly Kosher Jew food," Reles said.

"I was lookin for the pasta vazoo," Albert said chuckling, showing a set of bright, even teeth.

"Schmuck chef neva hoid a it," Reles said. "I tole him I break his knees he don make pasta vazoo. So he tries ta get veal parmesan past the rabbi. Ya know that's milkik and flashik. Rabbi back dere in da kitchen has a shit hemorrhage."

"Every religion gotta have respect," Costello said. "Hebew, Catolic, whatever."

"Catolic's a good religion," Pep said. "Cept don like confessions."

Albert, Costello and Gagie burst into laughter. Albert doubled up and tears came into his eyes.

"In the Catskills in July you can call it a Jewish Thanksgiving, right, Abie?" Mrs. Reles said.

"An we got a lot ta be thankful for," Lepke Buchalter said. "We got organization, good friends evywhere." He winked and smiled. "Especially in da government." There was a wave of chuckling laughter. "On da bench."

"In da cops," Albert said, still wiping his eyes.

"In da cops," Mr. Buchalter repeated. "Da unions. Da shmata bosses. Da bakers and dere bosses. Da ponies. Da numbers. Da banks." He looked at Gagie. "And right here in da Catskills tanks to Gagie."

Gagie blushed.

"He's doin one helluva job up heah, ain't he, Albert?"

"Da best." Albert looked toward Gagie and raised his glass. The others did the same.

"To the king of the Catskills," Albert said, drinking. The others did the same.

"We wuz smart sending him up heah, right, Frank?"

"We used our, how ya say, tuk ass," Frank said, pointing to his temple.

"Tuchas, Frank," Bugsy Goldstein said. "And yaw pointin to da wrong place."

Frank Costello howled with laughter and the others did the same.

"So we gotta lot ta be thankful faw, Lep," Reles said.

"America is a good place," Anastasia said. He raised his glass of scotch and everybody raised their own, turned to their neighbor and clinked.

"Da best," Mr. Buchalter said, winking. "Except faw dose bums La Guardia and Dewey. Dey gonna try ta make trouble and we gotta handle it right. Da Tammany boys are running scairt."

"No cojones, Lep?" Albert said. "We gotta lotta woik ta do."

"Sumbitch little flowa, dat La Guardia. Refawma, he calls hissef," Reles said. "Ya know his mudder was a Jew broad from Italy."

"We gotta loin him a lesson," Albert said.

"We ain't afraid of dose punks," Reles said. "Say da woid and we give 'em a trip ta Canarsie."

"Canarsie? Hell, we got lots a good lakes up heah," Gagie said.

There was a moment of embarrassed silence. Costello turned toward Gagie and seemed to give him an angry look of authority. Mutzie felt a moment of extreme tension come over the group. Reles covered his mouth and looked at the ceiling.

"I nevah said nothin, Frank," Gagie croaked. "What I meant was it's da beauty up heah, da hills and da lakes. Ya know what I mean?"

"Sure, Gagie, we know," Albert said.

"I mean I love dis area," Gagie continued.

"Sure you do, Gagie," Abie said patting his arm. "And we love ya ta love dis place, right, Frank?"

Costello blinked and a thin smile formed on his lips. The tension abated.

"I nevah had chopped liver at Thanksgiving," Anastasia murmured, and the festive air returned as people concentrated on their food and talked to their partners.

"So did you see *Saratoga* with Clark Gable and Jean Harlow?" Mutzie asked Albert. Pep had made it a point while they were dressing that she was to be especially nice to Mr. Anastasia. Albert, he told her, was a very important man and it was absolutely necessary that he enjoy every minute of his stay at Gorlick's. After dinner they were going to have a meeting and Albert and Mr. Costello were staying overnight.

"I ain't seen dat one yet," Albert said, smiling down at her as he ate his food. Conversation buzzed around the table and she could see that the people in the dining room continued to stare at them like they were royalty.

As they were finishing their turkey, Mickey Fine came to the table and introduced himself as the social director of the hotel, saying how honored he was by their company.

"I'm the tumler," he said.

"Not only that," Helen Reles said looking pointedly at Mutzie. Mickey ignored her remark and looked at Albert.

"Anyway I hope you enjoy your stay at Gorlick's. I hope Garlic didn't give you a room in which you stand up and a chain hits you on the head."

"He means da crapper," Albert said, laughing.

"He's really very funny," Mutzie said, winking at Mickey. "Some of the time."

"Well, I hope you all enjoyed the meal, folks," Mickey said.

"If there's any more I'll bust," Mrs. Buchalter said.

"Busting is absolutely prohibited. Not until after dessert," Mickey said.

Mr. Gorlick had come up behind him with a nervous look on his face. Mickey, seeing his look, retreated and started making rounds of the other tables.

"Is everything all right, folks?" Gorlick asked.

Mr. Buchalter made the everything's perfect sign with his fingers and Mr. Costello nodded. It was, of course, understood that they were going to have an important meeting later, but as far as Mutzie could make out there was absolutely no more talk of business and everybody behaved perfectly.

During dessert, Mickey got up and announced that the show that night would feature a special performance by him and a surprise guest. He looked toward the table where Mutzie was sitting. Helen caught Mutzie's eye and winked.

Mickey was the master of ceremonies. There was always a singer who belted out Tin Pan Alley songs and a small musical combo. The singer was so-so, but the audience was polite and reasonably attentive.

Then Mickey made his surprise announcement and Mutzie stood up. There was a round of applause.

"Ya nevah tole me," Pep said. He seemed angry but Mutzie wasn't sure.

"It's a surprise, like the tumler said, Pep," Mutzie said.

"Ya shoulda tole me."

"They were together rehearsing all week," Helen said, directing her remark to Pep.

"And he made me real happy," Mutzie said pointedly.

"I'll bet," Helen Reles said, shooting Pep a sarcastic glance.

Mutzie shrugged and walked up to the little stage.

"She's a looka," she heard Albert say. "I like dat, Pep."

"I'm very nervous," Mutzie told Mickey when she reached the stage.

"You'll be great," Mickey told her. She took a deep breath and steadied herself. She would show Pep how happy he had made her.

"Break a leg," he whispered.

"Hope that's all I break."

They began their rapid-fire routine. Mickey looked at Mutzie and began.

"Waiter, what's this fly doing in my soup?"

"Looks like the backstroke to me."

The audience laughed and Mutzie and Mickey gave them more and more. Their timing was flawless. Then Mutzie did a Jessel routine Mickey had taught her.

"Mama, how do you like the love bird I bought for the front room? What? You cooked it? You cooked a South American bird? A bird that speaks five languages? Oh, you didn't know. He should have said something."

The audience was in stitches and they continued their routines. Mutzie was no longer nervous. She looked at Pep, whose shoulders shook with laughter. Albert Anastasia was hysterical. Helen Reles looked unhappy.

"Darling, I dreamed last night you bought me a mink coat," Mutzie said. She felt that they were on a roll.

"That's nice. Next time you dream wear it in good health," Mickey said. More jokes followed to thunderous applause.

Their parody of "Makin' Whoopee," in which Mickey imitated Eddie Cantor and Mutzie made cute faces and acted as a foil was a great closer. He sang and she acted the coquette:

Now this place has the atmosphere
For little girls—who have no fear
For in the nighttime, why that's the right time
For makin Etzele, Petzele, Gaggele, Googele, Etzele,
Petzele Zetz
For in the morning, you wake up yawning
From all the whoopee you made till dawning.

The audience roared.

Mutzie came back to the table and Pep embraced her. Albert did the same.

"Ain't she sumpin," Pep said.

"Betta believe. And I loved da boy, too," Albert said. He looked over at Gorlick, who was grinning with pleasure. "You gotta good one here, Gorlick."

"They went together like cream cheese and jelly," Helen said so that they could all hear.

When they had settled down, the waiters served coffee and brandy. They lifted their glasses to a number of toasts. Suddenly, Mutzie felt Albert Anastasia touch her knee with his. Her leg froze. She didn't know what to do. She looked at Pep who was busy talking to Mr. Costello. She felt Albert's entire calf rubbing up against her.

Careful not to make a scene, she kept her leg frozen next to Albert's and tugged Pep's sleeve. He stopped talking to Costello and turned toward Mutzie, who forced her lips into a smile. As he rubbed Mutzie's leg with his, Albert talked to Bugsy's wife, who was sitting next to him.

"My leg," she whispered. "He's rubbing my leg."

"Good," Pep whispered back. "Rub him back."

"But Pep . . ."

"Anyting he wants, capish?"

She didn't know what to do. She looked around helplessly, but she did not rub him back. When he finished talking to Mrs. Goldstein, he turned back to Mutzie.

"Pep says yaw quite a girlie," Albert said.

"Me and Pep are, you know . . ." She had trouble getting the words out.

"So I heah," Albert said. "That's good. Pep got good taste."

His hand ducked under the table and grasped her thigh. An icy tremor shot through her. Her chest constricted and her breath seemed to come in gasps. But Albert's hand continued busily.

"I have to go to the ladies' room," she announced suddenly.

Albert squeezed her upper thigh.

"Hurry back," he said, winking. When he released her, she got up.

Her legs felt unsteady as she walked across the dining room. She was confused, unable to understand what was happening. Pep had told her to rub Albert back. What did that mean? He had promised, hadn't he? She was his, only his. She felt all eyes scrutinizing her as if she were naked. When she reached the lobby, she started toward the ladies' room. But before she could push open the door, she felt a hand on her shoulder pulling her back. It was Pep. He put his arm under hers and walked her out to the porch. It was a chilly night and that section of the porch was deserted. She immediately fell into his arms.

"Oh, Pep," she cried. "I was so scared."

"You my numba one?" Pep said. He gave her a deep soul kiss. After the kiss he said, "You was great wit dem jokes. Albert loved it."

"He got fresh, Pep. I didn't know what to do."

"I'm gonna tell ya. You'll do anyting for Pep, won't ya, baby?"

"Oh, Pep you know that," she said. Her fear was accelerating and her legs were wobbly.

"Anyting Pep wants you to do, right?"

He was kissing her neck and she felt his tongue slip into her ear. Her reaction was disgust. At that moment she heard movement on the porch. Pep stopped kissing her and shouted into the darkness.

"Get da fuck outa here."

From her vantage Mutzie caught a brief glimpse of a person. Mickey Fine. What was he doing here? Pep was turned in another direction and couldn't see him.

"Putz," Pep muttered.

The interruption seemed to change his mood. He grabbed Mutzie by the shoulders and looked into her face.

"Ya gonna be nice ta Albert tonight, Mutzie," Pep said. "Ya gonna do dis for ole Pep, unnerstand?"

"I am being nice to him, Pep," she said, her heart beating in sudden panic.

"I mean real nice, baby. I want ya should be Pep's present to Albert."

"I don't understand, Pep," Mutzie said fearing the worst.

"I gotta draw ya a pitcher?" Pep said, squeezing her shoulders. "I want ya ta show him all da stuff Pep taught ya. The good stuff. I want ya ta make Albert feel real good."

"You mean . . ." She could barely talk. "Pep. You promised. I can't do that."

"This don't count, Mutz. This is just business. Ain't got nothing to do wit you and me. He's onea da important bosses and he done good tings faw me and I gotta show respeck."

"I can't, Pep. Please, Pep. I can't. I want to be true to you, Pep."

She was pleading, begging, knowing that a reprieve was impossible.

"And ya betta be, Mutz. Ya betta. Hear me good. But dis fava has nothin to do wit you and me. Nothin. It's like . . . like I'm giving da boss a box of candy." He laughed suddenly at his joke.

"Please, Pep." She felt a sob begin deep inside her. "What about respect for me?"

"I respeck ya maw, ya do dis for me, Mutz. Shows yaw true love."

Love? The word has lost all meaning. She wanted to run as far away from this place as her feet could carry her. That was a hopeless dream.

"I can't, Pep. Please. You can't . . ." She felt him stiffen and she could feel him suck in a deep breath. He jabbed her chestbone hard.

"Now you listen, girlie. I want ya to fuck him, fuck him good. Give him anyting he wants. Youse my gift to Albert. Ya hold back and I getta bad report, we got problems, Mutzie."

Her body seemed to dissolve, and with it any shred of dignity. He was passing her around like the lowest kind of whore.

"I can't, Pep," she mumbled, but her courage was failing. Escape was impossible. She was trapped. Worse, she felt she deserved this fate. She had brought it on herself.

"No can'ts," Pep said, menacingly, putting a hand over her mouth. "No ifs. No buts. No talk." He raised a finger and waved it in front of her nose. "Ya wanna stay Pep's numba one, ya fuck Albert Anastasia tonight. Ya fuck him good. He don come down smiling, ya gonna be sorry."

She tried to shake her head in the negative, but he held it steady with one hand over her mouth and the other tightly grasping her chin. She felt helpless, humiliated, degraded. No, she decided, this is only a movie. We are acting out this scene. It is not real. Pep couldn't do this to his number one. Not Pep.

"Ya make Pep look bad, den ya say goodbye to dis pretty little face, got it? And that ain't all." He removed his hand from her chin and grabbed at her crotch. She squirmed in pain. "You ain't nevah seen what a baseball bat can do."

She closed her eyes. Hot tears brimmed over her cheeks. She felt utterly defeated as a person.

"Ya fuck who I tell ya to fuck, Mutzie. You're my numba one private stock. I catch you givin it away to somebody that ain't got Pep's okay, ya go into the shitter."

She swallowed to keep down her food, trying to focus on his words. Sudden she found herself dealing with one issue . . . survival.

"Now I'm gonna take my hand away from yaw mout and yaw gonna smile and give ole Pep one big kiss, ain't ya." She swallowed but did not give him any sign of consent. "Ain't ya," he repeated. She nodded. She was beyond resisting.

Slowly he released his hand over her mouth and pressed his lips to hers. She felt his tongue slide in and she tried her best to respond, afraid that any lack of response would make him do something terrible to her.

"Dat's my goil," Pep said. "Now ya take dat sweet liddle tush ta da ladies' room and get yourself lookin good and smellin nice faw Albert." He released her and she started to move toward the door, fighting with her legs, which tried to resist her movement.

"And Mutzie," he said. She stopped, obeying instantly, frightened, hoping she could hold her food down. "I wanna see ya smile, baby."

With effort, she turned and forced her lips to form a smile.

"Ats my numba one," Pep said.

She managed to reach the ladies' room, where she bent over

the toilet bowl and threw up. Then she washed and looked at herself in the mirror. Her eyes were swollen and tears had streaked her makeup. She no longer felt like a person. She wanted to leave this place, go home, disappear. But she knew that was impossible. Pep would find her and he would do those awful things that he had threatened. How had she come to this? She cursed her naïveté, her stupidity, her ignorance.

She washed her face, repaired her makeup and brushed her hair. Surely, there was some way out of this. Unless Pep was just playacting, which he sometimes did in their lovemaking. Once he had tied her up hands and legs and made all kinds of terrible threats and it had excited him greatly. But, of course, he had warned her in advance that it was only a game. What was happening now was definitely not a game.

Or maybe it was just a test of her loyalty. Maybe the idea was to prove her loyalty and her love for Pep by obeying his command. These Brownsville boys had a strange code of loyalty. Loyalty was an important consideration to these men, and the quality they valued most. So this was just a test, she told herself, a test to prove that she was Pep's girl, his number one.

The thought made her feel somewhat better and she was able to muster her strength and return to the dining room. The table was filled with bottles, glasses and cookies. Pep watched her as she came forward.

"Long time no see," he said as she slid primly into her seat. Albert looked up at her and smiled and immediately placed his leg next to hers and his hand on her thigh. She looked up at Pep, smiled, and put her hand on Albert's thigh. Had she any choice in the matter?

Jean Harlow would consider it all an act. If Jean Harlow could, why couldn't she?

7

E XCITEMENT RAN THROUGH THE DINING ROOM LIKE AN
electric charge. The big boys were at the hotel. Frank
Costello, Albert Anastasia and Lepke Buchalter, the
three biggest fish of all.

Naturally everybody was nervous. Mickey was doubly nervous since Mutzie was in their company, which only increased his
jealousy and his revulsion. How could such a beautiful, sweet
person be in the company of those gangsters?

His anger made him short-tempered and he had to fight with
himself to be funny. Gorlick had told him to skip their table on his
nightly round of tumeling, but he could not resist the temptation
to be there, as if to show Mutzie that he was alive, a somebody
in his own right. She had smiled and winked at him, a friendly
gesture, but it also told him that apparently all was well and that
Mr. Strauss did not believe the rumors about Mutzie and him
carrying on.

"You see," Mickey told Gorlick after the show with Mutzie.
"No problem."

"So far."

"Everybody loved it. And they loved Mutzie. She's a natural.

153

All the big boys. You saw. Anastasia was in stitches. Lepke and Costello loved it, and those boys don't smile much." He paused and searched Gorlick's face. "So I stay?"

"So far," Gorlick said again. "Doesn't mean people won't talk. That Helen Reles didn't look too happy."

"She's just a gossip."

He did not tell Gorlick about her advances.

Everybody knew that a big meeting was in the offing and there was considerable speculation among the help. The combination controlled all the rackets in Sullivan County: the gambling, the prostitution, the shylocking . . . everything. Something very important must be happening.

He made his usual after-dinner announcement about the events for the next day, including the Simon Sez session and other events for the kids.

"And folks," he thought of saying. "We have here the top crooks and gangsters in the nation. The inimitable Frank Costello, the mob celebrities Albert Anastasia and Lepke Buchalter and those fabulous killers Pittsburgh Phil, Kid Twist and Bugsy Goldstein."

As he spoke, he saw Mutzie rise and leave the table. She looked strangely troubled and unhappy. It could be his imagination, he decided, but he could not chase the idea from his mind.

Then he saw Pep get up and leave the table as if to follow her. He, too, looked as if something was wrong and it filled Mickey with anxiety. Maybe Helen Reles made some remark that had set things off. Or Mutzie had suffered some kind of intimidation or insult. What was it his business? he rebuked himself. Who was he? Her self-appointed protector? But he could not chase the feeling.

Unable to restrain himself, he followed Strauss when he left the dining room. But when he got to the lobby, he saw no one.

Then, suddenly, he saw them. The tall man seemed to be forcing her to walk with him, holding her unnaturally under the arm as if she were resisting him. Mickey quickly ducked behind a pillar in the lobby and watched them move out through one of the French doors to the porch.

His instincts had definitely been correct. Something was awry, rousing his sense of panic and danger. He came to the French door and eased it open. They were only a few yards away, slightly hidden in the shadows. They were locked in a tight embrace, which surprised him, and then he felt embarrassed over his proprietary interest in her welfare. She was, after all, another man's woman. He had no right to interfere. Still, observing them for a moment, the embrace seemed unnatural, although he didn't know why. A tremor of jealousy shot through him. How could she? A involuntary groan escaped from him. Pep raised his head, turned toward him and squinted into the darkness.

"Get da fuck outa here," he cried.

Mickey stood still and moved deeper into the darkness. He didn't think Pep had recognized him, and something compelled him to remain. Instead of going back through the French doors, he opened and closed them then flattened himself against the wall and hid in the shadows. He watched them, not daring to breathe. In the cool silent night air, their voices carried.

He could not make out every word, but the gist of it was clear. A chill shot through him. His lips chattered. His stomach knotted. What he heard horrified him, filled him with anger and loathing. She was to be passed around like a piece of meat. It was sadistic and inhuman. Don't, Mutzie, he pleaded silently. Don't let them do this to you.

They walked by him on their way back to the lobby, passing within barely inches as they moved through the French doors. He could smell her perfume. He wanted to strike out at this terrible man for what he was doing to Mutzie. Fortunately, he resisted the compulsion, but he resolved that he must find a way to get her out of Pep's clutches.

But resolve was one thing, execution another. He felt totally helpless. Too upset to eat, he could not go back into the dining room. It would be impossible for him to muster any humor. Behind the dining room were the gambling rooms with their rows of shiny slot machines and two tables, one for craps and the other for blackjack. The dealers and supervisor were quietly chatting and smoking in a corner of the room.

He waved to them, forcing a smile, but he had no desire to talk to them. Instead he moved through the casino to the private room reserved for high-stakes card games or high-level meetings. On one end of the room was a long oblong polished mahogany table. On the other was a grouping of leather furniture, a couch and three easy chairs.

He had often come here to relax on the couch during the day when he didn't feel like taking the long walk to his room. He threw himself face down on the couch. He wanted to cry. In fact, when he blinked, moisture dripped from his eyes onto the couch. If he was crying, it was out of anger, frustration and despair. Poor Mutzie. Poor him for loving her. Why couldn't he be indifferent, unaffected?

The fact was that there was no way to intrude. He would only make it worse for her. He tried to imagine himself confronting these gangsters, fighting them with the only weapon he felt strong enough to muster, moral courage. He snickered at his naïveté. Moral courage? Raise his hand to protect her, even his voice, and they would crucify him. From what he had heard and what he had seen with his own eyes, they were capable of the most cruel acts.

Hadn't he just watched Strauss show Mutzie a painful hint of what he had in store for her if she didn't obey him?

His mind raced for solutions. None came. Then, suddenly, he was aware of voices in the room. It was not long before he recognized them. Although he could not see them, they were obviously seated around the table. This was the business meeting that was the real reason for them getting together. The back of the couch faced the table. As long as he was still, they could not see him. But if one of them rose and walked to that end of the room, he would be visible.

For the first few moments of the meeting, he was too frightened to make sense out of their voices. Then it occurred to him that if he was suddenly discovered, even now with the meeting just begun, his life wouldn't be worth a plug nickel. Above all, he urged himself, he must stay calm, tamp down hysteria, keep his wits about him, think of this chance encounter as an opportunity. He heard laughter in his mind as he ridiculed himself. Some opportunity. An opportunity to sleep forever in a casket. It was only then, after the first flush of terror dissipated into mere abject fear, that he began to listen.

"Dead to rights," a voice said. "He's skimmin. One faw him. Two faw us."

"Cheez, Albert." It was Reles speaking. "Gagie. He don show nothin. Lives like a pig."

"A hozzer," Bugsy Goldstein said. "I seen da inside a his place. He got his stask locked away somewhere."

"Whaddaya tink, Frank?"

"I tink we gotta do him, Lep."

"Twenty yeahs I knowed da fuck," Reles said. "My right arm I'd give him. It hoits. Da man's a fuckin teef."

"Punk shitface." It was Pep's voice.

"We give him dis territory on yaw recommendation, Kid." It was Lep's voice.

"Fuckin teef," Reles said. "I'm embarrassed, Lep. Wois, I'm ashamed."

"How much ya figger?"

"Twenty, thirty grand he took off us."

There was a long whistle.

"People do dat, dey got no respeck for da organization," Lep said. He spoke softly, with an undercurrent of indignation. "I always liked Gagie. But we can't take dis insult. We gotta have da discipline in da organization. We gotta make an example."

"Human nature," Frank said. He seemed to speak with the greatest authority. "Whatsamatter with people."

"Youse is right. We gotta do him."

Mickey lay on the couch, listening, petrified. If he was discovered now he would also have to be "done." His stomach churned loudly. He wondered if they heard as he forced himself to stopped breathing.

"Pep'll handle it," Reles said.

"Pep does good woik," Lepke said. "Da best." There was a long silence. "Bad business," he continued. "We had to do tree last week. We're real proud of ya, Pep."

"Nobody does it like Pep," said Frank. "Neat, clean. No muss."

"Maybe we give Pep a raise on dis one," Albert said.

"Yeah," Lep said. "Double on dis one, Pep. Say five long faw yaw end."

"If you guys insist. Da old price was good, too."

"Don matter. Pep does it faw love anyhow," Reles said chuckling. "Right, Pep?"

"I enjoy my woik," Pep said.

"Make da fucker squawk before he goes," Bugsy said. "Double crossers are da woist kind."

"Da woist," Reles said. "A friend fucks ya it's da woist."

"Da question is when," Lepke said. "Frank, Albert and me gotta be outa here."

"Say Monday den," Pep said. "I'll stay ovah. We do him Monday night."

"I gotta go wid ya, Pep," Reles said. "Point a hona. We growed up togedda. Went to chader wid me. We did jobs togedda. Hell, he help me do Tommy Da Mick, Jack Moonface, and dat odder guy. Da wop." Mickey heard a nervous gasp. It was Reles.

"It's awright, Kid," Albert said. "Right, Frank? Deys family."

"We're all brudders," Frank said. "Wops, kikes, micks." He laughed and the men joined in. "The woild's changin though . . ." There was a long pause, as if the men were waiting for something more to come from Frank's mouth. A gangster's Sermon on the Mount, Mickey thought, too frightened to put a humorous spin on the idea. "Prohibition was nice clean fun and good business. Hell, everting was wide open den. Ya knew where ya stood. Tings are different now. We got refawmers. When ya get refawmers like Dewey and La Guardia and dem people on, da take get greedy. You watch. Someday da govament's gonna takes its piece. People got a natural feelin faw vice. Days gonna come when dere gonna legalize vice. Da ponies, da numbers, craps, cards. Maybe even broads. Drugs, too, someday."

"Nothins fawevah, Frank," Lep said. "Even da unions. What we gotta do is make hay while da sun shines. It ain't gonna shine fawevah."

"People don understand dat we really are da good guys," Albert said.

"We give a . . . a structcha," Lep said. "We go, foist ting ya

159

know a bunch of assholes start killing each udder in da streets like fuckin animals."

"Dat ain't civilized," Anastasia said. "To be civilized you gotta have a code."

"And da code says we do Gagie," Lep said.

"So me an Abie does Gagie on Monday night," Pep said. "We invite him out to Gorlick's for dinner. Send a wheelman. Right, Abie? Real buddy buddy. Den we drive him back to his house. Only we don't."

"Swan Lake is a good deep lake," Pep said. "Nobody goes."

"Dat's where we put whatzizname last year, right Pep? Da one we went tru da apple orchard."

"Boinstein's Orchard," Pep said. "I rememba."

"Was dat Schmutz Parker?" Reles asked.

"Naw. Dat was Benny Gold. Rope job. He was a fatso. Fish did good wid old Benny."

"Pep nevah fegets," Reles said.

"Ya gotta remvemba who ya do," Pep said. "And weah ya put dem." The men laughed.

"So Monday den," Albert said.

"We got someone up heah faw wheelman?" Pep asked.

"Dat redhead putz," Reles said. "He woiks faw Gawlick. Day call him Irish. I got him keepin an eye out. He wants a job to prove hisself."

Irish, Mickey thought bitterly. Mickey was certain that it was Irish that had stirred up trouble for Mutzie.

Suddenly Mickey heard chairs move. The men were rising.

"Ya still interested in my knish, Albert?" Pep said. He sounded barely inches from where Mickey lay on the couch. Again, Mickey stopped breathing.

"Fuck yeah," Albert said. "She know huh stuff?"

"Carta make liva pills?" Pep said laughing.

"Diden seem too anxious," Albert said.

"She's anxious now, Albert," Pep said. "Gives ya a problem slap huh aroun."

"Oh, yeah. Hell, I may slap huh around even if she give me no problem."

Both men laughed and moved away.

When he was sure they had gone, Mickey stood up. His knees were weak and his stomach felt as if he had swallowed a basketball. But he found the presence of mind to peek through a crack in the door before emerging into the casino. He noticed Goldstein, Lepke, Costello and Reles already at the craps tables.

Pep and Albert were nowhere to be seen. He rushed out of the casino, intent on finding Mutzie. He must help her. She had to leave this place at once. Go as far away as she could.

"Tumler. Where the fuck you been?" It was Gorlick, redfaced, obviously angry. "You gotta mingle."

"I don't feel so good," Mickey protested, searching the lobby.

"A tumler gotta mingle."

He wanted to tell Gorlick to take his job and shove it, but he hesitated and in the moment of hesitation he realized that if he was fired there would be no way to help Mutzie.

At that moment, he saw her. She was walking toward the big guest staircase with Albert Anastasia and Pep. His mind reeled. Ignoring Gorlick, he walked quickly across the lobby and blocked their way.

"Hear the one about the head?" he said.

What could he do? His only weapon was the joke, humor, tummeling. Not very lethal.

He exchanged glances with Mutzie, who looked none too happy.

"This guy has a son born with nothing but a head."

"Dat supposed to be funny?" Pep said.

It was, he knew, a desperate ploy, merely a stall, but he could not hold back. Mutzie started to speak, but Albert interceded. Mickey wished he could find some way to save her from what was happening.

"Den what?" Anastasia asked.

"He don stop," Pep muttered.

Mutzie looked at him with lugubrious eyes. Mickey continued.

"Goes into a bar, orders two scotches. One for his kid. One for himself. He helps the son drink and suddenly the son sprouts the beginnings of a torso."

"Jeez," Pep said. "Turns my stomach."

"I'm listening," Anastasia said.

Mickey wanted to string it out.

"Speed it up, tumler," Pep said.

"The father orders two more scotches. The kid sprouts arms."

"Go on. I nevah heard this one," Anastasia said.

"Orders two more scotches," Mickey continued.

"Two more den two more," Pep said, shaking his head.

"The son grows legs and is complete now."

"Two more, right?" Anastasia said.

Mickey nodded. He knew it was futile. Mutzie was trapped.

"Bartender puts two more scotches on the bar. Father and son drink. Suddenly the son falls over backwards dead . . ."

"Dis is funny," Pep said.

"Bartender looks over the bar at the dead son . . . says, 'He shoulda quit when he was ahead.'"

Anastasia roared.

"Dis is one funny guy," Anastasia said.

"Take a walk now," Pep said.

Watching Mutzie, he saw her eyes warning him and a tiny shake of her head. The message was unmistakable. Go away.

Mickey hesitated, watching Mutzie.

"Yeah, take a hike, Mickey," Mutzie said. It was her mouth talking, not her eyes. Maybe not her heart either, Mickey thought. He wanted to cry with helplessness.

"Ya hoid the lady, putz," Pep said. He grabbed Mickey and took a handful of shirt in his hand, drawing his face close to his own. "Maybe you wanna go faw a midnight swim." He pushed Mickey away and the three of them proceeded up the stairs.

Mickey turned and saw Gorlick. He was shaking his head and smirking.

"With his shmekel, he wants to commit suicide," he said gravely. Mickey straightened his shirt and walked toward where people were congregating. For Mutzie's sake he had to stay employed.

8

I T WAS NEARLY ONE WHEN SHE FINALLY GOT BACK TO HER
room. She was relieved to find that Pep wasn't there since
she was determined to pack up and leave this place. She took
her suitcase out of the closet and quickly began to pack.

She felt unclean, humiliated, degraded. Despite all her
efforts to put her mind elsewhere as Albert abused her, she could
not ignore the images of her degradation. Worse, she had per-
formed her indignities by acting as if she was enjoying them. Such
weakness in herself disgusted her. But she was genuinely frightened, terrorized by the thought of being maimed, or worse, if she
didn't comply to his wishes.

Whatever illusions she had had concerning the type of man
Pep was, they were shattered by this experience. His looks belied
his true self. Inside the handsome package of a man was a ruthless
maniac. There was no way to rationalize her predicament. She had
made her own bed out of false fantasies and hollow dreams. She
was a fool and she deserved her punishment.

"You take good care a Albert, Mutzie," he told her. "You do
dat fuh ole Pep."

She had nodded consent, even forced a smile, then Albert

165

had taken her arm and brought her to his room. Once inside, she tried to imagine that she was elsewhere, that she wasn't the real Mutzie. The woman in this room was someone else, a robot wearing her clothes. Unfortunately, her imagination couldn't stretch that far. This was simply an act of self-preservation, of survival. She had no illusions about what would happen to her if she disobeyed Pep. It was too horrible to contemplate. She steeled herself to get it over with as quickly as possible. Make believe it's a movie, she told herself.

Unfortunately, Albert's sexual appetite was not easily appeased. She had hoped to get it over quickly, but his reactions were slower than Pep's. It was awful, the most awful thing she had ever experienced in her life. She felt like a piece of dirt.

After a couple of hours, Albert had dozed and she had risen from the bed to get dressed. She had barely stood up when he grabbed her by the hair and pulled her back.

"Where da fuck ya tink ya going?" he shouted.

She started to answer, but he silenced her by pushing her face on his semi-erect penis.

"We ain't finished yet."

When he was finally satiated, he told her she was free to go and put a hundred dollars in her hand.

"Getchaself a nice dress, Mutz," he told her. "Ya been a good fuck. I'm gonna tell Pep."

Suddenly, as if a bell had wrung in her head, she decided that it was time to go, to escape. She would run, whatever the consequences. She had reached rock bottom, some netherworld run by the devil, a sick, primitive place. She vowed to fight her way back to civilization.

When Albert left, she went back to her room and packed some clothes, leaving everything in the closet that Pep had given

her. She hated the sight of those things. There was no point in crying, she told herself defiantly. Then she illustrated this defiance by
taking the hundred dollars that Albert had given her and flushing
it down the toilet.

What she needed most now was strength, determination and
courage. And speed. She had to get out of here and she knew it
wasn't going to be as simple as it sounded. Where could she go at
this hour? Back to Brownsville? Running out on Pep offered a
very unhealthy prospect. Suddenly she thought of Mickey. He had
tried to help her and nearly gotten himself hurt for doing so.

Suddenly the issue became moot. She heard Pep's voice in
the corridor. He was saying goodbye to Reles. Both men were
laughing. She closed the suitcase and put it in the closet, then
removed her clothes and got into bed, pretending to be asleep.

"All ovah oily," Pep said, putting on the light. She kept her
eyes closed. Sitting down on the bed beside her he slapped her
face to wake her. It was pointless to keep her eyes closed after
that.

"Albert like what he got?" Pep asked.

"He didn't complain."

"Ya did good, Mutzie," Pep said patting her arm. "I got real
big plans faw you."

"What sort of plans?" Mutzie asked.

"We gonna see Gloria tomorrow."

"Gloria?" She had met Gloria briefly and knew what she did.
A stab of fear shot through her.

"Hell, Mutzie. What ya got ya can sell. You wanna be a
schleper all ya life?"

She sat up in bed. Under the covers, her body trembled.

"How can you do this to me, Pep?" she asked, feeling the
tremor in her throat. She seemed barely able to get the words out.

"Cheez. I'm given ya a chance ta make some real moolah. Ya should be grateful ta ole Pep. I give ya a vacation here in da mountains. I buy ya tings. I treat ya like a fuckin princess. What I do ta ya, Mutzie?" His anger seemed to be accelerating. "Hell, I give ya an opportunity, ya spit in Pep's face." He got up off the bed and went to the bathroom.

"I can't do it, Pep," she whispered when he came back. No matter what, she had decided, there was no way she could do "that."

"Ye did it wid Albert. Dat hoitcha?"

"Yes," she whispered. "It did."

The remark triggered his anger and he ripped away the covers. She was naked. She felt deceived and vulnerable.

"I don see no scars," he said, grabbing her by the neck just under the chin and lifting her. She gasped, unable to breathe. "But if you wanna see scars, I can make em." Suddenly a knife had materialized in his hand. He pressed the point against her breast. "Maybe we chop off a nipple. Give ya a little remembrance from ole Pep."

She felt the cold steel against her breast. A nausea seemed to take hold of her and she gagged.

"Please, Pep. I've got to throw up."

His sense of fastidiousness made him jump away and she ran to the bathroom and threw up in the toilet. She felt totally dehumanized and helpless, like a caged animal whose rear legs had been tied together. Flushing the toilet, she watched the swirling water and wondered if she could drown herself in it. There seemed no point to living. If this was real life, she hated it, hated herself for allowing this to happen. Most of all she hated Pep and wished he would die. She searched her heart for the full impact of her hatred. She longed for the courage to kill him.

She stayed in the bathroom a long time and when she came out he was asleep. He lay on his back, his lips slightly parted. Even in sleep he was handsome. He looked so peaceful, so benign. Seeing him this way, it was incredible that he could be so cruel. Beside him on the night table was the knife he had threatened her with. All it would take was to find the courage to pick it up and plunge it into his heart.

But she couldn't. Even if it meant survival. It was too foreign to her nature. Violence, she supposed, was not a woman's thing. A pity, she thought. Pep deserved to die. He was corrupt, evil. If the situation was reversed, he would kill her without batting an eye.

Of one thing she was certain. She had to get away from him. But how? Where would she go? They had informers, contacts. Where could she hide? And if they found her? She moved to the window and looked out over the expanse of lawn to the peaceful lake, moonlight spangling its surface.

The sight calmed her. Above all, she needed to think this through. Perhaps, after awhile, they would forget about her, lose interest. What was she, anyway? Just one of Pep's whores, a silly romantic who had become entwined, like a fool, in their net.

As she stood there a chill swept her body and her teeth began to chatter. They had seen her as a fly on the wall, unimportant, a nonentity, and they had talked in front of her, said things, although it was difficult now to recall specifics. But they would remember that and wonder what they had said that might incriminate them in some way. It would worry them. They hated loose ends.

Her knees felt weak. She had to think this through without hysteria, without panic. But under no circumstances would she yield to Pep's wishes, join Gloria's troop of prostitutes. Oh my

God. The idea of it was making her sick again. She turned from the window and tamped down her nausea.

Tomorrow she would find a way out. She had to. There was no choice. She crept into bed beside Pep, her back to him, hoping he would not reach out for her. His touch, she knew, would make her skin crawl.

She slept the dreamless sleep of exhaustion and when she awoke the low rain clouds hung in the air, adding to her sense of gloom. Thankfully, Pep still slept and she was able to crawl out of bed without waking him.

When she thought about her plight in the light of day, she found that a vague plan had surfaced in her mind. One thing was certain. She did not wish to spend another moment with these people, especially Pep. Remembering that she had flushed the hundred dollars bill that Albert had given her, she rebuked herself for her lack of foresight. Emotion was one thing. Survival another.

Dressing in slacks and a sweater with extra underwear stuffed in her pocketbook, she put a brush through her hair and let herself out of the room. She wished to take nothing that would provide her any memories of this episode in her life. At that point, she told herself, she sincerely hoped she had a life.

There were a few people in the corridor, mostly chambermaids. The Reles boy ran up and down the back stairs bouncing a ball. He was a miniature version of his father with the same cruel, burning agate eyes and shuffling walk.

"Pep's coorva. Pep's coorva," the boy chanted as he stopped to look at her.

The derisive phrase triggered a burst of anger and she grabbed the boy and twisted an ear. He cried out in pain.

"You're a little snot-nose like your stinking father," she hissed. The boy looked at her with hatred.

"I tell my mudder and fadder on you, coorva."

She let go of him and hurried down the back stairs. Now that was dumb, she told herself.

When she arrived in the lobby the dining room had just opened and the breakfast smells of freshly baked bread and cake wafted through the air. She knew where Mickey would be at this hour. He would be conducting the obligatory pre-breakfast Simon Sez routine on the lawn to those intrepid early risers who enjoyed the bracing morning air.

Owing to the threatening weather, there were only ten people in the group when she arrived and Mickey was just getting started. It would be fatal, she knew, to show or accept any sign of confidentiality between them. Mickey's face brightened when he saw her slip into the back row.

"Simon Sez do this," Mickey said raising his arms skyward. The group followed. The object of the game was to ape the leaders actions only when he said "Simon Sez." Mickey watched her, his eyes locking into hers. Help me, she said with her eyes, hoping he would understand her plea.

"Simon Sez hands on hips," Mickey said. The group followed. "Simon Sez hands on heads. Simon Sez hands on shoulders. And straight out."

"You, you, you," Mickey said, pointing to three people who had moved to the wrong command. Mutzie had hesitated, then executed the correct action.

The group fell away by half, then by a quarter more. Then there were only three players left. She was concentrating, determined to stay until the end. Those disqualified from the game meandered toward the dining room, perhaps thinking that they had done their healthful daily dozen for the day.

"Simon Sez do this," Mickey said. "Do this." She moved slightly but he did not cite her as disqualified. Had he sensed her plea? She wasn't sure. "Simon Sez do this." He did a jumping windmill maneuver. "And this." He did a scissors maneuver which eliminated everyone but Mutzie. A good omen, she decided, as she moved toward the lake.

"Winner and new champion," he said. Those who remained as spectators applauded and he went over to give her the traditional winner's hug.

"Got to see you privately," she whispered.

"The boathouse," he replied.

She moved toward the boathouse and Mickey followed at a distance.

When she got to the boathouse, which was deserted at this hour, she quickly ducked through the door and stood waiting for him on one of the planks that served as the storage dock for the sailboats.

"I got troubles, Mickey," Mutzie whispered.

"I know," he nodded.

"No, you don't," she responded, thinking that he couldn't possibly know the extent of her problems. Suddenly, she felt afflicted by the idea that she was taking advantage of what she sensed were his feelings for her.

"That was me last night on the porch. I heard. I knew what was happening."

Suddenly, she was ashamed. She looked into his eyes, saw their devotion and it frightened her.

"I can't be here any more, Mickey. I don't know where to turn. I need help."

"Try me," Mickey said.

"I have no right to get you involved."

"I already am, Mutzie," he said, his eyes searching her face.

"You don't know what they can do,"

"Yes, I do," he said. It puzzled her. "Trust me. Let me help."

She hesitated, wondering how much he really knew and how much she needed to tell him.

"I have to get away from him," she said. The words came out like a confession.

"I could never understand how you got involved with that man in the first place," Mickey said. He spoke the words gently, but they still came out as a rebuke. "He's . . ." He seemed to stop short as if he were waiting to complete the sentence.

"I know what he is, Mickey," Mutzie sighed. "And I know what he can do to me." Images of her potential fate filled her mind, increasing the trembling. She saw her face and body puckered with acid burns. She saw herself moving slowly on crutches, her legs broken and useless. She saw herself garroted, flung into a lake, her legs encased in cement. Then she saw herself with her throat cut, the blood soaking her clothes, her eyes open in a fixed death stare.

"What is it?" Mickey said.

She opened her mouth to scream, but no sound came out. She was petrified with her own fear.

"I don't know what to do," she sobbed, leaning against him, feeling herself enveloped in his arms. "He wants to . . ." She swallowed with difficulty, then suddenly the words rushed out and she told him about Pep's plans for her, about Gloria. It was a full confession and it calmed her, although it did not fully chase away her fear.

"I'd rather die than have that happen to me," Mutzie said. "And I feel ashamed and disgraced."

"You aren't in my eyes, Mutzie," Mickey said.

"I don't even know if it's possible to hide from them. I'm sure I can't go home. That's the first place they'll look. So where could I go? Who can I trust? I'm just a sad, dumb, gullible girl." She thought suddenly of her fantasy life, her making herself over to look like Jean Harlow. Did Jean Harlow confront such horror in real life? She doubted that.

"But why would they want to harm you?" Mickey asked.

"Pep said he would, said that he had done it to other girls who didn't do what he said."

"Maybe he was just scaring you," Mickey said.

"Well, he certainly succeeded. Besides, you don't know them like I do. They do harm people, Mickey. They really do."

"I know," Mickey sighed. He paused, looked deeply into her eyes and patted her hair. "But please, Mutzie. Be strong. We'll find a way . . ." His voice trailed off.

"A way?" she asked eagerly, finding a ray of hope in his words.

"To get them," Mickey said. His tentative look belittled his pose of determination.

"Get them?" Mutzie said. "That's impossible. They control things. They have politicians and cops on their payroll. Nobody gets them. Except maybe . . ." She paused. "Each other."

"They worry about certain things," Mickey said. He nodded as if agreeing with some idea that had just occurred to him. "Yes. Certain things."

"Like what?" she asked.

"Not *what* but who."

"Who?"

"A third party who corroborates a crime," he said, his voice lowering an octave, as if someone in the empty boathouse might hear. He explained it to her.

"You mean a witness," she offered, still not understanding what he was talking about. The idea sent a chill through her. They had talked in front of her, described crimes. Some had even criticized her being around. But Pep had vouched for her. It occurred to her suddenly that they might think she knew too much. "Oh my God," she cried, putting a hand over her mouth.

"What is it?"

"I heard things."

"What things?"

"I'm not sure. I can't remember. But if they think I can, then I'm in deeper trouble than I thought. Pep would have to . . ."

"Please, Mutzie. We have to think things out," Mickey said. He looked at her but said nothing. She could tell he was trying to come up with a plan, a course of action. She felt a sense of hopelessness and guilt, guilt that she had gotten Mickey involved. After a long silence, he nodded his head in the affirmative as if an idea had occurred to him. For a moment she surrendered to optimism.

"We're going to witness a killing. You and I," Mickey said.

"What are you talking about?"

"A killing. I overhead them. They are going to kill a man by the name of Gage Monday night."

"Gagie? Him? He runs Sullivan County for them. Not Gagie. I know him."

Suddenly the idea of death, of killing, took on an even more sinister aspect, underlining her fear. They were going to kill a man who they considered a friend. If they could do that without a qualm, then surely they could do the same to a her without giving it a second thought.

"I can't believe it."

"Believe it," Mickey told her. "I remember what they said.

Swan Lake. Bernstein's Apple Orchard. I know where they're going to dump the body. Monday. Tomorrow night." He paused and she felt his gaze biting into her. "We're gonna watch it."

She felt a bubble of hysteria start somewhere deep inside of her. She seemed to track it in her mind as it grew and spread and burst into a kind of joyous laughter.

"Are you crazy, Mickey?"

"All tumlers are crazy," he said.

"You think they'll let us walk around if we tell the police that we saw them do that?" She hoped that he would interpret it as ridicule.

"They'll have to protect us, won't they?" Mickey said. He didn't seem particularly sure on that point.

"I told you. They own the police," Mutzie said.

"Maybe not all of them," Mickey shrugged.

She watched him for a long moment.

"This is a tumler's joke, right?" she said.

"I gotta believe there are some good people out there, Mutzie," Mickey said.

"Worse yet." She looked to the far end of the boathouse as if talking to someone. "Is this one an idealist or just a cooney lemel, an idiot?"

"That I can answer someday," Mickey shot back. She could tell it was a tumler line. "Not like the question that can never be answered with a yes."

"Like what?" she asked, playing her role.

"Are you asleep?"

"Not so funny," she said. "But funnier than your suggestion."

"You came to me for help," Mickey said. "So that's my help. This way maybe you've got a chance. Otherwise, if they're as powerful as you say they are, you'll spend your life running. That's a life?"

Of course, from her point of view, there was some logic in his argument. But from when she looked at it from his point of view, there was no logic in it at all. He would be jeopardizing his life for a perfect stranger. It was unfair and foolhardy. Maybe, of all the alternatives for her, the best would be go back to Pep, become one of Gloria's girls. What difference did it make? Her dignity had all but been destroyed, her dreams and illusions exploded, her body corrupted. In a few short months she had taken a roller coaster ride from elation to despair. Her mother was right. She should have married Henry, lived a safe, normal, conventional life. Her eyes filled with tears and Mickey embraced her.

"I'm not going to let you do this, Mickey," she said when she had calmed down.

"You got a better idea?"

"I'm going back."

She extricated herself from his arms and started to move along the indoor dock to the boathouse entrance.

"You want to throw your life away," Mickey shouted. "Okay by me."

"It's not your business," she said, turning to face him. He had not come after her, but stood instead beside one of the sailboats listing slightly in the lake's gentle swell.

"It is now," he called. "You came to me."

"It was a mistake," she cried back at him.

"Not for me," Mickey said. "I'm doing this for me."

"That's because you're stupid. A strange girl . . . a gun moll, that's what I am. Let's call a spade a spade. She bats her eyes at you and suddenly you're a regular Romeo. Well, I'm no Juliet."

"Let me be the judge," he said.

His response was oddly comforting.

"You're a schmo. Not a Romeo."

He laughed. "A regular rhymer. You want my job. The first girl tumler in the Catskills."

"Believe me, they see you with me, you won't have your job long anyway."

Yet she knew that her actions belied her intentions. He was right. It was no life. She would rather die than follow such a path. She started to move again, then stopped and called back to him. They traded glances for a long moment.

"You would be wasting your time with me," she said.

"So," he replied. "It's my funeral."

"For once you're right, tumler," she said, moving toward him again. Hers, too, she thought.

9

"**P**UTZVATIG," MICKEY TOLD HIMSELF AS HE LOOKED INTO one of the lobby mirrors on his way to the dining room. The derisive Yiddish expression brought on a broad clownish smile and a rumbling hysterical giggle. Of course it was crazy, he thought, but then again, wasn't it a noble act? There were few enough acts of nobility in the world. Were'nt there?

Noble shmoble, he told himself. It was love and he was being an exhibitionist, a show-off, offering this grand gesture to impress the woman he loved by saving her from a life of white slavery.

"Love can kill," he whispered to his image in the mirror. "Not only that. You don't look so good."

Yet he continued to linger in front of the mirror as if he were searching for something beyond his visible image, trying to mine heroic nuggets beneath the crust of himself, searching for a grail even more powerful and significant than love to justify his actions. Perhaps it was also revenge for what these animals had done to his father. Or maybe it was the very idea of these gangsters, their insult toward all Jews, toward all decent, law-abiding people who played according to the rules.

Who was he kidding? It was love, mysterious, illogical. Why

179

her? How come? The only answer that made sense didn't really make sense to the brain, only to the heart, which could not think. For love people do stupid things and this was one of them.

Suddenly, he remembered all the jokes he had told about love.

"Is it better to have loved and lost? Much better."

And the one that usually got the most laughs: "I've been in love with the same woman for thirty years. If my wife found out she would kill me."

Kill? It made him tremble. It's for love, he agreed finally. For love, you took risks.

"You're a bigger putz than I thought," he told his image in the mirror.

Mutzie had stayed behind in the boathouse until he had gone into the main building. He had given her the key to his room and detailed instructions on getting to it by using the back stairs, the "help" stairs. Then he had posted himself at an obscure area of the porch, watching her proceed.

He observed her as she moved quickly up the rise of the lawn. The overcast had darkened, deepening the green of the lawn, and it had begun to rain. Mutzie accelerated her pace as the rain quickened, running up the porch stairs to the safety of the overhang, then through the French doors. When he had ducked inside to the lobby, she had disappeared.

"I got news, tumler."

Gorlick's voice startled him. He had been looking in the mirror but only at himself. Now he saw Gorlick's image clearly. He forced himself into tumler high gear. To be fired today would call attention to himself. For the moment he needed this job. And then? He pushed any thought of the future out of his mind.

"I'm keeping you hired, tumler. Albert says you're the funni-est he ever saw. When Albert talks, I listen."

"He's God."

"Bigger," Gorlick said. "On top, I'm giving you a five-dollar raise."

"How lucky can you get, Mr. Gorlick? You make me feel like Samson."

"I know. I know. You'll bring down the house."

Mickey forced a laugh. "Stepping on my lines again, Mr. Gorlick."

"I'm entitled. I just gave you raise," Gorlick said, looking out the window. "Oy the rain. You'll really have to tumel them today. It rains on a Sunday, those that go back say the weather stank all weekend. Those that come up are worried they paid for lousy weather." He turned toward Mickey and pointed a stubby finger at his nose. "For you, tumler, this is the, how you say, the truth moment."

"Moment of truth," Mickey corrected.

"Whatever," Gorlick said. "So go tumel."

Mickey knew what rain meant. He would have to organize indoor games and shows to keep people from thinking about the weather. He had hoped good weather might have spared him that on this of all days.

He went into the dining room. Most of the tables were still empty, but stragglers were coming into the room at a slow trickle. He looked toward what he had dubbed in his own mind "the gang-ster's table." Mrs. Reles was there with her bratty son. Also Mrs. Buchalter.

"Top a the mornin, ladies," he said with a slight Irish brogue.

"Now he's a mick," Helen said. It did not seem to him to be a lighthearted remark.

"I thought you were very funny last night," Mrs. Buchalter said. "Very amusing." She was a chubby woman, overdressed for the morning with large diamond rings on her fingers, a diamond bracelet and a huge string of pearls over an ample bosom.

He could feel Helen Reles studying him with some hostility. He pretended not to notice. Some women, he knew, could not deal with rejection. He wondered if he had been wrong to refuse her invitation. But then, wouldn't that have set off a whole other set of dangerous circumstances? Like possessiveness, jealousy, spite. Not to mention the wrath of Kid Twist. He watched her pat her son's ear.

"Let me kiss the booboo," Mrs. Reles said, putting her lips against his cheek.

"Little guy get a clop on the ear?" he asked.

"Your girlfriend, tumler," Mrs. Reles said, turning to look at him. "She swatted my kid."

"Who?" he asked, hoping that he had hidden his sudden anxiety.

"Right here," the Reles kid said showing his red ear.

"I don't understand," Mickey said.

"That Mutzie," Mrs. Reles harrumphed, her nostrils inflating with contempt and anger.

"You mean Mr. Strauss's friend?" he corrected forcing an air of naïve innocence.

"Yeah," she snickered. "Pep's so-called . . ." She whispered the word "coorva."

"The one with me in the show?" he persisted, deliberately avoiding confrontation, determined to appear good humored, although he was burning inside.

"He's dumb like a fox," Mrs. Reles said.

With effort, Mickey maintained what he hoped was an

expression of vague confusion. It seemed to soften Mrs. Reles's blatant hostility.

"Not that this one didn't deserve it, probably," she said, pinching her son's upper arm while looking at Mrs. Buchhalter. "Anyway, Abie went lookin faw huh. Pep said she went out." She shot Mickey a sharp glance. "Ya seen her?"

He felt his mind turning over at double time.

"I think at Simon Sez," he said. "Yeah. At Simon Sez. But if I do see her again, I'll tell her that your husband is looking for her."

"Better say nothing until Abie cools off."

"That serious?" Mickey asked, sorry immediately for showing his concern.

"Nobody likes nobody to swat their kid, right, Ruthie?"

"Labele would go through the roof," Mrs. Buchhalter said. Or worse, Mickey thought.

"I'm sure everything will turn out hunky-dory," Mickey said patting the boys red ear. At that moment, he saw Pep and Reles come into the dining room. He knew he should have left the table, but he stayed out of curiosity. And panic.

"You find huh?" Mrs. Reles asked.

"Looked eveyweah, even in da ladies' can," Reles said.

"Ah, she'll be aroun, Abie," Pep said, but without much conviction, as if the subject were simply annoying and unimportant.

"No big deal," Abie said. "Alls I want is to tell huh to watch huh hands."

"Somtimes da brat desoives a belt, Abie," Pep said.

"Believe me, Pep, we do ouwa shaih. Don we, Hesh?"

Heshy made a face.

"Alls I did was call her a coorva," the boy said.

"He had it right," Helen said.

"Me, I wudda twisted his shmekel faw dat," Pep said.

"And I'd drop ya in Canarsie," Reles said.

It was more bantering than argument, Mickey thought. They often kidded around like that.

"Maybe ya should get married Pep, seddle down. Get a brat a ya own. Ony wid no coorvas," Mrs. Reles shot Mickey a surreptitious wink.

"Can't she keep huh trap shut, Abie?" Pep said. He was obviously working himself into a sour mood.

Throughout this conversation, Mickey stood rooted to the floor, unable to find the will to move, hoping they would continue to ignore him. No such luck. Pep's eyes suddenly drilled into him.

"Ya seen Mutzie, tumler?" he asked.

"She. . . ." He coughed to mask his panic. "I think I saw her at Simon Sez."

"And aftah?"

"I didn't see her. Maybe she went back to the room." He struggled to find something funny to say. "Unless she likes singin in the rain." He trilled the words from the song. It went over like a lead balloon.

"Yeah. Well maybe she went back up. I'll go see," Pep said. He turned to Abie. "I'll tawk ta huh about da kid. Only ya keep hands awf."

Abie smiled thinly, looked at his wife and shrugged while they all watched Pep walk purposefully out of the dining room. But it left Mickey worried. Was she safe? Thankfully, Gorlick was too cheap to have the help's rooms cleaned by chambermaids. Mickey smiled and gently squeezed Heshy's shoulder.

"He's a good boychick," Mickey said.

"When he sleeps," Reles said. Mickey forced a laugh and went to his table.

As he drank his coffee, Mickey watched the gangster's table. Pep came back, looking angrier than ever. Albert Anastasia joined them at the table, then Frank Costello and Lepke. One big happy family, Mickey thought bitterly. He also kept an eye out for Irish, who seemed to be perpetually watching him with sinister intent, hoping he would falter in some way.

Then he saw him. Irish smiled wryly and winked malevolently as he passed Mickey's table. Did these gestures augur anything imminent? Mickey wondered, remembering again that Irish would be the driver, the "wheelman" in the killing of Gagie that night. We'll see you in hell, too, Irish, Mickey vowed silently to himself.

When Irish went back to the kitchen and the people at the gangster table concentrated on their breakfast, Mickey filled his pockets with bagels and wrapped some lox and cream cheese in a napkin, which he hid under his shirt. Then he stood up and started to move through the dining room. Peripherally, he saw Pep watching him. His pores opened and perspiration ran down his back. He could not tell if Irish had seen him leave.

In the lobby, he walked quickly toward the back stairs, which he ran up two steps at a time. In his room, he found Mutzie sitting on the bed. His sudden entrance frightened her. Quickly, he emptied his pockets, put the food on the bed and opened the napkin.

"It's the best I can do, Mutzie," he said breathlessly, his heart pounding. "Now I gotta get back."

"Have you heard anything?" she whispered.

"Pep's looking for you. Reles, too. You smack their kid?"

"I twisted his ear. I wanted to do worse."

"I gotta go," Mickey said.

"Mickey . . ." she called to him as he reached the door.

"Lower," he pleaded, putting a finger on his lips.

"Are you sorry, Mickey?" she asked. He turned to look at her. She looked helpless, vulnerable. He wanted to hold her in his arms, comfort her.

"So far, no," he said, wanting to tell her more. They exchanged glances. "Just keep the door locked. I'll bring lunch later, okay."

She nodded. He opened the door a crack, then closed it as someone came past in the corridor. He waited and opened the door again. The corridor looked deserted and he ducked out of the room. Walking quickly, he reached the staircase.

He began to perspire as he walked through the lobby again. He felt flushed and out of breath. His heart pounded. He sat down at the table and tried to lift his coffee cup, but his fingers shook. Suddenly Gorlick was bending over him, talking into his ear.

"You seen dat girl?"

"What girl?"

"Don hand me, Fine."

"You mean Pep's girl?"

"The one you said you didn't shtup."

"You, too. I'm not a meshuganer."

"Yaw entitled to yaw opinion. Ya seen huh?"

"Yes, at Simon Sez."

He could smell Gorlick's foul, stale cigar breath as he hovered above him.

"She musta done something. Dey all been lookin faw huh."

"Yeah," Mickey said. "I heard them talking. She slugged the Reles brat."

"Dat it?" Gorlick asked.

"That's what they told me," Mickey said.

"Only dat. I thought maybe all dis had sumpin to do with dat schmeckel a yaws."

"I told you, Mr. Gorlick. No way. And I resent your attitude on this."

"But why would Strauss be so mad, den?" Gorlick asked, obviously puzzled. "Da brat don look any the woise for weah."

"It'll blow over," Mickey muttered.

"Sumpin's not kosher, tumler. Pep and Reles is stayin ovanight. And Lepke, Costello and Anastasia are coming back Friday night. Sumpin's happenin. Only I hope whatever is happening doesn't happen at Gorlick's." He had partially risen. Then he bent down and put his mouth closer to Mickey's ear.

"Anyting to do wid ya, I swear, Fine, yaw balls is gawn. Got that, tumler? Gawn."

"I don't like this talk, Mr. Gorlick," Mickey said, desperately trying to keep his emotions in check.

"What does it count what ya like?" Gorlick said. He straighted up and waddled through the swinging doors into the kitchen.

Soon the dining room grew more crowded. Mickey got up to make his usual breakfast announcement and his Sunday goodbyes with the usual jokes. As hard as he tried he could not keep the tremble out of his voice.

"I understand there wasn't a single roach in your room," he said, "Only married couples with large families." There was a trickle of laughter.

"We also have last minute exercises for everyone leaving. You bring down your own valises. Then we do bend overs in the lobby. You bend over the valises, then you open them and give Gorlick back his towels."

There was some polite laughter among the diners.

Because it was raining, he was expected to do a routine. It was the moment for Marsha to do the lines he had taught her and paid for in lieu of sex. They had done it a few times before. He pointed his finger at her as she passed and she nodded.

"How did you get in here?" he called to her.

"It's raining outside."

"How long can a person live without brains?"

"I don't know. How old are you?"

"Looks who's talking. She thinks she's a Lana Turner. Actually she's a stomach turner."

"And him," Marsha retorted. "Everybody thinks he has a good heart because the dogs lick his hand. If he ate with a knife and fork they wouldn't lick his hand."

"You notice how she talks slow. Before she could say, 'What kind of a girl do you think I am?' she was."

"Last night I dreamed my husband bought me a mink coat."

"Next time you dream, wear it in good health."

The audience tittered. She seemed to be waiting for more lines from him, but at that moment he saw Pep rise and move to a corner of the dining room. Irish moved to meet him. Their heads seemed to tip toward each other as they talked. Then their heads rose and they looked toward Mickey. He felt a thump of fear, quickly aborting the routine and announcing that after breakfast there would be games inside. Then he stepped from the raised platform and moved to the kitchen where Marsha had gone. She was starting to ladle oatmeal into bowls.

"You didn't get your money's worth, Mickey," Marsha said. "I was just getting warmed up." She winked. "I can get warmed up pretty fast."

"I need a favor, Marsha. And I need it now," Mickey pressed, his eyes searching for any signs of Irish.

"From little me?" Marsha said coyly.

"I need the key to your room."

"Finally," she said. She dipped a hand in her pocket and gave him the key. "I'll be up right after breakfast. Like I promised. It'll be on the house."

He wanted to clarify the request, but it was too late. Through the window of the swinging doors, he saw Irish coming toward the kitchen.

"You're a doll," he said, moving quickly past the busy cooks through the food storage area to a door that led to the outside. Then he ran to another exit near the rear of the hotel and scrambled up the back stairs.

Mutzie was startled by his return.

"Quick," he said. "No questions."

He gathered up the remains of her breakfast, wrapped it in the napkin he had brought up earlier and moved swiftly out of his room and down the corridor to Marsha's room.

"Pep thinks you're hiding me, right?" she asked.

"I don't know what he thinks. Just stay here until I come back."

He locked the door from the outside and was down the back stairs as fast as his feet could carry him. He started across the lobby to the dining room.

"You, tumler."

He turned. It was Pep. Behind him was the gloating face of Irish.

"He says . . ." Pep said, his head gesturing toward Irish, "dat if anyone knows where Mutzie is, it's you."

"Dey been pretty thick, Mr. Strauss . . . Pep," Irish said.

"I did what you told me, Mr. Strauss. You said keep her happy . . ."

Pep reached out and gripped him under one arm. Irish took the other and they moved him out to the porch.

"I been hearin tings bout you and Mutzie," Pep hissed, his eyes glowing with anger. He grabbed Mickey's windpipe and squeezed. "Ya shtup my Mutzie?"

Mickey gagged and tried turning his head. Pep's strong hand dug deeper.

"Where da fuck is she?" Pep scowled, suddenly releasing his grip. Mickey gagged and sucked in deep breaths.

"How would I know?" Mickey said, shaking his head vigorously. "And they're liars. We only did the show."

"Not what I heard," Irish said, sneering.

"And he's the biggest liar."

"Sure?" Pep asked. His hand grabbed Mickey's testicles. He squeezed. Mickey bit his lip, but resisted screaming.

"You wan I should pull dese out?" Pep said, his mouth twisted in a menacing grin. Mickey groaned in pain.

"Please. I don't . . ." Mickey could not go on. Pep released him and stuck a fist in his stomach pushing upward. Mickey writhed in pain.

"Ya gonna feed da fishes, tumler," Pep said.

"If I knew I would tell," Mickey managed to say.

Pep turned toward Irish.

"Whaddaya tink, Irish?"

Pep's attention obviously gave Irish courage.

"Maybe she's in his room," Irish hissed.

"Yeah, maybe," Pep said. They grabbed Mickey under each arm and dragged him forward and up the back stairs.

"Ya shit me, yaw a dead man, tumler," Pep said as they moved clumsily up the stairs.

"It's all wrong, Mr. Strauss," Mickey said, suddenly looking at Irish. "This bastard hates me. I wouldn't trust him as far as I can spit."

"Ya cocksucka," Irish shouted.

"You watch him closely, Mr. Strauss." Mickey said, remembering what was going to happen tomorrow evening, hoping he was undermining Irish's credibility. "He's a lying punk."

Irish reached over and pulled Mickey's hair. The pain was intense but Mickey did not give him the satisfaction of showing it. They reached the help floor and the men pushed him forward in the direction of his room. Then they moved down the corridor, passing the door of Marsha's room, where Mutzie was hiding, to Mickey's room.

"Open it, putz," Pep said. With a trembling hand Mickey managed to open the door. Then they pushed Mickey forward and he fell on the floor. It didn't take them more than a few seconds to discover that Mutzie wasn't there.

"I told you. This Irish is full of shit," Mickey said as he struggled up from the floor. "You'll see. He's not reliable. This is a perfect example."

"She ain't heah," Pep said. He turned to Mickey. "Ya bettah not be shittin me."

Then he turned to Irish and whacked him with a backhand across the face. "Goes faw ya, too, putz."

"He's a fuckin liar, Pep," Irish squealed.

"Up yaws," Pep said storming out of the room, leaving Irish alone with Mickey. They glared at each other.

"I seen ya wid her, big shot. Dis mawning. Near da boat-house."

"Maybe you should have looked there?" Mickey said.

"I did," Irish said. He took a step toward Mickey, who grabbed a pair of scissors that were laying on the table.

191

"Go on, Irish. Give me the pleasure."

Irish backed away. He pointed his finger, started to say something, then ran out the door.

Mickey threw the scissors on the bed. His hands shook. Was he capable of such an act? These men were. How could they? It was a question that answered itself. When it came to human beings, anything was possible.

After Irish had gone, he washed and changed his clothes, then moved cautiously into the corridor to Marsha's room knocking quietly.

"It's me. Mickey. Open up."

"Anything wrong?" Mutzie asked as he moved inside the room.

"They think I'm hiding you," he said. "Pep just worked me over."

"Oh my God," Mutzie said. "I'm so sorry, Mickey." She embraced him and held him tightly. "It's not fair." Her proximity calmed him.

"They are very bad people, Mutzie. Maybe we should burn bagels on the front lawn?"

"It's no joke, Mickey."

"We'll call in the Ku Klux Kleins."

"Be serious."

"Me serious. They don't scare me. They get too pushy, I'll put locks on their bagels."

A tiny smile broke through her gloom.

"Stay that way," he said, taking her hand. He opened the door. There was someone in the corridor. He waited for the person to disappear then ran with her back to his room.

"Now I've got you in trouble, Mickey."

"It's Irish, making accusations. "

"About us?"

"Guess he has a good sense of rumor," Mickey shrugged, his groin area still painful. His expression gave him away.

"Did Pep hurt you?"

"He insulted my dignity. Both of them."

She sat on the bed and put her hands over her face. Her shoulders shook with sobs. He sat down beside her and caressed her back.

"Better to laugh than cry," Mickey said. "It works, believe me."

After a while she stopped crying. "Now what?" she asked.

"We get outa here. Then, later, we get to Swan Lake, the place where they're going to do Gagie tomorrow." His plan, once vague, was beginning to grow in his mind.

"How are you gonna get to Swan Lake?" Mutzi asked. "We need a car."

He nodded.

"We'll borrow one from the guests coming in. I can drive."

"That's stealing," Mutzie said. Mickey waited for a joke line. None came. She seemed to grow sad.

"Who asked you?" Mickey winked, hoping to pick her up. "Here's one: Man gets thirty days. On what charge? No charge. Everything's free."

"You're impossible," Mutzie said, again cracking a tiny smile.

"Trust Irving," Mickey said.

She looked at him, puzzled.

"It's a Jewish bank. Used to be Irving Trust."

She shook her head.

So he was the boy whistling in the cemetery to keep up his courage. But despite the danger, he could not deny the secret pleasure it gave him to be part of this.

"We'll never get away with it, Mickey," Mutzie said.

"Who said?"

Another thought occurred to him suddenly, diluting his fear somewhat. He was on the side of what was right and right always wins. Right? In the face of such overwhelming virtue in his reasoning, how could they fail?

"Who are we, Mickey?"

"The good guys, that's who."

"You are. Not me."

"So now you're fishing for compliments."

"You're crazy," Mutzie said.

"You and Gorlick," Mickey sighed. "He called me a meshuganer."

"He's right," Mutzie said. Shrugging, she put her arms around him. "You're something, Mickey. Really something."

"So are you, Mutzie. So are you."

Her closeness thrilled him and he felt her kiss him on the cheek.

"It's a start," he whispered.

He left Mutzie in Marsha's room and came down to the lobby for the fourth time that day. The lobby was beginning to fill with people checking out. Most of the new check-ins would not arrive until later in the day. He would take one of their cars. That part he viewed as simple.

The boys who parked the cars kept the keys in a cabinet near the driveway in front of the hotel. All he had to do was watch one of them park, then put the keys of the particular car he had in mind in the cabinet. Sure, it was stealing, but this was an emergency, wasn't it?

Outside, the rain had gotten worse and people came into the lobby in raincoats and hats, stamping their feet on the porch to remove droplets of water. He saw the Buchalters, Albert Anastasia and Frank Costello being fawned over by bellhops as their luggage was brought out to waiting cars.

They were saying their goodbyes to Pep and Reles with much fanfare, embracing like ordinary departing guests. Except for the carful of Anastasia's body guard goombas that waited nearby, the scene struck Mickey as so normal and bourgeois, so far from the truth of these people's lives.

"Hey, watchacallit, c'mere." It was Albert Anastasia. He had spied Mickey and motioned with his hand for him to come over. He stuck a hand in his pocket and pulled out a thick wad of bills, peeling off a twenty.

"Faw da kicks, kiddo. Not so funny, but ya tried." He laughed and handed Mickey the twenty. Despite his sense of revulsion at touching anything of Anastasia's, Mickey took it and forced a smile.

"Everything runs hot and cold at Gorlick's," Mickey said. "Except the water in the rooms. That's cold only."

"Maybe he'll be cold alla time, too."

It was Pep who had come up behind them. Mickey turned and continued to maintain his false smile.

"Ya hidin Pep's doll?" Albert asked with mocking laughter in his voice. "Ya look in his pants, Pep?"

"It ain't funny, Albert," Pep said, scowling.

Mickey felt the sudden need to change the mood.

"How about this: Man reaches into his pocket and pulls out a cigar stubb. 'Oh no,' he cries hitting himself in the head. 'What happened' somebody asks. Man says, 'I think I smoked my penis.'"

Albert guffawed, then laughed for a long time. Finally, he took out his handkerchief and blew his nose.

"So she runs out on ya, Pep," Anastasia said putting a hand

on Pep's shoulder after he had finally stopped laughing. "What's it to ya; a crumb on ya lap. Ya got a mudderlode a quiff."

"Nobody runs out on Pep," Pep grunted, scowling.

"A regular brooder," Reles said, joining the group.

"This schmuck knows," Pep said, pointing to Mickey. "I'm watchin ya, tumler."

"Listen, I need all the audience I can get," Mickey said.

"It ain't funny," Pep muttered.

"Where's ya sense a humor, Pep?" Albert Anastasia turned to Mickey. "Ya think this little kikey stole huh from da great Pittsburgh Phil? Ya really think dat, Pep?" His hand was still on Pep's shoulder.

"Na," Pep said. "He's a punk."

"She was good, but I had bettah, Pep," Albert laughed. "What ya should do, call Gloria. Let huh send ya some prime meat. Clean da pipes. Memba you got tings ta do tomorrow tonight. Loosen up."

"Yeah, yeah, Albert. Don worry. I got my head in da job."

"Business foist, right, Pep?"

"Nothin bodders business, Albert."

"Bettah not. Ain't no percentage in it."

There was more tipping of the fawning help by Costello, Buchalter and Anastasia. Finally, they left the lobby like visiting royalty. Pep, Goldstein and Reles went out to the porch to wave goodbye to the three big cars as they headed along the driveway to the main road.

Mickey started to go inside, and once again he felt the ubiquitous eyes of Irish following him. He repressed a flash of anger by reasoning that as long as Irish kept his eye on him, he would not be searching for Mutzie.

As he entered the lobby Marsha suddenly appeared.

"I thought we hadda date," she said, her hands on her hips, her eyes accusatory.

"I was about to go upstairs."

With a peripheral glance at Irish, he grabbed her arm and moved her out of his line of vision.

"Forgive me, Marsha. Maybe later. It rains, a tumler works."

"It was raining when I gave you the key, Mickey."

"Garlic caught me on the stairs."

She probed him with an unbelieving skeptical stare.

"I think I know where she is." Marsha said. "They been lookin for her."

At that moment Irish strode into the lobby.

"Please Marsha. Trust me. I'll explain later." He started to move away, but she held his arm.

"Make like ya wanna, Mickey?" she said smiling lewdly, licking her lips with her tongue.

At that moment, Irish reached them.

"Don bodder, Marsha." He cut a glance at Mickey. "He used it all up on Pep's quiff. Ain't got none left?"

"You scumbag," Marsha hissed.

"Ya givin him da flat rate, Marsha, or da twofers," Irish said. He turned his malevolent eyes on Mickey. "Wassamata, ain't got enough from Pep's coorva?"

Irish was baiting him. He tried to hold his temper.

"Pay no attention," Mickey said. "He's a two bit punk wants to make like big time gangster. Only he hasn't got the stuff. Have you, shlonghead?"

He watched Irish flush red, his lips quivering. Intimidation and tough talk were apparently the only ways to deal with Irish. Thankfully, the method worked once again and Irish retreated quickly, but not before a parting threat.

"Ya keep lookin ovah yaw shoulder mamzer, cause Irish is watchin yaw back."

Mickey knew the threat was real. It also comforted him to know that Irish would be caught in the trap that he and Mutzie were preparing.

"Thanks, Marsha," Mickey whispered.

"Ya playin with fire, Mickey," Marsha said. "Ya betta get her outa here."

"We got a plan," Mickey replied.

"Betta be a good one," Marsha said. "But if ya ask me, pussy ain't worth dying faw."

"I'll remember that, Marsha."

"And I'll memba to pray for ya. Both."

Keeping the remaining guests amused through the morning was torture. Chaos reigned. Children ran in and out of the rooms. He tried his biblical routine. "So you know why they didn't play cards on the Ark? How could they? Noah kept sitting on the deck." Not a titter. He tried again. "Poor Abraham. Had to sleep five in a bed. How come? He slept with his forefathers. And Moses, you know, was the first tennis player in the bible. He served in Pharoah's court."

Still not a giggle. He couldn't blame them. It was the wrong time and the wrong energy. Especially on his part. He was think-ing of Mutzie, worrying now that a light might go on in Irish's unscrupulous head.

"Play some games, tumler," someone shouted from the unruly and restless group. He consented, but organizing games was nearly impossible. He tried a "Pass the Orange" game in which participants pass oranges from one to another using their chins and not their hands.

A woman participant got a crick in her neck and had to be

taken to her room. One of the children stepped on a fallen orange, squashed it and slid across the floor. He searched his mind for anything to hold their attention. But he could barely hold his own.

During lunch, he felt himself under continuous surveillance. The dining room, as always at Sunday lunch, was half empty. Pep seemed to glare at him. Irish shot him menacing glances. Mrs. Reles looked at him strangely. He felt persecuted. Most of all, he worried about Mutzie alone upstairs and he plotted getting hold of one of the box lunches the kitchen prepared for homeward bound guests.

"Go tumel them," Gorlick told him. He was in a bad mood. The weather prediction was for rain all week. Mickey didn't feel like tumeling. But he made his rounds of the dining room, cracking whatever jokes were not stifled by his nervousness. He tried to skip the gangster table, but Kid Twist called him over.

"My wop friend's a good tipper, eh, tumler?" Reles said.

"Mr. Anastasia was very generous," Mickey said. Pep still groused at him, but seemed less interested as he ladled sour cream over blintzes.

"Ya wanna piece of his action, Abie," Bugsy Goldstein chimed in.

Reles laughed.

"Yeah, protection for tumlers," Reles said. He looked at Pep and pointed.

"Especially from him."

It was meant, Mickey supposed, as good-natured joshing. Pep didn't crack a smile.

"Ya find her, tumler, ya keep her," Reles said.

"I find her I twist her tits off," Pep said, looking up from his sour cream and blintzes.

Reles clicked his tongue and shook his head.

"Comes ta love, Pep got no heart," Reles said sarcastically. "No heart."

Mickey hated hearing Mutzie disparaged, but he kept a smile pasted on his face and moved to the next table.

He made his announcements amid his usual patter of jokes. Luckily Sunday afternoons were absorbed with registering guests. Mr. Gorlick liked him to hang out in the lobby to tumel with them as they arrived. He also arranged for a movie showing in the social hall, taking care of the kids while the women who were left behind played cards.

His objective now was to arouse no suspicion, to carry on with business as usual, even knowing that he and Mutzie would not be coming back to the hotel once they had gotten out safely. His plan was still in embryo stage, but the outlines were coming into focus. He and Mutz would drive the stolen car to Bernstein's apple orchard, then get to a spot near Swan Lake that would give them a good vantage point to witness the deed.

Of course, it was an awful and dangerous prospect. He decided not to focus on that part just yet. He hadn't any idea what would happen after they witnessed Gagie's killing. He had it in his mind to tell someone, someone who could act against these fiends. Surely there must be some government authority in the state that might prosecute these killers on the strength of his and Mutzie's testimony. There had to be someone. They couldn't control everything. Or could they?

As the plan grew in his mind, his began to focus on his sense of mission. He would be the righteous avenger for his father's beating, the savior of the woman he loved. The thoughts energized him. There was one more thing he had to do. He had to get himself fired.

He got up and addressed the dining room crowd with a

string of jokes that got a good laugh. Then he launched what he hoped would be the clincher.

"Now let me tell you about Garlic." He looked toward Gorlick, who was eating vegetables and sour cream at his regular table. At the mention of the hated word, he seemed to misfire, getting his spoon to his mouth. Sour cream covered his chin.

"He hates me to call him Garlic. But when a man stinks, what do you call him? Mr. Fart?"

The audience roared, the joke enhanced by Gorlick's dripping chin and beet red complexion.

"When it comes to money, you've got to hand it to Garlic. He'll get it anyway." The audience roared, encouraging him. "Garlic has so much money he doesn't know which building to burn next." More laughter. "But I can tell Garlic wants me around. He keeps giving me postdated checks." The audience howled. "If he can't take it with him, Garlic will send his creditors. After all, he has something the creditors like, but he won't spend it. But he gives me plenty of exercise. Every time he gives me a check I have to run to the bank." He looked at Gorlick, whose face had gone from beet red to ashen. His eyes glared hatred.

What surprised him was that even Pep howled. Maybe, just maybe he was taking his mind off Mutzie. He knew he had succeeded in making Gorlick the laughingstock. The fact was that he, Mickey Fine, also enjoyed it immensely.

"Sorry, Mr. Garlic," Mickey said. "You wanted I should make them forget about the rain. Keep the checkouts down."

After the usual announcements about the evening's activities, none of which he would attend, he stepped down to some enthusiastic applause. When he looked around, he noticed that Gorlick had gone. But he had barely started to drink his coffee when Mildred Feinstein, Mr. Gorlick's cross-eyed assistant came to the table.

"He wants to see you in his office now," Mildred said.

"*Now* now? Or now later?"

"Now now. He's having a conniption."

Mickey strode out of the dining room, feeling jaunty and exhilarated. In his office, Gorlick sat slumped in his chair.

"An ungrateful mamzer I hired," Gorlick said.

"All right, then, we're even. A mamzer hired a mamzer."

"You remember our verbal agreement. No boss jokes."

"A verbal agreement isn't worth the paper it's written on," Mickey shot back.

"This schmuck will kill me," Gorlick said. He handed Mickey a check. "Go. Go. As fast as your legs will take you. I want to fumigate your room."

Mickey, hiding his elation, looked at the check.

"You deducted for room and board?"

"You didn't eat? You didn't sleep?"

"That's not very fair, Garlic," Mickey said. He knew he was gilding the lily and had expected the deduction.

"Mildred, throw this man out," he screamed. "And call around the other hotels. I need a new tumler fast. I'll pay double." He turned to Mickey. "Double. You hear me. Double."

"Easy, Mr. G, your heart," Mildred cautioned.

"If I die, he'll have it on his head for the rest of his life."

"And what will you have on your head, Garlic? A tombstone."

Mickey quickly about-faced and left the man's office, having accomplished his objective. He wasn't sorry and he could not deny the enjoyment he had had.

With surprising boldness he went back into the dining room, then strode into the kitchen and picked up a box lunch and went out through the storage area and up the back stairs to Marsha's room. Irish, he had noted, was busy in the dining room.

Mutzie looked pale and frightened and seemed to be losing heart.

"As my mother always said: Eat. Eat," he said. She appeared puzzled by his ebullience.

"Why are you so cheerful?" she asked.

"I just got a lot of laughs," he replied. "Best of all, I got fired." He explained how he had done it. "All part of the master plan. You see the logic? Now they won't suspect we left together."

"But you lost your job," she shook her head and clucked her tongue. "You put yourself in danger. You lost a job that meant something to you. You should check yourself into the nearest asylum."

"Actually, I'm more certain than ever that we're doing the right thing."

"The right thing, maybe. The dumb thing, for sure." She bit into an egg salad sandwich without apparent appetite.

"When you're on the side of the angels, why worry?"

"I don't mind being on their side. I just don't want to be an angel," she said.

"I need this competition," he laughed.

"I also don't feel too good about Gagie," Mutzie said. "He was always nice to me. A perfect gentlemen."

"Another killer. You said so yourself."

"I know," she agreed. "They just . . . it's all so strange. Their meanness. They have no conscience. I don't understand it. How can people kill other people?"

"Happens all the time."

"Yeah," she shrugged. "Like in the movies."

"Like in real life," Mickey said.

He had never really seen violence, except that terrible scene in his father's store. He did have a few scrapes as a kid, but nothing even approaching a fatality. These people seemed like beings from an alien land, engaged in conduct outside of the value system he had been taught. Considering the heinous crimes that they were to have committed, it seemed almost a civic duty to thwart them, even beyond the broader reason of helping to save Mutzie from a life of sexual enslavement. He reveled in such noble and heroic thoughts, remembering King Edward the Eighth's abdication speech in which he said he was giving up the throne of England for the woman he loved.

"If you don't stand up and be counted," Mickey said, "the bad guys win."

"Such a hero," Mutzie said, putting aside her sandwich. She sounded depressed, but he ignored it. Instead he told her about his plan, as far as it had developed.

"If they catch us, you know, we're gone," she said.

"A real gloomy Gus."

"Better a miserable life than none at all," she said. It was, of course, the nub of her depressive state and he let it pass. If she was having second thoughts there was no way to force her to go along with his plan. This had to be her decision. He had made his.

"Now I want you to try on some of my clothes and fiddle with them to make them fit. There's no way you can go back to your old room. And we've got to get the hell out of here."

He went back to his room and quickly picked out some of his clothes and threw them in his battered suitcase. Above all, he needed to find a car and make a safe exit for both of them. Like some of his comedy routines, he was obliged to make it up as he went along. The important thing for him was not to show her any indecision on his part. He came back to Marsha's room.

"I feel like I'm in a Marx Brothers comedy."

He gave her the clothes he had chosen and turned his back while she put them on.

Finally she told him it was okay to see her and he turned and saw a good imitation of a boy wearing his big brother's clothes. She had tucked up her bleached, Jean Harlow hair under a beret that he used as a costume for French imitations. He looked down at her feet and noted that the pants covered her tennis sneakers.

"Sam, you made the pants too long," he sang. She smiled and he felt that the song had lifted her spirits.

"Fact is you look beautiful as a boy," he said and meant it. She blushed. "A girl, too."

Their eyes locked for a long moment. Hers moistened.

"You think I'm worth all this, Mickey?"

"Yes, I do."

"I've been such an idiot." She hesitated. "I've soiled myself." A sob shook her chest and she turned away from him.

He wanted to reach out and comfort her, but held back. His mind was absorbed by his plan. He would station himself near the driveway and observe the guests arriving by car and make his move at the most propitious moment. He would drive the car to the road and park next to a stand of trees that would screen it from the hotel. He would wait there until Mutzie joined him and they would take off to scout the Swan Lake area in preparation for their nocturnal observations.

Mutzie listened intently as he explained the plan. Admittedly there were risks and he tried to calm her fears. Above all, she must appear natural, certainly not furtive or uncertain. She would use the back stairs, then make her way to a corridor near the lobby and duck out onto the porch. From there she would descend a side stairway to the lawn and make her way on foot to the road. He told her exactly where he had planned to park the car. He looked at his watch.

"Give me about fifteen minutes."

"I'm scared, Mickey," Mutzie said.

"Worse things have happened," Mickey replied, smiling.

Her face brightened. She apparently sensed he was throwing her a straight line.

"Like what?"

"Like the farmer who tried to milk a bull."

She clicked her tongue and shook her head, but it brought out a smile. Then he got serious again.

"Above all, talk to no one, keep moving and do not make eye contact," he warned.

She pursed her lips and nodded.

"I hope I can handle it," she said.

"You can."

He picked up his mostly empty suitcase, moved toward the door and turned.

"Such a pretty boychick," he said, then he let himself out.

The lobby was less crowded than earlier and he strode through it, heading for the driveway. He carried his suitcase, proof of his departure.

"I'm really sorry about this," a woman's voice called from behind him. He turned quickly. It was Helen Reles.

"Not your fault," he said curtly. "Garlic had a right."

"Screw him," Helen said. "Abie will talk to him."

"It's all right," he said quickly. Her hand touched his arm and squeezed.

"No, it's not," she said, putting on what she must have

thought was her most compassionate look. "I hope it wasn't me that made this trouble for you."

"Nothing to do with you, Mrs. Reles," Mickey said.

"I've given you a bad time. And I'd like to make it up to you." She bent closer to him. "Give me a chance to be nice to you."

"It's not your fault," Mickey protested.

"What can I do? I'm Jewish. I feel guilty."

Her eyes opened liked puddles and her lips seemed to have mysteriously moistened. Nor did he have any doubt about her intentions.

"I'm resigned to it," he sighed, searching in his mind for some way to dismiss her.

"C'mere," she said, leading him by his arm to an alcove in a deserted corner of the lobby. He stole a glance at his watch. Mutzie would be getting ready to leave his room. In the alcove, she nuzzled close to him.

"Gorlick is no problem. Abie will take care of it. No problem."

"Really, Mrs. Reles . . ."

"Helen," she whispered poking her breasts into his chest. "Believe me, boychick. I can help."

"I . . . I've already lined up another job."

"So what. You belong here. It's me that made the trouble."

"It never happened."

"Okay, so I was wrong." She patted his face. "But who could blame me, such a cutie pie." She bent her head and whispered in his ear. "Don't be a putz. I can fix it." She paused and watched him. "All I have to do is tell my Abie and all you have to do is be nice to little me sometimes. Believe me. You'd be in the clear. I swear it. Abie won't think nothing, cause Abie won't know nothing. I know how to handle that. I'll tell him that Heshy gets a kick out of you."

"It's okay. I don't need anybody's help."

"Everybody needs a little help now and then. Even me. Now and then."

Mickey nodded, then realized what his nod might mean.

She reached down and squeezed his crotch. He jumped back stunned by her gesture.

"Oy, can I make a lollypop outa you bubbala," she whispered.

"Please, Helen," Mickey whispered.

She pressed closer to him. "I promise you." She took his hand and moved it to her crotch and kept it there with the pressure of her arm. "I can send you to the moon. Come on. We gotta deal?"

He was saved from answering by someone coming in their direction. She released his hand and moved away.

"And don't worry about nothin. We'll work it out. Right?"

He felt trapped. By now Mutzie had to be proceeding to where he was supposed to be meeting her with the car.

"I don't know what to say," Mickey said. It was true, of course.

"Say mazel tov," Helen said. She patted the hand.

One of the guests passed by the alcove glancing at them briefly. When he had gone, Helen moved quickly toward him and kissed him on the lips, prying them open and inserting her tongue. He felt nauseous, but he let it happen.

"Now go," she ordered pointing to his suitcase. "Bring this upstairs. You ain't going nowhere." He hesitated and she said sharply. "Go before I go crazy."

He moved back to the lobby. She followed him and, guiding him silently with an upward motion of her chin, watched him, until he moved up the help-forbidden front staircase. Then she moved forward, ascended the first flight, watched him hesitate, egged him on again with her chin until he had no choice but to ascend the stairs to the top floor that housed his old room.

There was a window on the landing. Peering out, he could see Mutzie making her way along the path by the lakeside that would take her on the roundabout route toward the place where he was supposed to be waiting with the car. He started toward the help stairs, planning to descend, then realized that if Helen Reles saw him with his suitcase she would logically assume that he had double-crossed her. He quickly put the suitcase in one of the maid's closets.

Then he looked out the window again and his heart lurched. Mutzie was still moving across the path, trying her best to look unconcerned and casual in her oversized costume. True to his instructions she did not waver, looking forward only. But following behind her, stalking her like a predator, crouching, hiding behind trees and shrubs, was Irish.

He started to run down the corridor in the direction of the main staircase, which would be closer to the lobby entrance than the backstairs. There was no time for niceties of conceal-ment. Mutzie was clearly in danger. Another ominous surprise greeted him as he reached the top of the stairs. Pep was ascend-ing rapidly, accelerating his pace when he saw Mickey. He was certain that Irish had alerted Pep to what was happening.

Mickey saw his face, the killer mask firmly in place, the eyes burning with hatred. Turning, he dashed backwards down the corridor to the back stairs, hearing Pep's pounding steps behind him. With the banister for balance he moved quickly down the first flight.

"Where's the fire?"

He saw Marsha moving toward him, standing in the center of the narrow stairway, her face frozen in an attitude of surprise.

As he passed her, he nodded and smiled thinly, perhaps hoping to disguise his terror. He saw her head turn upward, surely seeing the menacing Pep descending on him.

As he ran, some anxious reflex made him turn. It was only for a miillisecond, but it captured the moment with all its harrowing portent. "Don't," he cried out, or thought he did, although he heard nothing. He saw Marsha stick her leg in Pep's path and heard Pep's angry curse as he tumbled forward.

Mickey did not look back as he ran out of the building.

10

S HE FELT LIKE A CHARACTER IN A MASQUERADE, SUDDENLY free from the burden of herself. It was liberating to be someone else. Not that she was totally free from anxiety, but walking along the lake in the shadow of the serene lush mountains, she was finding it difficult to maintain the idea that she was truly in danger.

Mickey had said to walk nonchalantly, casually, intent on the scenery, as someone who might be taking on a normal walk in the country. Viewing the lovely landscape made everything that she had experienced in the past few months unreal, like a. . . . She checked herself. She was afraid to think in movie terms. Believing in movies and the life they depicted had gotten her into all this trouble in the first place.

And yet hadn't she been rescued by the handsome prince? Handsome, she decided, was a word she would never use again. Pep was handsome, a pretty wrapper for the ugliness and cruelty that lay beneath it. She couldn't understand what had drawn her to him. Had she been hypnotized? It would certainly relieve her of responsibility if this were so.

No, she decided, getting involved with Pep was her own

fault, her own wicked stupidity and delusion. Pep was a cruel, selfish man, capable of anything no matter how terrible. She had denied this to herself, hadn't she? She had been used, abused, treated like garbage. The memory of her conduct disgusted her. Only a blind woman could not see the truth about these men. Pittsburgh Phil Strauss, Kid Twist, Bugsy Goldstein. She mocked these nicknames. They were stupid names, perverse names.

It was, of course, utter madness for Mickey and her to attempt to strike back at these people. All right, they both had their reasons. But they didn't have a chance. Besides, it was another fairy tale to believe that goodness could triumph against corruption. She had certainly learned that lesson the hard way. No, she would have to talk him out of it. Once they were out of this environment, he would be able to think straight.

She moved along the trail that led to the road down the hill from the hotel. She had gone over it in her mind a number of times. By now, he must have found the car and was waiting for her. With each step away from the hotel, she felt better.

Reaching the road, she followed the treeline that shielded the hotel from view and walked to the indentation that Mickey had shown her from his window. Freedom, she trilled inside of herself, as she skipped forward for a few paces, certain that just around the bend in the road he would be waiting.

But when she reached the spot, it was deserted. A mistake, she decided, walking upward over a rise to get a view of the hotel and what she imagined was his window.

"Expecting someone, boychick?"

She turned quickly. It was Irish, arms folded, smirking with arrogance. Swallowing hard, she felt her body begin to tremble. His eyes wandered over her clothes.

"Ten will get ya five there's no shlong in dose pants," Irish said, howling with laughter.

Few cars passed on the highway. She felt trapped and alone. Where was Mickey? Still, she would not say anything. She felt the strong desire to run, to escape, but she remained immobile, too shocked to act.

"Pep knows now I wuz right. Jes like I told 'em. Them two was cookin up sumpin."

He moved up the rise to where she was standing and reached out for her arm. She wrenched it away.

"Hey, Cooz," Irish said through his tight smile. "Ya ain't gawn nowhere no more. An I doubt yaw buddy's comin. Pep's prolly seein ta dat."

Her heart sank. There seemed no point in resisting. With her pants hanging over her snearkers, he could easily outrun her and he was undoubtedly stronger.

"You're lying," she said, her voice hoarse with agitation, searching his face for some sign of wavering. Yet her disbelieving mind continued to be alert elsewhere, her ears searching for sounds of rescue, of Mickey emerging with the car to save her.

"Fug I yam," he said, reaching out again. This time he was prepared and she was unable to shake his hand loose from her arm.

"Leave me alone," she cried.

"Won do ya no good, cooz. Ya an dat fuggin tumler are caput. Pep gets a hole a him, he'll bash his head in. An you. . . ." He flattened her against him and squeezed her breast. She bent her head and tried to bite his hand, but he managed to evade her thrust by smashing her in the stomach with his elbow, almost knocking the wind out of her.

"Bastard," she hissed, squirming in his grasp. But he held her fast.

"Youse think ya cun make Irish look like a dummy. Well ya got anudder guess, cooz. Befaw yaw finished you'll be beggin ole Irish to give him freebies jes ta save yaw ass."

As she struggled futilely to get free of Irish's iron grasp, she heard a car slow nearby. She continued to fight him. He started to drag her up the rise, sweating and grunting with the effort, his foul breath nauseating her. Then she heard the car stop somewhere nearby. To keep Irish occupied, she continued to struggle furiously and his blows to contain her grew more and more intense.

Then she heard him grunt suddenly and loosen his grip. Turning, she watched him slowly buckle to the ground and above him, she saw Mickey, rubbing his fist. The skin had split and his knuckles were raw and bleeding. Irish reached the ground where he squatted holding his head in pain, dazed.

"What did your big toe say to your little one?" Mickey said, wringing his fist.

"God, Mickey, I thought it was over for me," Mutzie said.

"There was a heel following you," Mickey said without missing a beat.

Irish groaned, his head slumped over his chest.

"You know what I've decided, Irish?" Mickey said.

Irish looked up, his palms cupping his sore head. He tried to get his legs to leverage him up, but soon gave up in frustration.

"Jesus, tumler. Ya hit me so hard," Irish whined.

"I did that because you're not a very nice person," Mickey said.

"Coorva'll getcha into maw trouble, tumler," Irish groaned as Mickey and Mutzie turned away.

Grabbing her hand, Mickey led Mutzie to the car, a dark

blue Chevy four-door sedan. Mutzie's sense of terror retreated.

Irish struggled to his feet. He no longer looked like a menacing figure.

"Ya both are in deep shit," Irish cried, shaking his fist. "I'll getcha fa dis." He continued to rub his head.

"Nobody can get in deeper than you, pal," Mickey said gunning the motor of the Chevy.

Through the rearview mirror, Mutzie watched Irish diminish and disappear in the highway dust.

From the car, Mutzie could get a clear view of the serene meadows with their background of sloping green mountains. The sense of movement in this beautiful setting calmed her. For the moment all sense of danger disappeared. She wanted to keep going forever, far away from these cruel people, and to treat these recent experiences as a bad dream, a nightmare.

Not far from Gorlick's, Mickey had made a turn onto a narrow secondary road and was speeding over a hard, dirt-packed road that bisected truck and dairy farms.

He gunned the car forward, ignoring the washboard bumps, warning her to hold on as the car rocketed forward, smashing insects on the windshield. Mutzie held fast to the hand strap on the door with one hand and clutched the back of the seat with the other.

Mickey piloted the car through a maze of crossroads, making sharp turns into other back roads, squinting ahead at the unmarked terrain. It was not the moment to question his plan. For her, there were few choices: either escape, or surrender to a dark future. Besides, she had thrown herself on his protection and he had sacrificed everything for her rescue. Above all, she owed him her loyalty. Perhaps her life.

For nearly an hour, Mickey drove and said nothing, then suddenly he turned into another bumpy road to what appeared to be a crumbling deserted old barn. Inside the barn the car ground to a halt and Mickey slumped over the wheel.

"Good a spot as any," he sighed. "This escaping business can be exhausting." The smell of old dung hung in the air. Then he turned to Mutzie.

"You okay?" he asked.

"Terrific."

She searched his face, looking, she supposed, for regrets. No point in asking him, she told herself. It was far too late for that. They were in the same boat now. She reached out and touched his face, which was wet with perspiration, moist and cool to the touch. She felt a deep surge of gratitude for what he had done.

He turned to look at her, his gaze deep with affection. Its obvious and deeply felt sincerity made her uncomfortable. She was, she admitted, very confused about sentiment, about feelings. She had trusted feelings and they had betrayed her. She wondered if gratitude was a feeling that could be trusted. It would be a long time, she decided, before she could ever again trust affection. And never again love. Never that. She wanted to tell him this, but held back, even when he took her hand from his face and kissed her palm. She let him, then gently, almost surreptitiously, removed her hand from his.

"We'll stay here for a while," he said, leaning his head back on the car seat. She did the same, looking up at the rotting rafters of the old barn, wondering if there were bats up there hanging upside down. Again the movie image, she thought wryly. She had never seen a live bat.

"Do you know where we are?" she asked.

"Vaguely," he said. "I was really following the arc of the sun. Swan Lake is west of here." Suddenly he patted his pocket as if he remembered something.

"What is it?"

He pulled his hand out of his pocket and brought out the twenty dollar bill that Anastasia had given him.

"This is it, Mutzie. All we have between the devil and the deep blue sea."

He shook his head and shrugged.

"I'll never forgive myself," Mutzie said. "I've ruined everything for you, for myself."

"Sometimes you can't predict, Mutzie. Like Noah said when it started to rain, 'I knew I shouldn't have washed the ark this morning.'"

"This is really serious, Mickey," Mutzie said.

"Tell me."

She searched her mind for other alternatives. There was only one. "Maybe if I went back." He looked at her and frowned. Their eyes met, but he did not respond. "I'm not worth it, Mickey. You mustn't throw your life away for me."

"I love it when people look at the bright side," Mickey said.

"No more lying to myself, Mickey."

"Mutzie," he admonished. "The only way out for us is to get them before they get us. Sure, they're bastards, vicious killers. They wanted to turn you into a prostitute. And they nearly killed my father. And if they get their hands on us, don't think about it."

"Get them? We haven't got a chance," she said. "They're too strong, too powerful. It's a crazy idea, Mickey. Who will believe us? We're nobodies. They're powerful. They control things. They kill people who stand in their way."

"We'll see," Mickey mused.

She studied his face.

"Now it's you starring in a movie. Who are you? Jimmy Stewart or Gary Cooper?" she asked.

He smiled and his eyes flickered.

"Buck Jones," he said. "He wears a big white hat."

"I don't like cowboy pictures," she said, realizing that he was all but foreclosing on her objections.

"I do. The good guy always gets the girl." He giggled nervously as if the words had been said without permission.

She felt herself flush.

"Not if he's dead," she murmured, thinking . . . the girl as well.

"In the movies, the hero doesn't die," Mickey said after giving the matter some thought.

"It's not a movie, Mickey," Mutzie said. She would have to continue to remind herself about that.

"That's the point," Mickey said. He seemed to become dead serious, more serious than she had ever seen him. They remained silent for a long time, each lost in their own thoughts.

"They'll find us, Mickey," she sighed.

"Not if we use our tuchas." He tapped his head.

"But if we see them do that to Gagie, and we tell what we saw, there would be no going back. They'll hunt us forever."

"Not if the law stops them."

"What law? They own the law."

She searched his eyes for some sign of wavering, found none, then sighed.

"It'll never happen. Who are we? Pishers," she said. It was harsh, she knew, but suddenly it became important to say it. He smiled.

"To me, you're not a pisher," Mickey said.

"Then you're blind. I'm soiled goods now," she said, remembering her mother's sermonizing about keeping herself pure.

"So call me Procter & Gamble," Mickey said.

She lay her head back on the seat. "I think you've lost your mind," she whispered.

"Actually, I'm a split personality. My psychiatrist sends me two bills."

"I wish I could laugh, Mickey. But I want to cry."

"Don't," Mickey said. "You need clear eyes to see what we've got to see."

Mutzie slept in the back seat and he slept in the front. They awoke at first light, hungry and uncomfortable. Her sleep had been dreamless, for which she was thankful. Then reality crowded in on her. She felt suddenly drained.

"You okay?" Mickey asked.

"Tell you later," she whispered, dreading the day. She got into the front seat and looked at herself in the rearview mirror.

"Doesn't do you justice," Mickey quipped.

"I don't need justice. I need mercy."

She knew what he was doing. Maybe he had a point. When in doubt, try laughter. He had taught her punchlines. She turned to him and smiled.

"Hey, Mickey, you have your shoes on the wrong feet."

"Hey, these are the only feet I have."

"What did the mother turkey says to her playboy son?"

"If your father saw you now he would turn over in his gravy."

"Feel better?" Mickey asked, starting up the motor.

She searched for a comeback line, but couldn't find any. "Getting there," she lied, dreading what they had before them.

They got back on the main road and searched for a store. After a few miles, they saw a general store with a single gas pump.

"Better gas up and get some food for later," Mickey said, parking the car next to the pump. And old man came out to pump the gas.

"Come on," he said to Mutzie and they got out of the car and went into the general store. A gray-haired woman wearing a flowered dress, scuffed high shoes and dirty anklets, squinted at them from behind the counter.

The woman got them milk, white bread and cut them a pound of American cheese and some baloney.

"Don't forget mustard," Mutzie said.

The woman behind the counter turned to face her. "She's a girl," the woman said.

"A girl?" Mickey said.

The woman studied them both impassively, not breaking a smile.

"Lots a funny stuff going round here these days," the woman growled. She turned her back on them, obviously removing a purse from a hiding place in her brassiere. Opening the purse she counted out one five and four singles and change. The woman looked after them as they left.

"Can you direct me to Bernstein's Orchard?" Mickey asked the man who had filled his tank.

"Bout ten miles up." He pointed with his chin. "Sign says where to turn."

The man was just putting up the nozzle. Mickey gave him a dollar for the ten gallons the man had put in the tank.

"Used to be only white people here," the man grunted.

"I know," Mickey said. "It really pissed off the Indians."

"I was meaning them Jews," the man grunted.

"Better keep that fly buttoned," Mickey said, looking at the man's crotch. "They're comin around to kosher your dick."

The man's jaw dropped. Mickey gunned the motor and left the man in a puff of exhaust.

"That was awful," Mutzie snickered.

"Pissed me off. He should have said those Jews instead of them Jews."

They found a spot in a stand of evergreens, made sandwiches and drank the milk.

"We were a good team," Mickey said suddenly.

Mutzie nodded. "I loved making people laugh."

"Nothing more satisifying," Mickey said. "For me, it has always been a kind of calling. Ever since I was a little kid."

"A born tumler."

"I think so. When you make people laugh, it's like you're giving them a gift." He paused. "Considering all the bad things, the things that make people cry. Laughter takes away the pain. At least for a little while." She felt him studying her. "We could be a team, Mutz. Like George and Gracie."

"Coulda shoulda," Mutzie said, thinking how awful their future looked at that moment. "From here, the life I lived in Brownsville seemed pretty good."

The entrance to Bernstein's Orchard had a faded sign stuck in the ground next to a narrow dirt road. They followed the rutted road past rows of apple trees heavy with half-ripe fruit. The afternoon sun had begun to elongate tree shadows on the ground.

About a half mile down the road, the apple trees ended, but the road continued in the direction of the lake, rising sharply into a high rocky plateau jutting out over the water. The road finally ended about fifty feet from the edge of the cliff. They stopped the car and got out, walking to the edge. Directly below them the lake was dark and seemed deep. Mickey picked up a heavy stone and dropped it, watching it disappear with a gurgling plunk beneath the inky surface.

"Bastards know their business," Mickey said, looking around him.

"How awful," Mutzie said, shivering, her lips chattering. She stepped back from the edge and started back to the car.

"Take a picture of it in your mind," he said. "And try to take in all the details."

She wondered suddenly if he was cold-blooded like all the rest of them. Did all men have this cruel streak in them?

Mickey drove the car back down the road, hiding it behind some trees at the edge of the orchard. It was growing dark swiftly now and the stars were beginning to sparkle out of the clear, dark, moonless night. With the sun down, a chill had begun and he put his arm around her shoulders as they sat in the car.

"I'm scared, too," he whispered.

"What will happen to us?" she asked.

He sighed. "Depends if we're bees or donkeys," Mickey said.

"Meaning what?" Mutzie said, nestling deeper into the crook of his arm.

"One gets the honey, the other gets the wacks."

She smiled and continued to watch the stars proliferate. He was right about humor. It soothed and chased pain, at least for a moment. With his free hand he fished in the back for the Milky Ways and gave her one while he took the other. They ate and it tasted good. Eating Milky Ways under the stars. She found it impossible to believe that something as terrible as murder was soon to happen.

"A long way from Brownsville," she said, thinking of her mother and father and their perpetual war. For her mother, life was stripped of all illusion, while her father found hope in his beloved socialism. She was certain that both of them would be ashamed of her now, as ashamed as she was of herself. Maybe this act of retribution that Mickey had concocted would redeem her, at least to herself. She wasn't sure. Condoning murder for a higher good was a troubling idea. Like a noble war. Her thoughts surprised her. She seemed changed, especially to herself, as if recent events had given her an entirely different persona and all the earlier illusions had vanished.

She must have dozed, then suddenly she was conscious of being shaken awake.

"Now," Mickey whispered. The moved out of the car. The only sounds were the usual country symphony of crickets. The air seemed to have grown less chilly, felt soft and smelled faintly of apples.

Hand in hand, they moved through the orchard until they reached the road that bisected it and followed it upward to the flat clearing at the top of the promontory. She let Mickey lead her to a thick stand of young evergreens, through which they could get a good view of area at the edge of the cliff.

Mickey made a soft bed of fallen pine needles and then they lay supine on their stomachs, watching the area like soldiers on lookout.

The sound reached them first as a distant irregular buzz, like a saw cutting through an unruly piece of pine, hitting an occasional knot, then smooth sailing until it hit a knot again. She tensed and was instantly alert, although assailed by the illusion that her heartbeat spread its sound over the orchard like a drummer on parade.

223

Beside her, Mickey lay on his forearms, like a predator waiting for its oncoming prey. She assumed his position, lifting her head and peering in the direction of the sound. In the distance, she could see the glow of the car's headlights as it bounced along the washboard ribbon of road.

Only then did she realize that she hadn't really expected it to happen, that it was simply one more expectation to be exploded by reality, Mickey's romantic fantasy, somehow intertwined by visions of heroism and adventure.

But now it came, shattering the improbable fiction, making what had gone before at Gorlick's the real illusion. Looking back on what had happened to her seemed completely without any relationship to real life, like a bizarre nightmare.

The car rounded a bend, briefly bathing them in light. They put their heads down until it washed over them as if they were prisoners on the run, to avoid being frozen in the searching beams. But the light quickly passed and their heads were up again as the car pulled up on the flat clearing a few yards from the precipice. She did not recognize the car, which suggested that it was stolen. Like their own.

The lights clicked off and the men got out of the car. The person in the driver's seat she recognized as Irish.

"Wait here, schmuck," she heard Pep say.

"Ya say it's buried aroun heah?" It was Gagie's voice, high pitched, anxious and exaggerated.

"Yeah, aroun heah."

It was Pep's voice now and she could see him clearly a few yards from where she lay, dressed improbably in one of his pinstripe suits and wearing his pearl gray hat. Then she saw Abie Reles step out on the running board carrying a shovel.

"Ya say Lepke tole ya this?" Gagie said.

"He drawed me a map, like I tole ya," Pep said. From experience, she knew by the pitch of his voice that he was irritated.

"Crazy place to put a bag a stones," Gagie said.

"Ten grand wortha stones," Pep said. As he said it, Gagie was watching Reles come toward them with the shovel until he faced both Pep and Gagie.

"Okay so we heah," Gagie said.

"Ovah dere," Reles said, and when Gagie turned, he swung the shovel and banged it with all his strength across one of his knees. The impact of metal against bone made a muffled ringing sound. Mutzie gasped and started to lurch backward. Mickey reached out and held her tight with one arm. Gagie dropped howling to the ground, clutching his knee.

"Ya done bad, Gagie," Pep said.

"Double-crossing mamzer," Gagie whined hysterically.

"Look who's talkin," Pep said, standing over the writhing Gagie. "Ya thought ya was gonna do me, right, Gagie? Diden bodder you."

"Was Abie who said . . ." Gagie began, but Reles came forward, swung the shovel over his head and banged him on the other knee. Gagie squealed in agony. Reles laughed.

"Me do Pep. He's like my brudder, schmuck. But dis is cause ya was a bad boy, Gagie. Woist is ta steal from ya buddies."

"No . . . I diden . . ." Gagie squealed.

"Lemmee, Kid," Pep said, reaching for the shovel.

"Be my guest," Reles replied with a chuckle.

Pep took the shovel and smashed it down on one of Gagie's feet. Again Gagie screamed. Mutzie gagged.

"I can't. . . ." she whispered.

"You gotta, Mutzie," Mickey said. "And you gotta remember everything. Everything." He spoke directly into her ear. Not that it mattered. Gagie was squealing in agony, filling the night with his screams.

"He gotta hava lesson," Pep said. "Right, Kid?"

"Givem a lesson on da udder one."

Pep lifted the shovel and smashed Gagie's other foot. He screamed in pain, then began to whimper.

"My wife and kids," he cried. "I nevah . . ."

"Hey Gagie," Abie said. "We take care a dem. Not to worry. We ain't animals. Right, Pep?"

"Yeah. We take care a dem. Man's family comes foist."

"My kid needs a fadder," Gagie pleaded. "So I made a mistake. Hey, we been friends fawevah. We did jobs togedda."

"Ain't friendship, Gagie. Jes business. Ya put ya fingahs in da till. We gotta set an example. Nothin poisonal. Right, Pep?"

"Shit no, Gagie. Nothin poisonal."

"I diden mean nothin," Gagie pleaded. "I give it all back. I swear on my mudder. Every shekel plus interest. Double if ya want."

"Ya shoulda tought a this befaw ya fucked us, Gagie," Pep said calmly as he leaned against the shovel. He lit a cigarette. Mutzie could see his face in the match's glow. It was unsmiling and menacing and she trembled at the sight. He took a deep drag then turned toward the car.

"You wanna show me now what a big man y'are, Irish?" He lifted the shovel. "Counta you today, I nealy broke my ass. I still hoit. Fuckin hooer that fat courva."

"Blame him? I tawt da broad tripped ya," Abie said.

"Wouldna bin dere it wasen for dat putz in da car. Was supposed to keep an eye out for that lousy quiff. Anyway it felt good to work dat fat cunt ovah. Evah see blue tits?"

"Oh no," Mickey whispered. "Not Marsha."

"Who?" Mutzie said.

"She helped us. Damn bastards. Just keep looking, Mutz. We got more reasons now."

"You fucked up a good waitress," Reles continued. "Ya feget we gotta piece a da place. Ya don do too good faw business worryin ovah this chickenshit. You and yaw goils, Pep. Get us all in hot water. Business foist, Pep. Ya tink too much wid yaw shmekel."

"Nobody fucks wid Pep," Pep muttered. Gagie, all but ignored, lay in voluble agony, groaning at their feet.

"Schmuck let 'em get away," Pep said. He looked toward Irish. "I ain't finished wid ya, Irish, putz."

"Dat's udder business, Pep. You and them knishes always getcha inta trouble. Top of it, Gorlick's also lost a good tumler. Who cared he got inta huh pants?"

Mutzie listened with disbelief. She looked toward Mickey who shook his head.

"No pussy don insult Pittsburgh Phil," Pep said. "Makes me look bad." He shouted toward Irish again. "Little putz is gonna findem, right, putz?"

"Fuck da quiff. Fine da tumler. My kid tinks he's funny. So does Albert."

"Well he ain't," Pep said.

"I seen ya laughin," Abie taunted.

"A minute I'll give ya dis shovel up yaw ass," Pep said, sounding as if he meant it. Again he turned toward Irish. "Come on, putz, show me yaw stuff. Wanna be a big man?" He turned to Reles. "I tink dis kid's a pussy."

Irish moved closer, to where they stood over Gagie.

"Come on kid," Abie taunted. "Ya only gotta hit 'em, not fuck 'em." He laughed his hyena's laugh.

Obviously scared, Irish came forward grinning, his face like a cutout pumpkin. Pep threw him the shovel.

"Jes swat him anywheres, kid. Make ya feel good." He looked down at the writhing Gagie. "We gotta make an example, Gagie. Don't we, Abie?"

"How else we gonna keep da boys in line? Shit, Gagie, we trusted ya."

"Faw once do sumpin right, kid," Pep taunted.

With some effort Irish lifted the shovel and raised it over his shoulder.

"Doesn't hoit," Reles laughed. "Unless ya miss an hit ya own shin." He roared again.

Mickey clutched Mutzie around the shoulders.

Irish hesitated, his face contorted. They could see the reflection of perspiration on his forehead.

"Putz's shittin bricks," Reles said chuckling.

Irish stood as if he had turned to stone. He licked his lips and they could see the whites of his eyes dancing in his head.

"Putz got no cojones," Pep said. "Maybe we do him like Gagie."

"Got da foist time shits," Reles said. "Feel a little wet in ya underweah, putz?"

Still Irish held the shovel on his shoulder while Gagie whimpered below him, pleading.

"I make it good. Gimme a break." he cried.

"Do him, putz," Pep shouted.

Irish started to lift the shovel, brought it almost over his head, then lay it back on his shoulder. She saw his face, anguished now, a twitch pronounced in his jaw, lips trembling, tears glistening on his cheeks. All the bravado and swagger had disappeared. He was a scared wretch, too frightened to rebel, and either too compassionate or cowardly to strike the blow. Although it had seemed impossible just moments ago, Mutzie felt sorry for him. His mean streak had limits. It was all sham and fakery. The poor bastard was not a killer.

Suddenly Pep kneed Irish's crotch, then quickly moved his knee away.

"Putz really pissed himself," he hissed, "rooned my pants."

He grabbed the shovel from Irish and lifted it over his head. Irish, made a meager and futile gesture put his arms over his face—less, it seemed, to protect himself than to hide his sobs. Unfortunately his shoulders gave away his sad condition.

But Reles reached up to stay Pep's forearm, his grip apparently like a clamp of iron.

"No freebees, Pep. We ain't gettin paid faw da kid. He ain't business."

Pep slowly lowered the shovel, but his anger wasn't spent. He kicked Irish in the shins. Irish yelped and fell to his knees. Pep, fuming, looked down, pushed Irish's hands from his face, and pointed a finger at his nose.

"No good fuck . . ." he began, then turned suddenly, lifted the shovel and brought it down on Gagie's shoulder. The crunching sound of bones breaking made Mutzie throw up into the pine needles.

"Look," Mickey hissed, lifting her head by grabbing her hair.

"Please, Mickey," she pleaded.

"We gotta . . ." Mickey began, then gagged himself. The sound he made was louder then expected and she quickly froze, watching the men now to see if they had heard. But they were too busy with their grisly work.

"Don kill me," Gagie screamed in agony.

"See, putz," Pep said, turning to Irish, who had managed

to stagger upright and was wiping away the tears with his sleeve.

Gagie's squeals became louder.

"Sounds like a cage a monkeys," Reles said.

"Ya makin too much fuckin noise, Gagie," Pep said.

"Pop im, Pep," Reles said, looking around. Mutzie froze. Kid Twist seemed to be peering directly at her. "Who knows who's out dere. People got ears."

"Don like da music, huh, Abie?" Pep said. Hurting Gagie seemed to have calmed him.

"Gets on my noives."

"Fuck you den, Abie, I shut it awf."

He lifted the shovel high over his head and brought it down full force on the still squealing Gagie. Again they heard the sound of crunching bone. Then Gagie was quiet, silenced forever.

"Tink he's done?" Abie asked, bending over the inert body.

"Maybe we give him coupla shots fa good measha," Pep said repeating his pulverizing of Gagie.

"Ya making a mess, Pep," Abie said. He turned to Irish. "Ya go get da slot."

Irish hesitated, his head down, watching Gagie's pummeled corpse with disbelief.

"Putz don listen," Pep said. He raised his foot and kicked Irish in the backside. It seemed to be more playful than mean, as if Pep had fully satisfied his sadistic bent and was now tranquil. Almost. Beyond her disgust, Mutzie was furious with herself for ever getting involved with such a vicious animal. She wished she had the guts and the strength to rush up and strangle him. The impulse startled her. Given the opportunity, could she have done it? Or opt out, like Irish?

Irish limped back to the car, opened the trunk and pulled out what looked like a slot machine, which he wrestled out of the trunk and manhandled over to where Gagie lay.

"Now go get da rope," Abie ordered.

Irish went back to the trunk, took out a length of rope and brought it back to where the men stood over the battered corpse.

"Now what ya do is tie dis piece a shit ta da machine," Pep said.

"I like dat touch, Pep," Abie said. "Weight him wid a slot. Wait'll Albert heahs. He'll getta laugh, right, Pep?"

"Woith it, jes ta see his face," Pep said, watching Irish tie the body to the slot machine.

"Not like dat, putz," Pep said, pushing him away. Pep bent down, fiddled with the rope and pulled a knot together. "Like dat. Ya wanna be in dis business kid, ya gotta know knots."

"Gotta know a lotta tings," Abie said. "Like not pissing ya pants. Dis is business. Dey ain't people. Dey is shitbags. Ya loin dat ya can do anybody. It's like a mental ting. Feget dere poisons. What ya see dere is a shitbag." He tapped his forehead. "Ya say ta yusself, I ain't gonna kill a man. I'm gonna kill a shitbag is awl. Like in a waw. Da udder army is shitbags. Nobody cries faw a shitbag."

"Anybody kin kill a shitbag." Pep said.

"Dat's our business, killin shitbags," Reles pointed out.

"Dollahs faw killin shitbags." Pep turned to Irish. "Dollahs, putz. Which ya ain't gonna see faw dis job. Ya ain't entitled."

"Ya coulden do it cause ya tought dat Gagie dere was a real poison," Reles said. "Me, I coulden kill a real poisen edder. Only shitbags. Business is all. Catch my drift, putz?"

Irish shrugged and nodded. "Next time . . ." he mumbled, clearing his throat. "You'll see. Jes gimmee anudder chance."

"We give im dat, right, Pep?" Reles said.

"I give im da sweat offen my balls," Pep said.

"Aw, comon, Pep. Anudder chance. I got a liddle woozy is awl. One maw. I kin do it." He raised his arm in a swearing gesture. "May I drop dead," Irish pleaded.

"Drop dead?" Pep said with a chuckling gurgle. "Who's gonna pay faw you scumbag. You ain't worth even a fin."

"Aw, Pep. . . ." Irish whined.

"Ya don't do nothin right, putzvatig. After dis job ya find them two you lost. Heah me. Ya ain't comin back ta Gorlick's less you bring 'em back wid you. Heah me good. Uddawise we give ya yaw balls for breakfast."

"I find dem, Pep. You watch."

"Nuff a dis crap. Let's put dis shitbag away," Reles said. He stood up straight and walked to the edge of the precipice.

"Maybe toity feeta wawta," Pep said. "We got some udda shitbags down dere to keep im company." He looked at the body on the ground. "Won't be lonely down dere, Gagie," Pep said.

Grunting hard, the three men pushed the body to the edge of the precipice then tipped it over. After a moment of silence they heard a splash, then nothing. Pep went back to the spot where he had dropped the shovel then flung it into the water as well.

"Gagie was a good boychick," Reles said.

"Till he went bad, became a shitbag," Pep laughed. He turned toward Irish. "Ya wanna not become a shitbag, putz. Ya find dem two . . . udderwise youse a shitbag, capish?"

"I'll find 'em, Pep. You watch . . ." Irish began.

"Ya know yaw a nudnick wid dat, Pep," Reles said. "Cantcha just feget it."

"I ain't finished wid dose two," Pep said. "Not wid him needer." He stuck a finger in Irish's chest.

"An ya know what we do wid shitbags. Abie here knows I ain't kiddin. You find 'em." He moved his head in the direction of the lake. "Plenny room down dere."

"Waste a energy," Abie said. "A piece a ass ya can always git." Reles shook his head. "Schmuck don feget nothin. How many times I gotta say it." He raised his voice. "Ain't in the business plan. Wese pros."

"I gotta score ta settle."

"Score shmore, Pep. We gotta nuff on our plate widout dat."

"I get my mitts on em, dey go on Pep's plate like a toikey. Evah see what dey do to a toikey on Thanksgiving?"

"Yeah, I seen it," Abie howled. "Only it ain't Thanksgiving."

"I cut it up good. I give ya da last part ovah da fence, Abie. Hers not his."

"Ovah and ovah. Ya give me a pain in my kishkes, Pep."

Pep grunted and pushed Irish forward, toward the car.

"Come on, putz. Weah outa heah. Ya drop us at Gorlick's and ya ain't gonna come back till ya bring 'em back alive like Frank Buck."

Irish limped swiftly to the car and restarted the motor. Pep and Reles got in and Irish maneuvered the car toward the road. Again the light washed over them and they lowered their heads.

Soon the car was heading back toward the main road. Slowly the sound faded and disappeared and it was silent again. They hadn't noticed the gathering of clouds that covered the starry night. It grew colder as they lay on the mound of pine needles, huddled together and speechless.

Mickey was the first to speak.

233

"I think we got Pep's attention."

She started to agree, but before the words could come, she vomited.

11

I N BERNSTEIN'S ORCHARD THEY HUDDLED IN THE CAR ALL
night, both of them too traumatized to find the energy to
move. Mickey was too terrified to think clearly, nor could
he find of a joke in his mind to chase away the utter gloom that
had descended on them both.

The night was chilly and Mutzie nestled herself in the crook
of his arm. Her body trembled and she sobbed quietly, remaining
unresponsive to his attempts to draw her out of herself.

What he had witnessed stunned him, despite the condition-
ing to the gangsters' cruelty he had received when they had beat
his father. They were totally without mercy or humanity. Human
beings became "shitbags" in their peculiar system of logic. And
once they had been transformed into "shitbags," they became
garbage, objects to be discarded like empty tin cans or stripped
chicken bones.

If there was the slightest doubt in his mind about the course
of action he had chosen for them, there was none now. He was
certain that he would remember every detail. The question now
was who could be told, who had the power to act and bring
these people to justice. Nor did he have any doubts that if he and

Mutzie were ever found, they could expect no mercy.

Pep had made it quite clear what he would do if he caught up with them. And there was no reason to believe he would be dissuaded by Reles or anybody else. The man was a maniacal killer, a ruthless monster. There was also an odd disconnect growing in his mind. The idea of Jewish gangsters seemed somehow against the grain, an aberration. Maybe this was a reaction for all those centuries the Jews were kicked around and treated like dirt. A sense of ethnic shame was beginning to seize him. Jews were not supposed to do this to each other. The idea gave impetus to his mission.

Sometime around dawn, Mutzie stopped trembling. He had dozed and her sudden quietude awakened him. Her eyes were open and she was watching the gray stripe of impending dawn through the windshield. The weather had cleared and the sun's morning rays painted the tops of the orchard's trees with a golden glow.

"I'm afraid all the accommodations I could offer is this luxury lodge," he said hoarsely.

"At least there's a good view," she murmured.

"A beautiful spot. Here the hand of man has never set foot."

"Now what, Mickey? We saw them do this. Now what?"

"We have to tell people," Mickey answered.

"But who?" she whispered tremulously.

At that point he had no idea about what to do next. Going to the police, considering how the combination had probably corrupted them, seemed fruitless, probably dangerous. He remembered Irish's words "dey own everybody." How else could they get away with gambling, prostitution and, worst of all, murder?

Then it occurred to him that the wiser course would be to go to the state capital in Albany and, hopefully, find someone who would listen to their story, someone beyond reproach, someone who could take action. He wasn't sure how the idea of Albany had entered his mind; perhaps it was all those election signs along the road featuring candidates for state office. He had noted that Governor Lehman was seeking a second term, a source of pride since Lehman was a Jew.

"They can't own everybody," Mickey reasoned. "Maybe we can find someone in Albany." It was more of a place than a plan, but not too far upstate from where they were.

"I don't know, Mickey," she said. Discouragement and fear had begun to sink in.

"All we need is one good man in a position of authority. The proof is undeniable. Gagie's body is at the bottom of Swan Lake." He paused. "Unless the fish have a feast and make all gone."

He did not want to frighten Mutzie with his uncertainty and the possibility of failure. Up to then it hadn't been an option. There was, of course, the risk that they would run into a corrupt official, someone on the combination's payroll who would turn them in, make them "shitbags." It was not a comforting thought.

"Remembering," Mutzie said, shivering. "That will be bad enough. Telling will be worse. Sometimes the memory plays tricks."

"Like Rabinowitz," Mickey said determined to raise their spirits. When in doubt make funny. Laughter was therapy. His new idea was filling him with renewed energy.

"Rabinowitz?" she said, obviously trying to jump start her own optimism.

"Guy runs over to Rabinowitz. Says, 'You've changed. You used to be six feet. Now you're shorter. You used to have black hair. Now it's red. You used to have blue eyes. Now they're brown. What happened to you, Rabinowitz?' Guy looks at him and says, 'I ain't Rabinowitz.' . . ."

"'Oh,' he says," Mutzie interrupted. "'You also changed your name.'"

"You heard it."

"From you." She cuddled closer to him. Her nearness sparked his confidence.

"Sometimes there are miracles," he whispered. When in doubt there was always the supernatural.

"I don't believe in miracles, Mickey. Not any more."

"The truth is still the truth. We saw it, Mutzie. With our own eyes. The important thing is that we do what's right. No decent person can live with this and do nothing. We'd never forgive ourselves."

"And I have a lot to forgive. For me, that will be the hardest part," she said, raising her eyes to his. Her face seemed radiant, less fearful, as if she had finally resolved something within her. He wondered if she was offering her lips for a kiss. But somehow any response on his part seemed inappropriate to the moment. Not now, he told himself, although he wanted to with all his soul.

"You're a good person, Mickey," she sighed, offering a tiny chuckle.

"So are you, Mutzie."

"Then tell me, if I'm so good, how did I get us into this? A few weeks ago we were strangers. You were a lot better off than now. I feel so guilty."

"Like the Jewish mother on jury duty. They sent her home. She had insisted she was guilty."

"I wish I could laugh, Mickey. It's like we're whistling in the graveyard."

"Better to whistle. Above all we must avoid being a permanent resident."

She shrugged and was silent for a long time, before she spoke again. "What do you make of Irish?"

Irish's actions had been a surprise. He had expected the little turd to enjoy the experience.

"First time jitters," Mickey said, wondering if his own hatred of Irish colored his conclusion.

"I don't know. Maybe there's a decent streak in him somewhere."

"I doubt it," Mickey said, remembering Pep's admonition to find them. One might conclude that for Irish that could really be a matter of life or death. Whatever Irish's motives, Mickey and Mutzie's testimony, if it could ever find a receptive audience, could certainly send him to prison. In an odd way, he wished that Irish had participated in the killing. That would make it possible for him to join the others in getting the electric chair. The irony of it suddenly jumped into his mind. It was Irish who had given him the weapon, told him about third party witnesses. His stomach reacted to the thought by turning itself into a knot.

His mind remained busy trying to come up with a course of action. Albany was still a possibility, but it seemed to grow more and more remote. He felt certain that the combination's contacts reached all the way up to the state capital. And even if they found an honest man among the state politicians, then what? Witnesses were certainly routinely murdered by these monsters. It was not a happy prospect.

Was doing the right thing worth risking his future, their future, their lives? At the moment, he found himself dealing with too many negatives, too many obstacles. Maybe they had already crossed an invisible Rubicon.

To add to their dilemma, they had run out of food and their

money was almost gone. And they were both tired and grungy. Still, Mickey started the car and headed to the highway with no fixed purpose or plan of action.

They stopped at a gas station and bought another dollar's worth of gas and picked up a free map of New York State. Studying the map, he considered the route northward. Canada was a possibility. Then he traced the route to Albany, which was much closer. He borrowed a pencil from the young teenager who pumped the gas and marked the route. It would be no more than an hour at the most. Still, he was wasn't sure.

"At least I know where we are," he sighed.

"Where?" Mutzie inquired.

"Up shit's creek without a paddle."

Not far from Bernstein's Orchard, they found a camp-ground. The sign out front said a dollar a day. They paid their fee and headed into the grounds. They had coffee and doughnuts at a small canteen and parked the car in one of the camp spaces, the most obscure one they could find. Then they showered in the community bathhouse and bought some basic toiletries.

Somewhat refreshed, they walked hand in hand through the wooded trails, contemplating their options. Around the lake, children played and adults cooked on stone grills. Later, when the sun went down, they sat by the lakeshore and watched the stars spangle the lake. Considering the danger they were in, Mickey felt oddly content.

"No second thoughts?" Mutzie asked, revealing what was on her her mind.

"None," he replied, believing it in his heart.

"I have. Many. My mother was right. I had foolish dreams."

"What's life worth without dreams?" Mickey sighed, wondering if his heart had sidetracked his dreams. Feelings have no logic, he decided.

"It was my choice," he whispered. She squeezed his hand.

Mickey had no doubts about what he felt. As best as he could define it, he was in love. Why else had he risked everything for her? Despite the danger, he felt enobled, as if he was proving his love by his sacrifice. And yet, her gratitude was his greatest fear. What he wanted most was her love and the proof of it.

He wondered what thoughts might be going through her mind. She had grown silent and he chose to respect that. He sat with his back to a tree and she leaned against him, nestling in the crook of his arm. He could feel her heartbeat. Still, he sensed a barrier and was reluctant to transcend it.

"Is it possible to cleanse oneself?" she said.

"Are you planning to jump in the lake?"

"If it was only that easy."

"Besides, first you have to be dirty," Mickey whispered.

"I am. Very."

"Not by my inspection." He caressed her head. "Maybe I should look in your ears."

She didn't react and he knew his words were a futile gesture.

"I'm scarred for life, Mickey."

"Scars heal," he said, caressing her shoulders. "As for life, that's what we're trying to prolong."

She shook her head in response. Again he concentrated on the danger they confronted and what action they should be taking. After a long silence, her steady breathing indicated that she was asleep.

"Sleep peacefully, my darling," he whispered, closing his eyes.

It was still dark when he awoke. She had stirred and was standing up.

"My God," she said. "I wasn't sure where I was."

Mickey stood up and they headed back along the trail to

their campsite and the car. Before they reached it they saw spears of light crisscrossing through the woods. As they got closer, they saw two policeman studying the license plate on the Chevy. They heard voices, then stopped all movement.

"This is it," one of them said. "Matches."

Apparently the man at the entrance had written down their license. Mickey realized that he had forgotten that the car was stolen.

"They gotta be around here somewhere," Both policeman washed the beams of their flashlight into the woods. Mickey and Mutzie backed against the trees, holding their breath.

"Maybe they're at the lake," one of the policeman said, continuing to shine their lights into the woods and along the path that led to the lake.

"Let me pull this," the other policeman said. They heard the tinkle of metal. Mickey figured they were disabling the car.

"Let's go," one policeman said.

They moved down the path to the lake, playing the flashlight beam in front of them. Mickey grabbed Mutzie's arm and moved through the woods. They found another path that intersected and headed out in the direction of the main road.

They moved quickly but cautiously and by the time they reached the road the sun was just beginning to rise through the trees. They continued to walk along the road. There was little traffic except for some trucks that passed by occasionally, going either way.

"We still have our thumbs," Mickey said.

A truck passed and they both held up their thumbs. It didn't stop.

"We look like two bums," Mickey said. They were still not very far from the entrance to the campground. Another truck passed on the other side of the road. Again they put out their thumbs. The truck didn't stop.

"Maybe if I was wearing a dress," Mutzie said. "Like Claudette Colbert in *A Night to Remember*. It won an Oscar."

"I'm no Clark Gable," Mickey said, remembering Gloria's comment.

A few more trucks passed. Whenever they saw a car or a truck they ran to the side of the road on which it came. It didn't matter which direction. Avoiding the police was all Mickey could think about. It wasn't simply the fear of the police, but the knowledge that the combination and the police were probably partners in crime.

Finally, they saw a milk truck and ran across the road with raised thumbs. The truck ground abruptly to a halt.

"Ya coulda got killed," the driver shouted.

"One way or another," Mickey replied winking at Mutzie.

The driver scowled and shook his head in puzzlement, then looked them over and reluctantly motioned for them to get in. They scrambled up in the seat beside him. The driver gunned the motor. Through the side mirror Mickey saw the police car turn into the road, moving in the opposite direction.

"Where you headed?" the driver asked.

"Wherever you are," Mickey asked

"Albany," the driver said.

Mickey and Mutzie exchanged glances. They both nodded.

"Albany it is," Mickey said.

12

I N THE EARLY MORNING RUSH, TRAFFIC WAS HEAVY IN ALBANY. Thankfully, the driver wasn't a talker and they both dozed much of the way.

"All over, people. I gotta make deliveries."

When the truck stopped at a red light, they thanked the driver and got out.

"You sure are a lifesaver, mister," Mickey said.

But after the truck had melted into the traffic, Mickey felt disoriented. It was one thing to rely on the serendipity of fate and quite another to translate it into an action. Mickey dipped a hand into his pocket and assessed his finances. He had four dollars and change.

"I was saving for a rainy day, but one good drizzle would wipe us out."

They stopped at a one-armed beanery, ordered coffee and split a ham sandwich. Mutzie looked pale, forlorn, unhappy and very misplaced in men's clothes.

"You ready to be a girl again, Mutzie?" Mickey asked.

"It didn't bring me that much luck when I was."

He sensed her depression. Her spirit was diminishing and he had no plan to bring any hope.

Over her objections, he made her buy lipstick and rouge at Woolworths and persuaded her to buy a skirt, blouse and sandals in a a small store that advertised cheap prices in the window.

"Magic," Mickey said when she emerged from the dressing area. She had put on make-up and brushed her hair, which fluffed out her Jean Harlow bob. Observing her, his heart seemed to overflow with feeling. She looked a lot younger than she had looked at Gorlick's.

"I'm a girl again," she said.

"Thank God," Mickey said, eyes locking into hers. They stared at each other for a long moment. She was the first to turn her eyes away.

"Now what?" she asked.

"Not what. Who." He felt an idea emerging. "Being tired, broke, hungry and desperate has its good points."

"Name one," Mutzie said.

"Motivates the survival instinct."

Grabbing her hand, he led her in the direction of the state capital building. But as they got closer, his pace slowed. There was something terribly intimidating about the structure, its façade gleaming in the sun and the New York State flag flying from its summit.

Again, the memory of Irish's words surfaced in his mind. *Whereyabeen. Dey got New Yawk in de palm a dere hands.*

And yet with Mutzie at his side, he was able to continue to muster some sense of the heroic. Or was he pretending? His gaze washed over the people who passed them. The streets and the people of Albany seemed oddly different. It suddenly occurred to Mickey that he was in strange territory, alien territory. They had emerged from the ghetto, from Brownsville, from the Borscht Belt, from the safety and commonality of a purely Jewish-oriented world.

Not that there weren't gentiles in that comfortable world of Jewishness. Certain of them didn't count as foreigners, like those Italians who lived on the fringes of the Jewish neighborhoods. Even men like Albert Anastasia and Frank Costello, or the odd gentile that seemed to have taken on the characteristics of a Jewish person, like some of the clerks in the stores or even the teachers in the Brownsville schools.

Even those cruel and brutal Jewish gangsters, who he had vowed to bring to justice, seemed less strange to him than the people walking the streets in this town. There was, he knew, a certain faulty logic in his observations. It was his bounds that were Jewish, his world, certain parts of Brooklyn and Manhattan and, of course, the Catksills. The Bronx, too, but that was far away, an hour by subway, eons beyond his home borders. The "City," by which he meant what everyone called the heart of Manhattan, had its share of goyem. But somehow it seemed more Jewish, less alien.

It surprised him. He had never thought about it in this way. Until now.

"Funny, they don't look Jewish," he said suddenly.

"I was thinking the same thing," Mutzie said.

"Were you thinking also that maybe we're traitors?"

"It crossed my mind," she said. "Then I remembered what I saw. Somehow. . . ." She hesitated. Her tongue darted over her lower lip, caressing it for a moment. "It makes me feel sick to my stomach. Jews aren't supposed to do things like that."

He nodded agreement. In this alien environment it was clear that everything in his and Mutzie's world was measured by "Jewishness." Es ist gut fa de yidden? Is it good for the Jews, was the bottom line, passed down from parent to child, as ingrained in their psyche as the tiniest nuance of anti-Semitic attitude or jargon.

247

He was confused by this larger issue. It was troubling, although it did not negate his disgust at the horrors they had witnessed and the desire to set things right. We owe it to ourselves to cleanse our own house, he assured himself. This new idea renewed his confidence.

"Afraid?" he asked as they moved forward again toward the state capital building.

"Yes," she answered, squeezing his hand.

"Remember. Every silver lining has a cloud around it."

She pursed her lips and looked up to the sky in mock exasperation. As they walked to the capital, he began to feel uneasy. Perhaps the combination had their people here, watching for them. He felt uneasy, unsafe, paranoid.

"I feel like everybody is watching us," Mutzie said.

"It's like going for a long walk on a short pier."

Inside the capital, they made their way through the elaborate marble corridors to an area marked "Office of the Governor." It was crowded with people sitting on chairs theater style, apparently waiting to be called to meet someone on the governor's staff. Perhaps, he decided, they might find a person in the governor's office who was not tainted. But who? On the wall was a large photograph of the Governor. No, Mickey protested to himself. Corruption could never reach that far. No way.

There was a directory at one end of the reception room with names of various officials, none of whom were familiar except the name of Governor Herbert Lehman. Below his name was a roster of assistants and departments that meant little to either of them.

Mickey was afflicted suddenly with galloping discouragement and frustration. His grandiose plans to achieve justice seemed to deflate. No miracle had arrived. He felt helpless.

A gray-haired woman with a tight, unsmiling face wearing

rimless glasses sat at a reception desk. She seemed formidable and imperious. Every few minutes the telephone would ring and she would call out a name in an officious manner, peering at the waiting supplicants with icy superiority. A person or persons would rise and make their way to the desk, where she would scrutinize them and hand them a form that she had scribbled on, and the person or group would enter whatever inner sanctum awaited through large ornate double doors.

"Maybe this is the wrong place to start," Mutzie whispered.

"Perhaps I should ask for the office of the state police," Mickey mused. He had not seen any reference to the state police on the directory. At that moment he spotted a uniformed state policeman standing near the wall. He was observing the people in the waiting room. Mickey felt the policeman's eyes wash over him.

"Maybe he's one them," Mutzie said. "Looking for us. Maybe the word is out."

Mickey grabbed Mutzie's arm and they started toward the exit, when suddenly the came face to face, literally, with a recognizable face, a kindly, round bald man's face. The governor, Herbert Lehman! Behind the governor walked a state policeman. The man looked so ordinary, so normal.

To Mickey, it was the wished-for miracle.

Without thinking, as if by rote, he blocked the governor's path. "Mr. Governor," Mickey cried. "Just the man I need to see."

The governor looked at him, frowning warily, and the state policeman was quick to act, his hand reaching for his pistol holster.

"No, please," Mutzie shouted. "He means no harm."

"Step aside, sonny," the state policeman growled.

"I need you, sir," Mickey said, fighting for composure. His knees shook. "We've witnessed a killing."

The governor looked at him, puzzled.

"It's true, sir. By gangsters."

"Leave the governor alone," the state policeman said, his hand remaining on the holster.

"Please, sir," Mutzie pleaded. "Let us tell you. It's true. We need your help. We don't know who to trust."

"One more time," the state policeman said. "Move aside."

"Please, sir. It's a matter of life and death. Just give us a few minutes to tell our story."

"You're our only hope," Mutzie said. Her eyes met the governor's, who searched her face, then looked toward Mickey.

"A matter of life and death?"

Mickey nodded. "Ours."

The governor frowned and shook his head.

"Give us a chance, Governor. Please," Mutzie begged.

Governor Lehman contemplated their faces. He had a grandfatherly look, soft and compassionate.

"It won't take long," Mickey said, his heart thumping in his chest. He searched his mind for a joke. None came. "I wish I had a joke," he blurted.

"A joke?" the Governor asked, perplexed.

"He's a tumler," Mutzie said. "You know . . ."

"I know," the Governor said, offering a hollow chuckle.

"Show him, Mickey," Mutzie said.

"Really, Governor," the state policeman said. "You should be going." The governor looked at Mickey, expectant.

"Okay. Okay." Mickey thought for a moment. "Having one wife is called monotony. Terrible I know. Here's another. If the money is really yours, how come you can't take it with you?" Mickey felt sweat break out on his back. The governor didn't crack a smile.

"Now you see why I am currently unemployed." Mickey

shrugged. "And unfortunately what we have to tell you is not exactly a laugh riot."

"Is it that important?" the governor asked.

"Very," Mutzie said.

The governor looked them both over again and shook his head. "Follow me," he said, murmuring. "What a politican will do for a vote."

"Hey, that's good, sir. Maybe you should be a tumler."

"I am," the governor said.

Governor Lehman was kindly and understanding, grandfatherly with, as Mutzie's mother might say, a nice Jewish punim. They followed him to his elaborate office where he sat at his desk and they sat on two chairs directly facing him.

The governor smiled, then put his hands together in a finger cathedral, leaned back in his chair and nodded to Mickey to begin. He listened intently to Mickey's story, shaking his head in disgust periodically and occasionally nodding agreement as Mickey made suggestions and comments.

These people must be stopped, Mickey told him. They are killers, racketeers, ruthless, cruel, cynical men who corrupt everything they touch. He and Mutzie had witnessed a horrendous crime, he explained. They had seen this horror with their own eyes. Mickey had not spared the governor any of the details. At each gruesome turn in the story, Mutzie nodded in emphasis.

The governor shook his head in despair.

"How awful," he said.

The comment seemed a cue for Mickey to delve into those details of personal experience that he and Mutzie had undergone. He spoke of his father's brutal beating at the hands of Pep and Reles, and how it was well known that they bribed cops, judges and politicians.

"And we want to help. To tell people what we saw."

Then Mickey turned to Mutzie and, with delicacy and careful self-censorship, indicated how Mutzie had narrowly escaped condemnation to a lifetime of prostitution.

"Think of how many other innocent young women have been treated like this, Governor," Mickey said.

"Appalling," the governor responded, blowing his nose to mask his emotion.

Mickey told the governor what he had learned of the terrible corruption in the city, in Sullivan County, the gambling, the prostitution, the alleged payoffs and bribes. Of course, he admitted, he could not know individual details.

"There are people who believe that the corruption goes all the way to the state government."

The governor suddenly sat upright and with the flat of his hand banged on his desk.

"Not in this office," he said with passion and indignation. "Never."

"If we thought that, sir," Mickey said. "We would not be here."

Their testimony, Mickey told the governor, would be the opening wedge to break this evil gangster combination, and remove their stranglehold on many of the legitimate businesses of the state.

"We are not as naïve as you think, young man. Believe me, we are working on it. But we need proof, evidence. Tom Dewey is using every resource," the governor said. Again, he slapped his desk.

"Governor, the worst part is . . ." Mickey hesitated, shrugged and glanced at Mutzie. "The worst part is . . ." He lowered his voice. "Many of these gangsters are Jewish, like us."

Governor Lehman nodded lightly, pursed his lips and a frown creased his forehead. His bald pate turned slightly red.

"Our own people," Mickey reiterated. "It's a disgrace."

The governor turned his eyes away and studied his hands. Then he looked up lugubriously. "Not a pretty picture," he said.

Mickey's remarks had clearly agitated the governor. He tensed for a moment, then leaned back and again made a cathedral with his fingers.

After a long hesitation, Mickey then explained how he and Mutzie were in grave danger as material witnesses to this crime, citing the number of the legal code. The governor nodded.

"Who can we trust?" Mickey asked.

"You can trust me," the governor insisted, picking up the telephone on his desk.

"Not the state police, Governor," Mickey warned.

Governor Lehman rubbed his chin. He appeared deep in thought. Then he reached for the phone and whispered into the speaker. Within a moment a man appeared. He was youngish, serious-looking with horn-rimmed glasses and a professional, all-business air.

"This is Allen Morgan, one of my aides. He is working very closely with Mr. Dewey."

Morgan nodded. The governor introduced them.

"These young people have a story to tell Morgan. And they must be protected."

Mickey felt vaguely uneasy. Could he be trusted? Mickey wondered. There was something about the man's demeanor that roused Mickey's gut instinct unfavorably.

The governor studied Mickey and Mutzie for a long time. Then his look grew vague, as if he were looking inward.

"We mustn't make any mistakes on this one," he said. "I need to think this out."

"Of course," Mickey agreed. Think what out? he wondered.

"But I want you both close. I'll arrange for hotel rooms at the Strand, which is a block from here." He leaned back in his chair. "Mr. Morgan will arrange things."

Arrange what? Mickey asked himself.

13

STANDING BY THE WINDOW OF THEIR STATE-SPONSORED hotel room, Mutzie could see the state capital façade shimmering in the moonlit night. For the first time since she had left Gorlick's she felt hopeful and safe.

The events of the last few weeks flashed into her mind in scenes strung together like in the movies. She was sitting in the dark, traveling on a roller coaster of emotions as each episode replayed itself in her thoughts.

Indeed, some of these episodes were so painful to recall that she told herself that they must have occurred to another person, just as her Jean Harlow makeover had made her feel like that other person. The truth of it was that no person could every escape from their real selves, however they changed their physical appearance.

If Mickey had not intervened in her life, she would have become one of Gloria's girls, bartered like a commodity, to be used and reused until, finally, used up, humiliated and enslaved, she would be tossed away like a piece of garbage.

She wore nothing but panties, and although the night was warm, she felt a chill and a layer of goosebumps broke out on her flesh. On her way back to the bed, she caught a glimpse of herself in the mirror. She shook her head in disgust. How she hated her Jean Harlow hair. Never again. She would let it grow in, become the old Mutzie again.

In bed, she forced herself to concentrate on the good episodes, those that did not bring her pain. In those episodes Mickey was the star, courageous, clever, resourceful. What was it in her that inspired him to become her savior? Was she worth such devotion? She doubted it. Nor could she deny to herself any longer that there was more to his actions than simple revenge for what they had done to his father. Not that that wasn't important. But his sacrifice had gone far beyond that. He had deliberately put himself in danger. Life-and-death danger. Why?

Of course she suspected the real reason. Yes, she had barricaded her heart, had tried to eliminate any hint of romantic sensibility. Feelings like that had only brought her grief and despair. And yet, alone in this moonlit room on a summer's night, it was impossible to dissimulate from herself. Despite all her efforts to eliminate such notions, she knew his reasons. Worse, she knew that she had allowed herself to feed these notions by her consent, just as Pep had done to her, except that Pep had done unspeakable acts.

Still, wasn't this acquiescence on her part an unspeakable act? Wasn't she taking advantage of Mickey's feelings for her? Love, as she had learned through bitter personal experience, makes one foolhardy, clouds one's judgment, rationalizes stupidity, makes one a slave to emotion. She threw herself on the bed and curled under a blanket but still could not stop herself from shivering.

Despite the guilt-bashing she was giving herself, she felt

nothing but admiration for the way in which Mickey had conducted himself with the governor. It was an awesome performance on Mickey's part. After all, the governor was a very important man. She lived in agony that she might be called upon to tell her part of the story and she was certain that she would make a botch of it. Not Mickey. He told his story as if it had been carefully rehearsed beforehand.

Had she told him that, she wondered? They had been exhausted when they checked into the hotel. The governor had, exercising his own sense of delicacy, reserved adjoining rooms. She assumed that his generosity included room service and they ordered hamburgers and cokes for dinner.

She continued to toss in her bed for awhile, then drifted into a kind of sleep in which her mind insisted that it was awake. Images of people materialized in the room, larger than life-size. She heard voices, scraps of conversations, Pep speaking.

"I told ya, I told ya," he screamed at her. "Ya do Albert. I bust ya ass . . ." She saw his face grow in front of her eyes, like an expanding balloon, his mouth opening to a giant tongue that came forward toward her, the flesh torn, blood spouting from its wounds, pouring warm and slimy over her body.

Then, from the ceiling of the room, she saw a shovel descend, coming at her, then Gagie's pleading screams, and Pep's tongue whipping her, crashing against her body.

"Mutzie. Mutzie."

It was Mickey's voice, muffled, as if it were far away. Then it was coming closer and she was striking out, flailing at him with her arms.

"It's me, Mickey. Mickey."

His voice was insistent. Her eyes opened and she saw his face, close to hers, not in focus. "Oh my God," she sighed, when reality returned. He was holding her. Her body felt cold, her flesh clammy.

"You're freezing," Mickey said. He had lifted her into his arms and was warming her flesh with his.

"A dream," she sighed, relieved at its discovery.

"Some dream," Mickey whispered. She felt his breath in her ear. "It's okay now."

"Jesus, Mickey." She clung to him, her head resting against his bare shoulder. His hand caressed her hair.

"It will turn out fine, Mutzie." Mickey whispered. "Heck, I did."

"They'll find a way to . . ." she began, ignoring the joke. The dream had undermined her courage, made her vulnerable again.

"You heard the governor," Mickey whispered. "He said he would find a way to stop them. And he's the governor. He has the power."

She continued to cling to him. He was on his knees on the bed, his arms cradling her. "I don't want to die," she said. Her fear seemed beyond curing.

"Me," Mickey whispered. "I don't believe in death. That's why I want to be cremated."

She let the vague humor pass, feeling the comfort of his strong arms as he held her. "You can't imagine. . . ." she began, but was stopped by a sob that bubbled out of her chest. She wanted to explain how much she owed him, how wonderful he had been to her, how little she deserved his sacrifice.

"Don't," he said, as if he understood what was going on in her mind. Then, suddenly, as he held her in this long silent embrace, she sensed something more than simple gratitude and affection. It was confusing in an odd way, since she had honestly felt that that side of her had died. She became aware of her nakedness, her breasts pressing against his chest.

And of something else. He was wearing undershorts, but his reaction was obvious.

"I'm only human," he said.

"So am I," she whispered.

He eased her down so that she lay on the pillow, although he continued to hold her in his embrace. Then he moved his body so that his face touched hers and he kissed her deeply on the lips.

"You're so. . . ." she began when their lips had parted. "So clean."

"Clean?"

"And I feel so . . . so soiled."

Yet she felt a kind of resurrection in his arms, as if the grime of her recent life was being washed away by his kisses. He caressed her nipples with his tongue and she felt her growing arousal, but when he reached for the elastic of her panties, she reached out and stayed his hand.

"If you won't, I'll understand," he whispered.

"Understand what?" she asked, suddenly defensive, oddly disturbed. She answered for him. "Gratitude. You think this is for gratitude."

"I was hoping for genuine desire," he whispered.

She wanted to show him that part of her, but found herself holding back, not cleansed enough. Not yet.

"You don't think I'm a . . . hooer?" she asked. At that moment an image flashed in her mind. Her with Pep. Her with Albert Anastasia. Her stomach lurched.

"I love you," he said.

"You mustn't say that," she replied, pressing a finger against his lips.

"I'll say the truth when I mean it, Mutzie. I love you. I've loved you from the moment I saw you. And I think I will love you forever."

"That's ridiculous," she protested. Then relenting. "Even knowing what . . . what I've done?"

"It won't work, Mutzie. I love you. I can't help myself. I love you."

He kissed her lips again, and she responded with fervor. It was hard to assess her own feelings. Certainly she felt desire. All the physical signs were present.

Again he found the elastic of her panties and she raised her body to help him take them off. She wondered if there was something she should say. But no, she decided, she would wait. Was this about love?

"I'll be careful," he promised.

She knew he would.

14

THEY BOTH SLEPT PEACEFULLY UNTIL THE SUN STREAMED in through the windows. The telephone rang in his room and he jumped out of bed and ran to answer it.

"One moment, please, for the governor," a crisp female voice said. In a moment, he heard the soothing voice of Governor Lehman.

"I hope you both slept well," he said pleasantly, grandfatherly.

"Oh, yes," Mickey said. "Like tops." Spinning all night, he thought happily.

He sensed a longer silence than might be expected, then heard the clearing of the governor's throat. The hesitation was worrisome.

"Morgan will be coming in the door shortly," the governor said.

"Morgan?"

"The young gentleman you met yesterday," the governor explained pleasantly. "He will explain everything."

Explain everything? Mickey asked the question of himself, frightened suddenly at the obvious answer. Now Morgan knows. Who else knows?

"It was, of course, wonderful meeting you, Mickey, and please give my regards to your girlfriend. Yours is the kind of idealism and good citizenship that will clean up this state from the evil predators . . ." His voice droned on, but Mickey wasn't listening. His words seemed so institutional, as if he were addressing an Independence Day picnic.

"You are both an inspiration," the governor concluded.

"But, Governor . . ." Mickey managed to stammer. He was conscious suddenly of Mutzie standing in the doorway wrapped in a sheet, watching him.

"And good luck to you," the governor concluded. He heard the phone click. He continued to hold it in his hands as he glanced at Mutzie. Their eyes met.

"'Good luck,' he said."

"Is that bad?" Mutzie asked.

Before he could answer, a sharp knock sounded at the door. Mutzie was startled and the sheet nearly slipped out of her hands.

Mickey went to the door.

"Who is it?"

"Morgan," the voice behind the door replied.

"Him?" Mutzie whispered, looking at him curiously.

"The governor said he was coming," Mickey explained, not wishing to alarm her.

Mutzie cocked her head and frowned.

"I'm not sure I liked that man."

"Ditto," Mickey said.

She shrugged and with an expression of disgust retreated back to her room, closing the adjoining door.

"Be right there," Mickey called, hastily putting on his pants and shirt. He opened the door a crack to validate that it was

Morgan. It was. The man smiled. It wasn't warm, more pro forma than sincere. "May I come in?" he said politely.

Mickey nodded, waiting until he passed by him into the room, then looking into the corridor, which was deserted.

"I wasn't followed," Morgan said, trying to mask his sarcasm.

"It would seem not," Mickey said.

"May I sit down?" Morgan asked, surveying the room with finicky distaste. There was a single upholstered chair in the room. Morgan took it, leaving Mickey standing.

"And your friend as well."

"Mutzie," Mickey called.

"In a minute." she replied from the other room.

"After all," Morgan said. "What I have to say concerns both of you."

"Reminds me what I told the governor: Like the Irishman said to the chiropodist."

Morgan looked puzzled.

"Me fate is in your hands."

"Yes. That is amusing," Morgan said.

Mickey studied the man and shook his head.

"Now I know why cannibals get depressed."

"Oh, another," Morgan said.

"They get fed up with people."

"That is droll," Morgan said.

Mutzie came into the room, running a comb through her hair. He noted that her skin was red in spots from his ardent kisses. Morgan got up and pointed to the chair.

"Please," he said. Mutzie sat down. Morgan paced the room with an air of self-importance. Mickey leaned against the wall.

"I told the governor I would be as precise . . . as articulate as

263

possible. He wants you to have a complete understanding of his position."

"Good opener," Mickey said bitterly. "Better keep your legs crossed, Mutzie. Notice I'm standing with my ass to the wall."

"Above all, you mustn't misunderstand what I'm about to say. The governor is prepared to take certain steps. . . ." Morgan hesitated, bit his lip, looked out the window for a moment as if looking for an escape hatch, then continued. "The point is that this is an election year. Any precipitous action on his part could be misinterpreted."

"We're talking here of killers, gangsters, corruption in New York State," Mickey blurted.

"Exactly," Morgan said.

"We're both witnesses. We can put these killers in the chair."

"And you will, believe me. You will. It's just that the timing is all wrong at the moment. There are political considerations. But once the governor is reelected all the stops will be out. He will build his campaign on the theme of fighting crime and corruption in the state."

"Not now?" Mickey asked. "Like tomorrow?"

"After he is reelected."

"And in the meantime?" Mickey asked. He was appalled. The governor had seemed so sincere, so righteous and protective.

"Let me finish," Morgan said. "It will all fit together."

"Like the book Darwin wrote."

Morgan looked exasperated.

"The Origin of Feces."

"That's not very funny," Morgan said.

"Neither is your joke," Mickey said, adding. "The one I suspect is coming."

"You are not listening," Morgan said.

"What I'm hearing are dirty words. You and the governor should wash out your mouths with soap."

"Maybe with lye," Mutzie said.

"It's simply not the time to throw a grenade into state politics. We can't admit the extent of the corruption you allege. People will think it began in Governor Lehman's administration, that he is responsible. Don't you see that?"

"I was talking about murder. We saw a murder happen. We can put those men away."

Morgan reddened, obviously verging on anger, his sense of detachment quickly dissipating.

"We all agree on that point. But we have to consider the political realities."

"Like what?"

"Those gangsters are Jewish. They'll think he is starting a vendetta against them."

Morgan sighed.

"This is so complicated. Mr. Lehman is a German Jew. His people came to America in the middle of the last century. Those from Eastern Europe came later. They are mostly uneducated, lower class. They think the German Jews look down upon them. It's, well, it's a class thing. They're considered mockies."

"Kikes. Sheenies," Mickey said.

"To those types of Jews these gangsters are considered heroes. It will look like he's coming down too hard on them." He paused. "Do you understand?"

"And he thinks they won't give him their votes," Mickey said. "That is ridiculous."

"No, Fine. Politics. Even if I explained it, you might not truly comprehend. Ever hear of Tammany Hall? They used to run things in the state and New York City and they work hand in hand with gangsters. Now the reformers have arrived. La Guardia is Mayor. Dewey, who has been appointed to root out corruption, will most likely be elected district attorney. Their days are numbered. The election will be over in a few months. Then he will go after them with a vengeance. I promise you . . ."

"Listen to him," Mickey shouted.

"I don't understand any of this," Mutzie said.

"I'm also Jewish," Morgan said with an air of pride.

"Morgan?"

"Morganstern," he said, pointing a bony finger at Mickey. "You think it's easy to elect a Jewish governor? More than three-quarters of the state is non-Jewish. And we need every Jewish vote."

"You just lost mine," Mickey said.

"I'm giving you reality, Mr. Wiseguy. We are dealing here with people who have corrupted the whole process of government. They have burrowed in. The governor is an honest man and he knows how deep these people have penetrated. They are organized. Once the Governor is reelected, he'll blow the lid off these kike gangsters and their wop cohorts. I promise you—"

"Kike gangsters?" Mickey snickered. "From a putz named Morganstern yet."

"You people are as corrupt as they are," Mutzie said. She shook her head in disbelief. "I'm ashamed of you, Morganstern."

"You remind me of the guy who returns to the old country to visit his Mama . . ."

"I have to listen to this?" Morgan said. He began to pace the room nervously.

"Mama asks, 'Where's your beard?' Guy says, 'In America nobody wears a beard.' Mama asks, 'You still observe the Sabbath?' Guy says, 'In America we work on Saturday.' Mama asks, 'You still keep kosher?' Guy says, 'I eat out a lot.' Mama says, 'Boychik are you still circumcised?'"

Mutzie chuckled, laughing derisively at the pacing Morgan.

"I'll ignore that," Morgan said. "I told you that I was Jewish in good faith."

"There is no good faith here," Mickey replied.

"None," Mutzie sighed.

"Oh yes there is." Morgan took out an envelope from his jacket pocket. "Two thousand dollars of good faith is in here."

"They're bribing us," Mickey said, as if he had no regard for the money. Schmuck, he told himself, money is money. They were flat broke. Was this part of the miracle, he wondered, or the first stage in his being corrupted?

"They're as bad as them," Mutzie sighed.

Morgan hesitated for a moment. Then he smiled. "We don't murder people," he said smugly revealing his own patronizing manner.

"Not directly," Mickey muttered.

"We'd suggest you take the first train that will get you as far away from New York as you can go. Maybe California," Morgan said, ignoring Mickey's comment. "After the election, notify us and we'll come and get you. You'll get all the protection you need. Then we go to work on these killers." He smiled and lifted his hands palms up. "What we're talking about here is merely temporary postponement, that's all. Just until the election is over. Seems pretty reasonable to me and the governor. After all, he can't be of help if he doesn't get reelected. He'll then be in a powerful position to really do some good. If he's defeated, he won't be able to help."

"And meanwhile they have the greenlight to kill more people," Mickey said, fuming. "I think I'm going to throw up."

"On him, I hope," Mutzie said.

Morgan's glance passed from Mickey to Mutzie and back.

"I think you're both being unreasonable." He waved the envelope. "This should more than cover you both until the governor is reelected. I think it's quite generous. It comes from the governor's personal funds. Believe me, he is a big-hearted and compassionate man. This is purely a temporary political decision. Politics is all about the greater good."

Their deliberate silence had made him expansive. Mickey was certain Morgan felt he was being convincing.

"And if we go to the press?" Mickey said.

"You could." Morgan agreed. "But I doubt if you and this young lady will be alive much after any story appears. At this point no one knows what you and your girlfriend have witnessed. Tell the press about it and you'll be a nice juicy target."

His smugness was turning arrogant now. But he was expressing a certain logic.

"How do we know you told no one else?" Mickey asked.

"I give you my word," Morgan said.

"That's not worth too much," Mickey said, shooting a glance at Mutzie who nodded. "An anti-Semitic Jew who thinks some Jews are kikes."

"Okay. Mockies then." Morgan said. "You know what I meant, grubby, low-class Jews."

"Like us," Mickey said.

"You've totally misunderstood me," Morgan said.

"You know why the Jews wandered in the desert for forty years?" Mickey said in falsetto, hoping it would emphasize his ridicule. "Somebody dropped a quarter. "

"This man is a maniac," Morgan said, addressing Mutzie.

"All tumlers are," Mutzie said.

"You know what happens when a Jew with a hard-on walks into a wall?"

"I'm not going to listen to this," Morgan said.

"He breaks his nose."

"Jesus . . ." Morgan sighed.

"A good Jewish boy. He lived at home until he was thirty. He went into his father's business. His mother thought he was God . . . and he thought she was a virgin."

"We're trying to help you both," Morgan said. "Can't you see that?"

"What I see. . . ." Mickey said, his anger reaching the boiling point. "What I see . . . is politicians . . ." He groped for a word. "Evil. Pure and simple. Evil. It's sickening." He moved as close to Morgan as he could get without losing focus. "Who knows how many others they'll kill between now and the election?"

"You can make an argument," Morgan said. "That they only kill bad people like themselves."

Mickey shook his head. He was beginning to feel despair now. He felt betrayed, violated, totally disillusioned. He looked toward Mutzie, whose expression seemed to mirror his own thoughts.

Morgan put the envelope on the dresser.

"We didn't expect that you'd like this hard lesson in political science. But believe me, it's the best alternative under the circumstances. "

"Will you get the fuck out of here," Mickey said, his anger rising at full throttle, "before I . . ." He wanted to take the man by the throat and squash his Adam's apple with his bare hands. But Morgan was apparently quick to see there was danger in his staying and swiftly disappeared from the room.

It took Mickey some time before he could get himself under

control. He stared out of the window looking at the capital with rising disgust.

"You didn't learn this in civics," he muttered.

"No, we didn't, Mickey," she agreed. He felt her breath on the back of his neck as she came up behind him, embracing him.

"I feel so damned helpless," Mickey said. "In a worse pickle than before."

"Look at the good side," Mutzie said. "Two thousand dollars is nothing to sneeze at."

"But they won't know what we saw," Mickey said.

He felt her kiss the back of his neck.

"And maybe . . . well, maybe . . . when the Governor is re-elected . . ."

"Don't bet on it," Mickey said. "They could be part of it."

Mutzie looked out of the window, then, after a long pause, turned to face him.

"I don't want to be a part of it any more, Mickey," Mutzie said.

"And them?"

"Forget about them. Put them behind us." She came forward and put her arms around him. He felt the warmth of her embrace. "We can start fresh, clean."

"Mutzie. They'll always be behind us. As long as we live. And what we saw will haunt us forever."

He felt a growing anger. He wished he could laugh it away. He felt small and powerless. This "lesson in political science" had upset him. Getting reelected was all that really counted for a politician. He felt himself drifting away from the larger issue, their own survival.

Mutzie continued to cling to him. He looked down at her and kissed her hair.

"Does it really matter . . ." he asked aloud, "if they get caught or not?"

"It matters," she replied. "But not if it hurts us."

Her words sounded cynical, but also wise and mature. He felt his sense of idealism, of justice, collapsing.

Maybe, in the grand design of things, all this happened so that he could find Mutzie. Maybe everything else was unimportant, extraneous, an exercise in self-righteousness. Who cared, really, if gangsters chose to kill each other. Morgan was right.

"I think you have a point, Mutzie. Let's get the hell out of here."

"California here we come," she cried with excitement.

"Become an act," Mickey said.

Mutzie nodded and smiled.

He looked at her as if it were a cue.

"Doctor you have to help me."

"I have some dimes stuck in my ear."

"How long have they been there?"

"A couple of years."

"Why didn't you come to me sooner?"

"I didn't need the money."

Mickey made the circle sign of approval with his fingers.

"Widow goes to a séance,' Mickey began. "She contacts her husband."

"Honey is that really you?" Mutzie retorted.

"Yes, my dear."

"Are you happy?"

"I'm happy."

"Happier than you were with me?"

"Yes, my dear."

"Heaven must be a wonderful place."

"Who said I'm in heaven?"

They both laughed.

"What a team," Mickey said. "Why waste our lives worrying about those monsters? We'll start fresh. You and me."

"Like George Burns and Gracie Allen."

Putting a hand on her chin, he lifted her face, put his lips on hers and kissed her deeply.

"Why save the world? Better we save each other."

"Better that," she agreed.

Despite his happiness, he felt a vague stirring of guilt. She must have sensed something.

"What is it?"

"This being Jewish. I tell you Mutzie, it's a cross to bear."

15

THEY SAT ON A BENCH OF THE ALBANY BUS STATION WAITING for the bus to New York City. From there they would take a train to California. For the past hour they had concentrated only on practical considerations. The envelope with the cash was in Mickey's back pocket.

Mutzie had called her mother in Brownsville and Mickey had called his parents. Such periodic calls were a ritualized condition of Jewish family life. The obligatory call home, no matter what, no matter where, no matter when. She had called her mother every week since leaving home. The conversation was inevitably pro forma and only marginally accurate.

"I don't want you to worry, Ma," Mutzie said. "But I left Gorlick's."

"You left a good job?"

"I got a better one," she lied. No point in explaining. The absolute truth, her relationship with Pep, her life at Gorlick's, her flight with Mickey would not be within her mother's comprehension.

"In the Catskills?" her mother asked.

"Not far," she told her.

"In the mountains it gets cold. You should dress up warm."

"Of course, Mom."

"And watch out for the shmendricks. They all want to take advantage."

"Don't worry, Mom. I can handle myself."

"Of course, I trust you. But these shmendricks, they're a tricky bunch. They tell a nice Jewish girl lies."

"I can see right through them, Mama."

"Maybe if you're lucky you'll meet a nice fella."

"I think I have, Mama."

From where she stood at the pay phone, she could see Mickey. He was sitting down, his head pitched slightly over his neck. He was dozing.

"Jewish?"

"Of course, Mama."

"A professional man?"

"Very," Mutzie said.

"Mazel tov," her mother said. "Can I stop worrying now?"

"Yes, Mama, you can stop worrying."

She pictured her family living their lives in their narrow world. Still, family was family and she felt a certain sense of obligation and guilt for betraying their values.

"Seymour okay?"

"Seymour is Seymour."

"How's Papa?"

"Papa is Papa. His hobby is the pushcart. His job is complaining." Mutzie could sense that her mother was getting wound up in her own perpetual complaint.

"Mama, this is long distance."

Thankfully the operator came on and asked for more change.

"So you be a good girl. When will you call again?"

"Soon, Mama. Soon."

She came back to where Mickey was sitting. He was still dozing and it gave her the opportunity to study him. Last night when she had observed him sleeping, he looked like a little boy— a good, gentle, sweet, innocent Jewish boy. Again she berated herself about her earlier feelings for Pep. How could she? What madness had possessed her? The images of those moments with Pep filled her with revulsion, self-guilt and, above all, shame. Perhaps time would blur them.

At that moment, she was certain that her destiny lay with Mickey. She had felt both comfort and pleasure in his arms. Perhaps, too, in a perverse way, her experience with Pep had made her better for Mickey, more giving, more expert in other ways. Life, she was discovering, was a learning process. Living required practice honed by experience. Goodness and loyalty and devotion were essential between a man and a woman. In Mickey's presence she felt comfortable and, despite the current situation, secure. Mickey would never betray her. Never. And, she vowed, she would never betray him. Never.

She leaned over and kissed his forehead. He stirred, blinked and smiled, immediately awake to her presence near him.

"You call your Mama?" he asked.

"No matter how much we fight, when you call you know they love you. And you love them." Mutzie sighed. "If she knew what had happened to me she would have had a conniption."

My parents would plotz, Mickey thought, if they knew my present circumstances. He had called earlier reassuring them that everything was good and he was happy with his job. "That's no job," his father had said.

She looked at the big clock above the ticket booth. The bus

to New York City was scheduled to arrive in a half hour. They still had only the clothes on their backs. They planned to buy a wardrobe when they got to California.

"Do you know anybody in California?" Mutzie asked.

"Not a soul."

"Be starting over," Mutzie said.

"Sounds great to me," Mickey said, taking her hand and holding it up to his lips to kiss them. They sat for a while, then heard the call for their bus over the loudspeaker. Getting up, they started for the announced gate.

"Sos its da great white way fa da two loveboids," a voice said behind them. Irish. Unmistakably Irish. Turning, they saw his grinning, ugly, freckled face, his green eyes burning with victory.

"Gotcha," he rasped. "And I got dis."

He looked downward and they followed his gaze. He showed them a gun that he had withdrawn halfway from his side pocket.

"Big deal," Mickey said, but she could tell by the unsteadiness in his voice that he was taking the threat seriously.

"Pep'll getta laugh," Irish said. "Two loveboids on da lam." He let out a high-pitched, falsetto giggle. "I knew I would catch up wid youse. Ya people are so stoopid."

She wondered what he meant. It flashed through her mind suddenly that the governor and Morgan might have betrayed them. Wouldn't be surprised, she told herself, thinking how little trust and loyalty she had discovered in people during the past few months. Yet reason told her to give the governor and Morgan the benefit of the doubt, which she did reluctantly. She was certain that the same thought was running through Mickey's mind.

"Maybe you should come with us, Irish," Mutzie said, remembering his conduct at the murder of Gagie. Mickey gave her a sharp look that quickly telescoped the message: Make no references to what they had witnessed. The knowledge that other people had seen his humiliation might light a violent spark, especially if the humiliated man had a gun in his hand.

"Whafor," Irish said. "I got it good up heah."

For a brief moment, she thought she detected the slightest hesitation, a brief flicker of uncertainty.

"I got ma ticket back to Gorlick's," Irish said, certain he was being cryptic. She knew exactly what he meant. He was playing the hero now, fulfilling Pep's assignment.

Again the loudspeaker blared, telling passengers that the bus to New York City was at the gate. It was obviously last call. Mutzie contemplated making a run for it. She glanced toward Mickey, seemed to find consent, then futility as Irish, expecting such a move, put himself in front of them and the gate. He had brought the gun from his side pocket and put it inside his shirt, pointing directly at Mickey's stomach.

"I putta hole dere no alka seltzer gonna help it, tumler," Irish said.

"It's broad daylight," Mickey said. "People will see. You could be identified."

"An you can be dead, tumler."

"You got a point," Mickey said.

"I awso got a car, " Irish said. "So why doncha walk through the front entrance, loveboids."

Mutzie looked at Mickey, who shrugged acquiesance. No point in resisting, not yet, his attitude told her. But she knew his mind was turning over, looking for a way out.

"Think this is gonna give you points with the boys?" Mickey asked.

"Betcha ass," Irish said. "Gonna give you points, too. Sharp ones."

Mutzie shivered remembering Pep's reference to a Thanksgiving turkey. Irish pushed Mickey roughly on the back and Mutzie kept pace. As they walked, Mutzie saw the bus pull out of the station and with it her dreams for their new life.

They stopped in front of a massive black Packard, which she recognized as the car they had seen bring Gagie to Swan Lake.

"I see you're stealing gangster movie cars these days, Irish."

"Stealin caz is yaw line, tumler," Irish quipped, enjoying his comeback with a chuckle. He ordered them to turn around and clasp their hands behind them. Mutzie felt her hands being tied together.

"Where did you learn those knots?" Mickey said. Remembering Swan Lake, Mutzie understood the reference.

"Get in," Irish ordered, pushing them into the back seat. He came in after them carrying more rope. "A coupla knot tricks Pep taught me," he muttered, as he tied their legs together using a fancy knot that traveled from their calves to their ankles.

"Nice'n cozy, loveboids," Irish said. Before he backed out of the car, he looked at Mutzie and leered. He was close enough for her to smell his bad breath. She grimaced with disgust.

"You should change your diet, Irish," Mutzie said.

As if it were a response, he reached out with both hands and squeezed her breasts. "Always wanted to do dat," he laughed.

"Only way you could was to tie me up," Mutzie shot back.

"Maybe you wan I should untie yaw legs. Give you a shot of the Irish."

"How thrilling," Mutzie said.

"Oh yeah," Irish said. "Jes ask aroun."

"We did, Irish," Mickey said. "The reviews were all bad."

"Up yaws," Irish said poking Mickey in the chest.

"As eloquent as ever," Mickey sighed.

"An no maw lip outa youse," Irish scolded. He got into the front seat, started up the car and maneuvered it through the streets. Mutzie's mind continued to race with scenarios, possibilities. Irish wasn't a brain trust. Surely there was some way to outwit him.

She studied his eyes in the rearview mirror, waiting for a glimpse of them that might reveal how he could be thwarted. She had seen his most vulnerable side in Bernstein's Orchard, the cowardice, the fawning, the inability to act out the ultimate cruelty. Did that mean that the man had a soft center? A weakness? Certainly he was a braggart, an exhibitionist and capable of a vast array of petty cruelties. She had also seen him as mean-spirited, as a stooge and flunky. Indeed, she was surprised that she had retained so much information about this terrible nonentity of a man. What was the real key to him, she wondered?

Suddenly Irish fiddled with the rearview miror and locked into Mickey's stare.

"Whatcha lookin at, tumler?" Irish said.

"I'm waiting for your horns to sprout," Mickey answered.

"I always tought your jokes was dumb."

"Dumb. That's your franchise, asshole. If I gave you a penny for your thoughts, you would have change coming."

"Dats funny?"

"You've got brain damage, Irish. Your head got hit by a napkin."

"Who's smarter, putz? Me, or you an her in da backseat tied up?"

"They gonna graduate you from wheelman to killer?" Mickey asked in what was an obvious probe, indicating that an idea was brewing in hi's mind. She knew exactly what Mickey was searching for.

"Ya got a big tongue, tumler," Irish said, his eyes darting between them in the rear view mirror. "Good faw some tings, eh, baby. Bad for udders." He broke out into high-pitched laughter.

"Big joke," Mickey said.

"Gotta admit, even wid da dumb jokes, ya were one good tumler. Gorlick's tearin his hair lookin for anudder one."

"Maybe he'll hire me back," Mickey said.

"Not when Pep gets tru wid ya. Unless ya can tell jokes tru yaw tuchas." Again Irish broke up with laughter.

"That's the way a proctologist tells them," Mickey muttered.

"What's a proctolomecallit do?" Irish asked.

"What I'm doing now," Mickey said.

"Wassat?"

"Looking at an asshole."

Irish didn't laugh, but kept his eyes on the road and was silent for a long time. The car moved out of Albany and slid into the highway going south.

"What did we ever do to you, Irish?" Mickey began.

"It don matter. Like dey say. It's business."

"And what do you get for it?" Mutzie asked.

"I make my bones is what," Irish answered defensively, on the verge of anger. "Shaddup. You give me a pain in da tuchas."

"She wasn't inquiring about your mental state," Mickey said. It was clear that Irish didn't catch the insult.

They were silent for a long while.

"I guess you think you're pretty clever, finding us. You think you'll impress the shit out of them." Mickey said, obviously searching for a way to engage their captor, find his weak spot.

"Betta believe," Irish said.

"Come on, Irish," Mutzie said. "Brag about it."

"Ya ain't as smart as ya tink ya are," Irish said. He opened the window, cleared his throat and spat out a wad of phlegm.

"Youse a schmuck, tumler," Irish continued. "I tole ya. We got people evywhere. We put da woid out. Cops found da hot car right? We knowed about that. And we got people up here watchin faw us. Youse was spotted even when you got da gas for da hot car. Youse was easy. Why ya come up here is stupid. I tole ya dey own all the politicos, the cops and da judges."

Mutzie and Mickey stared at each, passing signals by blinking. Apparently the combination had not discovered that they had talked with the governor about the murder at Bernstein's Orchard.

Except for the politics of Morgan's explanation, which she didn't quite understand, Mutzie felt, even under these terrible circumstances, oddly relieved. The governor and Morgan were not in the corruption loop.

"In their eyes, you're just a punk, Irish," Mickey said cautiously, suddenly emboldened. "A flunky with no balls."

"A yellow belly," Mutzie shot back. Mickey nodded his approval. "Big talk. But no guts."

"I got guts," Irish muttered.

"Lily-livered."

"They're playing you for a sucker, Irish," Mickey said.

"You've got no future with the combination," Mutzie said with a cunning glance at Mickey. "They're looking for real killers, not big talkers."

"Youse shut yaw traps. I don need this shit," Irish said, beginning to rankle. Perhaps she had succeeded a bit, Mutzie thought.

"I got a business proposition, Irish," Mickey said. "You always liked do re mi."

Mutzie caught his message instantly. The two thousand Morgan had given them.

"An ya ain't got none."

"Suppose," Mickey said, "that I knew where to get my hands on a thousand smackers."

"Yeah. So?"

"Could we call it square?" Mickey pressed.

"Ya mean buy me off?"

"Something like that," Mickey said.

"I don believe ya got dat kind of shekels."

"That mean no deal?" Mickey asked.

Irish scratched his head, as if he were hesitating.

"Ya bullshitting me, tumler?"

"He's not," Mutzie said. Worth a try, she thought.

"Okay, I got a better offer," Mickey said. "I'll give you fifteen hundred, just for Mutzie. You let her go an . . ."

"No way," Mutzie said, suddenly troubled.

"Please, Mutzie," Mickey said. "Let me do the talking."

"Both or nothing," Mutzie said, firmly, and meant it. No more. Mickey had sacrificed far too much already. At least with her beside him, they might have a fighting chance. Or he might, which suddenly looked far more important than her own future. He had been too good, too kind, too selfless. It wasn't fair.

"Look, Irish. The offer stands. Fifteen hundred and you let her go. You still got me."

"Yeah. I gotcha. The ting ya don got is moolah."

"Just turn this baby around," Mickey pleaded. "What are we, a half hour from Albany? I'm telling you, I have it stashed. Look, all you lose is an hour. Half hour there. Half hour back."

Irish was silent for a few miles and neither of them said anything, not wishing to disturb his hesitation. Then suddenly, he gunned the motor and pulled the car into a filling station. He skipped the pumps and parked at the side of the attendant's cabin.

Then he got out and opened the rear door, sticking his head in.

"Yaw sayin ya got fifteen hunert in cash ready ta go?" Irish asked.

"In Albany," Mickey said. "And it's yours if you let her go."

"I'm not going to let you do this, Mickey. It's both or nothing."

"Thas what dere lookin for," Irish said, seriously. "I come back wid you it's half a loaf."

"Worse than if you came back with neither of us," Mutzie said. She remembered Pep's words on the banks of Swan Lake: *An ya don come back widdout 'em.*

"Maybe if I say yes, I get a bonus off dis little coova." Again he reached out and squeezed Mutzie's breast. "Shove in my farewell regards."

The idea was repulsive but she did not respond.

"Take the dough and just cut out, Irish. Hell, you'd have enough to go to California." Mickey looked at Mutzie and shrugged.

"Ah don wanna go ta Californa. Ah like it heah. Wid dem."

"Go to Florida, then. Where ever." Mickey paused while Irish contemplated. "Well, what do you say, Irish?"

"It doesn't matter what he says, Mickey. " Mutzie said. "I'm not going without you."

"Come on, Irish. Is it a deal?" Mickey pressed.

"Make it two thou, Irish. Two thou for both," Mutzie said.

"No," Mickey said.

Again Irish hesitated. He bit his lips and rubbed his head.

"Two thou is it?" He scowled, scrunched his eyes, and shook his head. "I don even believe one thou. Ya aint even got dat."

"Two thou for both," Mutzie repeated. Mickey looked at her and shook his head.

"Don't. You can't trust him, Mutzie."

"For both," Mutzie said. "Then you split. Home free. Let us go. And we take our chances."

"I dunno . . ." Irish said, obviously greatly tempted.

"Just for her then I won't give you no trouble," Mickey said. "Just let her go. They'll be impressed when you bring me to them. After all, I'm the one that engineered the whole escape. I'm the one that made Pep lose face. I'm the one they really want."

"Don't flatter yourself," Mutzie said.

Irish's eyes flitted from one to the other. He was obviously confused.

"It's both or nothing," Mutzie repeated.

"Mutzie, please," Mickey begged.

"Deal?" Mutzie asked.

"I'm tinkin," Irish said. His eyes looked from one face to another. Then he lifted a finger. "You say the money's back in Albany?"

"Half hour there. Half hour back," Mickey said.

Suddenly Irish uttered a Bronx cheer.

"This is one big loada crap. I ain't that stupid. Screw ya bot."

"Sorry about this, Mickey," Mutzie said.

"Don't listen to a word she says," Mickey pleaded.

"There's two thousand in an envelope in his back pocket."

"That wasn't very smart," Mickey said. His face had gone ashen. Irish reached into Mickey's back pocket. It was empty.

"Poverty's no crime," Mickey muttered.

"Lyin shitbirds," Irish said, slamming the door shut.

16

MICKEY AND MUTZIE AVOIDED ALL EYE CONTACT and Irish muttered curses to himself. A few miles from Gorlick's Irish parked next to phone booth near a country store and without a word got out to make a call.

Only then did Mickey maneuver himself to get the envelope that he had tucked into the space between the seat and the backrest of the leather seats.

"Don't ask," Mickey whispered as his tied hands moved the envelope to Mutzie's bound hands. She managed to lift her skirt and with effort stuffed the envelope in the rear of her panties.

"What better place," Mickey whispered. "Call it mad money." She didn't laugh.

"Maybe it will come in handy," he said, shrugging. He was thinking in miracles again. "That was dumb what you did before, telling him about the money," Mickey said.

"Where you go I go," Mutzie said. "Whatever happens. It really wasn't any of your business in the first place." She softened her voice. "But I'm not sorry, Mickey. I just think we have a better chance together than apart."

"I wonder if we have a prayer either way," Mickey said glumly.

They were quiet for a few moments, looking at each other.

"Close your eyes," Mutzie whispered.

"What for?"

"I want you to imagine me kissing you and I'll imagine the same." She watched him close his eyes and she closed her own. "Imagining?"

He nodded.

"We kiss deeply. I'm in your arms."

"I'm there."

"Yum," she said.

"Yum yum."

"Because I care about you, Mickey. I care a lot about you. And I know how you feel about me. So please, no more sacrifices. If you were smart you would have bought yourself out. Not try for me." She paused and smiled at him knowingly and nodded. In a way it was an old issue and they both knew it. "The least you could do now, Mickey, is promise me: No more acts of martyrdom on my behalf. It's too late for that."

Mickey thought for a moment, then nodded and blinked moist eyes.

"Maybe I was just trying to get rid of you," Mickey said.

"Not that cheap."

"Remember what the circus manager said to the human cannon ball when he wanted to quit?" Mickey smiled.

"You can't quit," Mutzie shot back. "I'll never find another person of your caliber."

"So you know that one."

"You taught me," Mutzie said. Despite everything, she felt oddly happy.

By then, he saw Irish make another call. He hung up, went

into the country store and came out with a paper bag. He was eating a Milky Way.

"Pep hadda good idear."

"I can't wait to hear it," Mickey muttered.

"Two boids wid one stone."

Mickey contemplated the cryptic remark. What was in store for them was ominous.

"I'm really scared, Mickey," Mutzie said.

"No talkin. I heard enough a yaw lip already. Woise, I fell faw it. How da hell would you guys geta holda two grand?"

When they reached Gorlick's it was nearly four in the morning. Most of the help and guests were still asleep. Irish parked the car in the parking lot, then turned around brandishing his gun.

"Heahs the deal. I untie ya and ya do as I say or I got pumission from Pep ta blow holes in ya heads. Unnerstand?"

"Who's arguing?" Mickey said. Remembering Swan Lake, Mickey doubted he would have the guts, but this was no moment to take chances. Irish came around to the back seat and untied them. Mickey helped Mutzie out of the car. They could barely stand and had difficulty walking, but after a struggle they managed to mount the back stairs.

Irish led them to the room Mutzie had shared with Pep. He held the brown bag he carried from the store.

"Not there, please," Mutzie begged. Irish manhandled her through the door, threw in some candy bars he had bought at the store, then locked it with a key. Mickey's heart lurched.

"You mustn't hurt her."

"Hoit huh? I jes give her some eats," Irish guffawed.

"Such a humanitarian," Mickey sneered.

"Ya do anyting stupid, she gets big trouble. Capish?"

Mickey nodded. His heart was breaking with fear for Mutzie

and for himself. He couldn't imagine what was in store for them, but it certainly did not augur well. His memory was seared with the threats made against them by Pep during the horrendous episode at Swan Lake.

Irish led Mickey to his old room and pushed him inside, then threw in the remainder of the candy bars.

"Gotta feed da monkeys."

"Now the apes are in charge of the zoo."

"Heahs da game plan, schmucko. Albert and his top goombas are comin here lata for a sit down with some of ow boys. Dere's sumpin goin down, but da ting is dat ya gotta be dere to make 'em laugh. Da boys want Albert and da rest ta be happy, unnerstand?"

Mickey was more interested in Mutzie's fate than his own. "And Mutzie?"

"Ya do good, dats all I know. Pep takes care a Mutzie. Da idear is ta make Albert and his boys happy. Get my meanin?"

He felt sick to his stomach. Terrible images of Mutzie being used and abused by those monsters flashed through his mind.

"So go ta sleep, schmucko and we discuss this lata."

He heard the door lock from the outside. For a long time, he paced the room, his head spinning with ways to evade the fate that seemed to await Mutzie. And himself. Finally, exhausted, he lay on his bed and tried to sleep, only to be interrupted by terrible dreams.

Sometime in the afternoon, Irish appeared at his door.

"Ya gotta see Gawlick," Irish said.

"First Mutzie," Mickey said.

"Feget it. And watch yawself with Gawlick. All he knows is ya gotta make Albert laugh. Ya open ya trap bout anyting else, ya start prayin for yaw lady friend."

"And if I refuse?"

"Ya ain't got no choice."

Gorlick was in his office which, as usual, was filled with cigar smoke. Irish left them alone.

"You remember what I told you, boychick, about a schmuck with a schmuck. Do I need this tsouris?"

"So why am I here, Mr. Gorlick?"

"Because you are a not bad tumler. Sometimes funny. Do I know? You make people laugh."

"Especially certain people. Right, Mr. Gorlick?"

"Especially," Gorlick agreed. He stuck the cigar in his mouth and puffed, then chomped down on the sucking end that stained his teeth brown. "Which is why I have decided—against my better judgment, Fine, but because I am a man with a big heart—I am going to give you a gift of one more chance."

"I'll say this, Mr. Gorlick, when you give a gift you'll stop at nothing."

Mr. Gorlick took a deep puff from his cigar and blew out a perfect smoke ring. "I hope you learned your lesson, if you get my meaning."

Mickey nodded. But his mind was elsewhere as a plan of action began to take shape. All he could think about was how he could help Mutzie.

"Absolutely," Mickey said.

"Remember, it's only a trial period."

Mr. Gorlick pointed his cigar at Mickey as if it were the barrel of a pistol.

"Lock up that schmeckel, tumler. What's in another man's bloomers is not your business."

"A wise saying, Mr. Gorlick. God couldn't have said it better to Moses."

Gorlick looked at his watch.

"So go start to tumel. You're back on the payroll."

It crossed Mickey's mind to refuse. After all, he did have the upper hand. Gorlick had found no replacement. But his new plan was contingent on his acceptance.

"You're a one-man royal family, Mr. Gorlick. A prince of man."

"Only a prince?" Gorlick said with a Cheshire cat grin.

Irish was waiting for him outside of Gorlick's office.

"Ya should kiss my tuchas, tumler. I got yaw job back. I should getta cut." He laughed. "That is, if Pep leaves anything left to cut."

17

MUTZIE FELT UTTERLY DEFEATED, TRAPPED AND WORRIED about Mickey. She had barely slept, preferring to curl up in a chair rather than use the bed that she had shared with Pep. The shame of it was almost too painful to bear. Soon, she supposed, Pep would arrive and her ordeal would begin. Remembering what they had done to Gagie, she dared not contemplate what they would do to Mickey. As for herself, she decided, she would do anything they asked of her if only they would spare Mickey.

Perhaps, she wondered, she might buy his freedom with the two thousand dollars Mickey had given her. It was her only bargaining chip, and a very long shot. Not wishing to carry it on her body, for obvious reasons, she stuffed the envelope in one of her high heel shoes that had remained in the closet.

Suddenly, she heard a noise at the door, and it was opened by Irish. He carried a tray, on which were a sandwich and a glass of milk.

"I brung ya some eats," Irish said, putting the tray down on the dresser.

"I'm not hungry," she murmured.

"Hey, lady, ya gotta keep up yaw enegy. Pep will be heah soon and Albert and his goombas may want to share some of the action. Ya gotta stoke the fires." He laughed and winked. Mutzie looked at him with revulsion. He came closer and as she started to back away, he grabbed her and pushed her close to the bed.

"First, Irish wants a little nosh," he said, manhandling her to the edge of the bed and pushing her down. Despite her struggles Irish dropped down over her, straddling her body.

"Make nice to Irish, baby, and Irish gonna make nice to ya," he whispered, his sour breath floating past her nostrils. She tamped down her nausea and he tried pressing his lips against hers. Quickly, she turned her face away and his lips found her cheeks instead.

"Never," she told him.

"Oh yeah?"

He pressed her body full length against his, crushing his groin against hers. His arousal was unmistakable, as he grabbed at her robe, forcing it open, reaching between her legs. Controlling her panic, she became rigid as she searched her mind for some way to thwart him. He began to open his belt.

"Going to wet your pants now, Irish?" she said calmly. "Like the other night at Swan Lake."

His body stiffened against her and his hand slowly withdrew from her flesh. Mutzie knew she had hit the mark, remaining silent as the meaning of her words sunk in. He had stopped pawing her and it was apparent that he was no longer aroused.

"Wha did ya say?"

"Gonna pee in your pants, like when you, Pep and Reles killed Gagie?"

She said it deliberately, moving her head back so that she could get a clear view of his expression. It was like watching the air go out of a balloon. His face sagged and his complexion turned gray, pasty. His lips began to tremble. It was the moment to be relentless and she pressed on.

"You peed in your pants, remember? Pep kneed you there and got his pants wet. Remember that?"

He started to say something, but his throat had clogged with hoarseness and he had to cough it clear. "Yaw in deep shit, lady," he managed to say, but the words lacked conviction.

She rolled away from him, stood up and tied her robe. He sat upright on the bed and made no move to stand. From her vantage, he looked whimpering, abject.

"No. You are," she said, shaking her head from side to side, feeling the sense of confidence and command that had crept into her voice. "And them." She cocked her head and made a directional motion toward the door, her meaning clear. Standing over him, looking down at his stunned face, she felt a kind of renewed sense of herself. She watched him as he rose to his feet, hoping she looked haughty and superior.

"I see your boner went south," she sneered, pressing her advantage.

"Fuck you, hooer."

"That's something you'll *never* do."

His complexion had become chalk white. He reached into a side pocket and pulled out his revolver. His hands shook.

"I see you got a replacement for the one that doesn't work."

He waved the gun threateningly, but she felt no fear. "Ya jes makin up stories," he croaked, but his words seemed hollow, tentative.

"And there's more, Mr. Tough Guy," she said, pausing to savor his discomfort. "You helped tie a slot machine to Gagie's body, a kind of practical joke, very practical. He sunk like a shot."

"Who tole ya that crock?" Irish muttered.

"Joke's on you, Irish," Mutzie said.

He was obviously trying to make some sense of her revelation. A line of perspiration had sprouted on his upper lip and his gun hand trembled as he brought it up to his face to swab away the moisture with the back of his hand.

This ploy had come to her suddenly and she wasn't certain how it might play out. She had, of course, prevented her abasement, but now she needed to expand her victory.

"Who tole ya that crock?" he asked again. It was obvious that he was trying to rally his courage. "Ya betta answer," he said, but his voice was more of a whine than a command.

She offered nothing more than a harrumph, as if his question was an annoyance.

"Sumbody's shittin ya. Bet ya tink Irish is stupid."

"More a sucker," she said, watching him.

"A sucker?"

Obviously searching to regain his poise, he squared his shoulders, tightened his belt, then flipped up his pants with his elbows.

"Nobody plays Irish faw a sucker," he hissed.

"And Pep kicked you in the shins when he got his knee wet," she said, forcing a giggle of ridicule.

He brought back his gun hand as if to whip her face with it.

"I saw it, you idiot," she said, pointing her finger under his nose. "And unless you're going to kill me, you had better not touch me again."

He had already checked his swing, lowering the gun down to waist level but still pointing it at her. His hand, she noted, continued to tremble.

"Hooer," he mumbled, nostrils flaring. His face had flushed with anger and confusion.

"I'm an eyewitness. I saw it. I knew what was going down and I watched. "

"How come?"

"Me to know and you to find out," she said. "Tell me I've got it wrong."

Irish frowned and swallowed hard. His eyes nervously explored the room, as if he were looking for someplace to run. He seemed thoroughly frightened and confused, unable to set a course of action. The hand that held the gun grew more uncertain and tremulous.

Watching him, she was surprised by her own fearlessness. But she had sensed that he was not going to pull the trigger. Hasn't got the killer instinct, she decided, remembering his behavior at Swan Lake. Besides, at this point she had nothing to lose.

Finally, he shook his head. Then, as if acknowledging to himself that he was not a killer, he lowered the gun and shoved the barrel into his belt.

"I got lots to tell," she whispered.

"Who ya gonna tell, hooer?" he said, trying to salvage some semblance of bravado. "Ya ain't gonna live long enough."

She felt the first trill of fear, but shrugged it off. "We'll see," she said.

"I diden kill nobody," Irish said. She caught a whiff of pleading in his voice.

"You're a lot of obnoxious things, Irish," Mutzie said pointedly, as if searching for some common ground with him. "But you're no killer."

"Ya saw dat. Aw, I can't kill nobody. I ain't goin to no hell."

It was an extraordinary admission, Mutzie thought, as if his entire façade had collapsed, revealing the frightened little boy within.

"I can put you all in the chair," Mutzie said.

"Not from six feet under."

"You going to tell them, Irish?"

"Who's ascared now, hooer?" Irish said, managing a smile, as if his courage was making a comeback.

"Thing is, Irish. I wrote it all down and it's in a safe place. Anything happens to me or Mickey. . . ." She made a slicing motion with her hand across her neck and watched him. In what movie had she seen this? She wasn't sure.

"Am I in what ya wrote?" Irish asked, clearly panicked.

"Hell, you're one of the main characters, Irish."

Now that she had gained his attention, she needed to embellish the point. Suddenly she remembered Morgan's words and the names of the people he had mentioned. "Here's the story Irish. The combination's days are numbered. Tammany Hall will be broken. Dewey will be the next DA in New York City and he'll be going after all the killers like Pep and Abie and Bugsy. La Guardia is the reformer. And when Lehman is reelected, it will be all over for the pack of them."

She wasn't sure what any of it meant. She had never had the slightest interest in politics. But watching the confusion in Irish's expression, she knew he was trying to make sense of what she had said. She hoped she sounded as if she knew what she was talking about.

"Sooner or later, they'll all get the chair," she reiterated, as if passing the sentence herself. "You got a yen for an electrical massage, Irish?"

"So where is what ya wrote down, hooer?" Irish said, brightening, as if he had come up with a flaw in her explanation. His mind had been slow to grasp it.

"Safe," she sneered.

"Ya tink Pep will believe dat?"

"Do you?"

Again, he was reaching for courage. She could tell he needed more persuading. His face was a kaleidescope of doubt and uncertainty, and he seemed to be struggling with his thoughts. Her mind groped for something that might put more force behind her assertion, and a new idea emerged.

"Maybe I'll tell Pep that it was you who told me the story about what happened to Gagie at Swan Lake. They think you're a loose cannon anyway. Like you were bragging about what a tough guy killer you are. Making yourself the big man."

There was no mistaking his surrender. She knew he fully understood that Pep would believe her. He went through a gamut of nervous ticks. He rubbed his chin, flipped up his pants again, bit his lip, but he was clearly defeated and frightened.

"Ya gonna take me outa what ya wrote?"

"Depends."

"And don tell Pep what ya said about me tellin?"

"That also depends. You got us here. Now get us out of here."

"What am I supposed to do? I tole Pep I was bringin ya both in," Irish said. "Dere's no way outa dat." He shook his head. "And at dinner dey want da tumler ta tumel, to make Albert and the boys feel good. I brung da tumler to Gorlick. I hear there's a lot goin down today, a big meetin."

"And after dinner?" Mutzie asked.

Irish shrugged. He was sweating profusely now and blinking nervously.

"I'm for dessert, right, Irish? Right?" A surge of cold fear gripped her.

He started to pace the room.

"Gotta tink, hooer," he muttered.

Suddenly, she stood in front of him. He stopped his pacing and she slapped his face as hard as she could. He was stunned. Her red handprint splashed over his cheek.

"If I ever hear that word out of your filthy mouth again, Irish, you're toast. Capish?"

He looked as if he was about to collapse. Unfortunately, she didn't have the pleasure of seeing it.

At that moment, she heard the key in the door and Pep stepped into the room.

18

FROM WHERE MICKEY STOOD IN AN OBSCURE CORNER OF the lobby, he could see the guests moving into the dining room. He was too depressed to work up any enthusiasm to mingle with them. His mind dwelled on what he imagined was going on with Mutzie in Pep's room. Yet he knew he had to keep these thoughts at bay while he concentrated on his plan.

As he stood there, plumbing his memory, reciting in his mind the jokes he would tell, he caught a glimpse of Helen Reles stuffed into a gold lamé dress. She was roaming helter-skelter in the lobby, obviously looking for her errant obnoxious son. As she passed him, Mickey caught her eye. He put a finger over his lips and beckoned her with his eyes.

"Oy, Mickey, are you in deep doody," she said. "You got Pep mad, boychick. Not smart, you taking away his coorva."

"What do you hear, Helen?"

She looked at him and patted his cheek.

"Believe me, boychick. I would have taken good care. You wouldn't have nothing left for anyone else."

"What can I say, Helen? I fell in love."

"Love? That's only in the movies, dummy. I coulda shown you real love, boobala. You woulda had love you could die for."

"I know, Helen. I guess I missed out."

"Not too late." She winked then took his hand and put it over her right breast. "Beneath this dollink is a beating heart. Oy, I'm getting hot."

"Helen, please. What do you hear?"

"I can tell you that Abie doesn't like this business of Pep with the goilies. With Abie it's business foist. And your little love knish was stupid. It's a matter of respect. Not as bad as the wops, but when it comes to private pussy, Pep goes bananas. I can tell you that they're gonna pass her around like an hors d'oeurve. So she'll be one of Gloria's hooers. Look, she had eyes wide open."

"Will they hurt her?"

"Not like they hurt that waitress hooer that helped you. She'll be in the hospital for a month. You may be, but I hope not. I'll talk to my Abie. They won't hurt huh. Not where it shows. Okay. Tell you the truth. I don't approve. But now they got real tsouris. La Guardia, Dewey, the government ain't foolin around no more. Soon gambling up here will be kaput. Albert, Lepke, Costello, Bugsy, Pep, Abie. The whole comibination. I mean everybody is worried. I can tell you they ain't in a good mood." She put her mouth close to his. "My Abie. He's got plans."

"I got plans too, Helen," Mickey said.

"Plans, shplans, dollink. In your head you should have one plan. Run. By yourself. Run now. As far as you can run. Oy, such a boobala. If we had the time I would give you a farewell shtup you could remember for a lifetime. Listen to Helen. I been around these guys forever. Put on your sneakers, sonny."

She heard a noise and spied Heshy annoying people at the other end of the lobby.

"Bye bye, boychick," she sighed, then left to get her son.

He felt himself rooted to the floor. He had heard Reles try to reason with Pep at Swan Lake with little result. Besides, he had seen them both in action at his father's store. These men had no pity for anyone.

19

EP GLARED AT HER WITH COLD, HARD EYES. SHE HUDDLED within her robe, expecting him to lash out.

"I dun good, right, Pep?" Irish said, cutting a glance at Mutzie. "I brung 'em here like ya said."

"Give him a medal, Pep," she said, refusing to cower. At any moment, she expected him to beat her. Instead he looked her over like some prize horse.

"You sure are a looker, babe," he said, showing his good teeth in a wide smile. "Ya gonna do good as one a Gloria's hookers. Fifty a pop. Maybe double dat."

She confronted him silently, assessing his attitude, waiting for the right moment to insert her request.

"Dey wasn't easy to find," Irish said. "I got 'em in Albany."

He turned toward Mutzie and chuckled.

"Who'd ya wanna see, the governor?"

For a brief moment, she feared he might have found out.

"Fat chance," Pep smirked. He shook his head and came closer, but instead of smacking her as she expected, he raised his finger and shook it at her. "No fuckin hooer runs out on Pep, less I kick yaw ass out foist."

Again Irish and Mutzie exchanged glances. Irish was chalk white with fear. Mutzie braced herself, gathering her courage. She figured it might be the moment.

"I'm really sorry, Pep. I did a very stupid thing. I was lonely. You know what I mean. You left me alone a lot. I missed you, really missed you."

Pep continued to glare at her, his gaze narrowing.

"You've got to forgive me, Pep. Look, the tumler is just a dumb kid. He doesn't mean a thing to me. He was like. . . ." She cut a quick glance to Irish. "Like a toy, Pep. That's all he meant to me. Like a toy. You were always my number one. I swear it, Pep. Only you. So I made a mistake, okay?"

She saw his confusion and wasn't sure what he expected from her. Suddenly he turned toward Irish.

"Get da fuck outa here, Irish." He laughed suddenly. "Befaw ya pee in ya drawers."

"Sure, Pep. Sure. I'm leavin."

Mutzie watched him leave, bowing and scraping. He quickly disappeared from the room. "Anyting ya want, Pep," she said. "Anything."

She opened her robe and Pep looked her over from head to toe.

"You are one great piece, Mutzie. Da right goods. Only we ain't got time now. We gotta get down for dinnah wid Albert and Frank and Lepke. And I wantcha to walk in dere like a fuckin queen. Dey gotta know dat nobody cuts out on Pep."

"Sure, Pep. Anything you say."

He opened a drawer, took out a clean shirt and began to change clothes.

"You got to do me this favor, Pep."

He did not respond, buttoning his shirt in front of the

mirror. She embraced him from behind and looked at herself and him in the mirror.

"I'll do anything you ask, Pep. I promise. Anything. I'll be nice to Albert and anyone else. I promise. I'll give them the best time ever, but don't hurt that kid. He's just a dumb tumler. You know, a lotta laughs. I swear, Pep. On my life. I swear to you. We never did anything. I swear. In fact . . ." She searched her mind for authenticity. "I think he's, you know, a fagele."

Pep stopped buttoning his shirt.

"Ya kidden me?"

"I mean it, Pep. You had it all wrong. He gave me a line of stuff and I was lonely, Pep. It was awful, a terrible mistake. Can you ever forgive me?"

"Yeah, yeah," he muttered putting on his tie.

She felt she was making headway now. He seemed to be responding.

"So you won't hurt him?" she asked cautiously.

"Ya want me to kiss him? Make him gimmee a blow job?"

He laughed and she noted that his mood was changing for the better.

"It's more my fault than his, Pep. Give him a break. He just went along for the ride."

"I'll tink about it," Pep said. "Maybe if he makes Albert feel good, like yaw gonna do lata. Ya know. Lots of laughs. Maybe we only break one kneecap." Pep roared.

She felt her stomach lurch. There seemed no limit to his cruelty. The fact was that what she was doing filled her with remorse. She could think of no other way out.

And yet, she could not see herself in this debasing role. She could never muster the indifference to pull it off. Never. But if she saved Mickey, she would find a way to endure it. Or worse.

She went into the bathroom and put on her makeup, then opened her closet and picked out a dress. It was then that she remembered where she had put the two thousand dollars. For a moment she was uncertain what to do, but decided finally to transfer the envelope from her shoes to her brassiere. Of course, she had no clear idea of what she was going to do. Of one thing she was sure, she would never be able to live with the knowledge that Mickey might suffer because of her. At this point, she felt trapped, but the money, the idea of freedom that it stood for, did provide her with some last vestige of hope.

Fully dressed, she put her arm in Pep's and they proceeded out of the room.

"You're my number one, Pep," she said as she walked with him down the stairs, her legs wobbly with nervous dread.

20

CROSS THE LOBBY, MICKEY SAW SOME OF THE MEN HELEN had mentioned. This time neither Lepke nor the Italians had brought women. Beyond them Mickey saw a number of bodyguards, big, beefy, swarthy men with hard cruel eyes, placed within hailing distance. Then he saw Pep and Mutzie come down the staircase. His heart beat so hard he thought it would explode.

Mutzie had put on makeup and was wearing a tight dress with a high neck that showed off her curvy figure. She looked ravishingly beautiful. He felt a sob rise in his chest and dared not speculate what had occurred in Pep's room and what would be in store for her future. She had her arm through Pep's and he seemed to be parading her through the lobby, showing her off, conveying the macho message that he had tamed his lady, put her back under his control.

He thought of Helen's advice. Run! By yourself! No! He would move ahead with his plan, whatever the consequences. Without Mutzie, he could not save himself.

Stepping into the lobby, he forced a big smile and strode over to the men, avoiding Mutzie's eyes.

"Hey, dere he is," Albert Anastasia said. "Da funny man. Hey, funny man got a joke fuh Albert?"

Without missing a beat, Mickey had a joke ready. "Hear about the rabbi who opened a discount temple? All you can pray for a dollar."

Albert laughed. "I love dem Jew jokes. Got any more?"

"A friend visits a rabbi in a hospital. He is covered with bandages. 'What happened,' the friend asked. 'I saw a bear in the forest and converted him. I preached God's word, read to him from the Torah.' 'So why are you in the hospital?' Rabbi says, 'I shouldn't have started with circumcision.'"

Everybody howled, Albert the loudest. Mickey showed his teeth in an empty smile. He exchanged glances with Mutzie, who nodded. He detected the sadness in her eyes. Pep looked at him and snarled.

"Lata, tumler," he snapped, with a sinister glance at Mutzie.

The grouped moved into the dining room and were shown to a big round table by a fawning Gorlick. As before, Mutzie was seated next to Albert. Pep smiled and put his arm around Mutzie, squeezing her shoulder. Mickey was furious as he followed the group into the dining room.

"You did good, tumler," Gorlick said. "Keepin Albert happy."

"He likes Jew jokes."

"So tell em," Gorlick said, taking a big puff on his cigar and blowing out a smoke ring, his tell-tale sign of satisfaction.

The waitresses fanned out and began serving the food. He kept his eyes on the group's table, where the three gangster bosses toasted each other. Mickey stood in a corner of the dining room, waiting for his moment to tumel the crowd. Posted around the room were the steely-eyed bodyguards. Irish looked forlorn, his complexion ashen as he stood near the dining room entrance.

Mickey watched Pep make a big show of his power over Mutzie. He kept his arm over her shoulder as he ate with his free hand. Once, his gaze met Pep's. It was ominous, frightening. He was gloating, flaunting his power over her. Mickey's rage percolated deep inside of him. It was time. He strode to the stage.

He desisted from making the usual announcements and spoke, as usual above the conversational buzz of the diners.

"Hey, make funny," Albert shouted. "What's da woid?"

"Tumler," Helen Reles cried.

"Yeah, Toomler."

Mickey held up both hands attempting to quiet the crowd.

"That's a famous person over there," he called out to Anastasia. "How'd your dago?"

The laughter was sporadic. He noted that Albert looked confused.

"You know how you can tell an Italian airplane?" Mickey paused. "It has hair under its wings."

He saw Anastasia frown and looked around the table. Gorlick shook his head. He seemed to be in pain.

"You know why so many wops are named Tony?" Mickey went on, gesturing to his forehead. "To NY. Get it? Tony."

He felt himself on a roll now. The audience was paying attention. Anastasia and Costello were frowning, their faces frozen.

"You know why Italians don't get circumcised. They're afraid of brain damage."

The audience howled. Gorlick rushed to the stage and called to Mickey, "Stop this."

"Let him go, Gawlick. Get outa his face," someone in the audience yelled. Gorlick froze puffing furiously on his cigar.

"Yeah, let 'im go," another person in the audience screamed. Others chimed in.

"You know who showed up when Christ was born? Mary, Joseph, Jesus and 32 wise guys."

"How come Italian men have moustaches?" Mickey went on in rapid-fire delivery. "So they can look like their mamas."

Anastasia stood up, furious, his face red.

"Fuck you," he screamed.

The diners turned around. People shouted.

"Sit down. This guy is hilarious."

"Throw him out," someone cried.

"You know why Italy is shaped like a boot? You think they could fit all that shit in a tennis shoe?"

As he fired off his jokes, he watched the group table. Anastasia and Costello were standing. The others were trying to quiet him.

"Fuckin Jew bastard cocksucker," Anastasia shouted.

Some men in the audience moved forward threateningly. Suddenly Anastasia's bodyguards became active, drawing guns.

"I want that fucking Jew boy's ass," Anastasia shouted.

Mass confusion erupted. Bullets were fired at the ceiling. People screamed and were rushing out of the dining room.

"I'm gonna burn this Jew shithole to the ground," Anastasia roared as his bodyguards made a circle around him to protect him from the now surging crowd.

Suddenly Gorlick's voice shouted in his ear.

"What did I tell ya about wop jokes, schmuck?"

Before Gorlick could say anything more, one of Anastasia's goombas hit him in the stomach and he doubled over. As the melee continued, someone shut off the lights and plunged the dining room into darkness. Mickey ran in the direction of where Mutzie was seated. Apparently she had shrugged herself free of Pep's embrace.

"Mickey, where are you?"

He heard her voice over the din and ran toward it.

"Mutzie. Mutzie," he cried.

"Where is that sumbitch tumler?" Pep's voice roared above the crowd.

"Putz." It was Helen Reles voice. He felt her hand on his arm. "Betta get the fuck outa here, boobala."

"Where is Mutzie?"

"Ya don't listen, boychick," Helen Reles said.

Again he called out for Mutzie.

"I'm gonna bust yaw balls." It was Pep's voice, coming closer.

Then he smelled smoke and somebody yelled, "Fire!" Mickey felt the crowd surge around him, pushing toward the exit.

"Mickey!"

He heard her voice over the melee and rushed towards it. As the dining room emptied, he was able to follow the sound. Then she was clinging to him.

"He's going to kill you, Mickey," she cried.

"I know. And I don't want to be around when it happens."

He grabbed her hand and tugged her in the opposite direction of the surging crowd. The smoke grew thicker. He tried to find his way to the kitchen entrance.

Suddenly he felt a sharp tap on his back. It hurt but he didn't cry out.

"Grabahold schmuck," Irish said.

"You kidding me?" Mickey cried, brushing him aside.

"Do it, Mickey," Mutzie said. "I'll explain later."

The smoke was getting thicker.

"Listen to her, tumler," Irish said, grabbing Mickey by the upper arm and pulling him into the kitchen, which had emptied out. He led them through the door used for kitchen deliveries.

313

When they were outside, they breathed in the fresh night air. Irish started to run, then stopped and looked back.

"Ya comin or ya wanna be fitted faw a coffin?"

"Come on, Mickey, please," Mutzie coaxed grabbing his hand and pulling him forward.

Confusion raged everywhere. People were screaming. Mothers clutched their children, who wore pajamas, and ran from the burning building. In the distance Mickey heard the sound of fire engine sirens. A burgeoning crowd gathered at a safe distance watching the flames and smoke rise from one side of the building.

Irish was jogging in front of them into the parking lot. Behind them Mickey could sense people running. They reached the car in which they had ridden the night before. Irish jumped ino the driver's seat.

"Get da fuck in," Irish shouted.

Mickey opened the rear door and Mutzie jumped in. Still not fully comphrending what was happening Mickey paused briefly and looked back. One end of the building was completely engulfed in flames lighting up the sky. People filled the area outside and watched the burning building as if it were a fireworks display.

Mutzie tugged at his arm and he jumped into the backseat just as Irish gunned the motor and sped out of the lot. He did not turn on the car lights and instead of heading for the main road drove the car in another direction through a bumpy swath into the woods. Then he turned on the car lights and, driving cautiously to avoid hitting trees, eventually turned onto a one-lane secondary road.

"You trust this shemegegy?" Mickey whispered.

"I hoid," Irish said gaining speed as they hit an asphalt road.

"Not now," Mutzie said, drawing Mickey's hand to her breast where he could feel the envelope.

After a half hour of driving, they reached a small town. Irish stopped the car in front of a bus stop beside which was a man in a ticket booth.

"Now get outa here," Irish said, reaching behind him and opening the door. "Go."

Mickey and Mutzie exchanged glances.

"Are we supposed to thank him?" Mickey asked.

"Memba what ya promised," Irish said.

"I remember, Irish," Mutzie said.

Mickey noted a long unexpected pause pass between them.

"I ain't gonna wish ya good luck," Irish snapped, turning his head toward the windshield. "Ya got it aready."

He gunned the motor, made a U-turn and headed back in the direction from which they had come.

Mickey turned toward the ticket seller.

"Where to?" the man asked.

Mickey turned to Mutzie and smiled.

"Hollywood."

"Ya trying to be funny?" the man said.

"You got it, buster. I'm a tumler," Mickey said. He squeezed Mutzie's hand and winked.

Epilogue

MANY OF THE GANGSTER CHARACTERS IN THIS STORY are based on real people who populated the brutal crime scene in New York in the thirties. Dubbed by the press as "Murder Inc.," their reign of terror in the New York underworld is well documented. Pittsburgh Phil Strauss, known as "Pep," got the electric chair, along with Bugsy Goldstein, on June 12, 1941. "Lepke" Buchalter got the chair on March 4, 1944. Abie "Kid Twist" Reles, who snitched on his pals, fell from a high floor of the Half Moon Hotel in Coney Island while being guarded by six law enforcement officers just as he was about to testify against his fellow gangsters. Albert Anastasia was shot while getting a haircut in the Park Sheraton barbershop on October 25, 1957, and Frank Costello died of a heart attack in a New York hospital on February 18, 1973 at 81.

As for the Catskills, the era dominated by those famous hotels such as Grossinger's, the Concord, the Nevele and numerous others and were collectively known as "the Borscht Belt," have passed into history along with the famous "tumlers" who arguably invented contemporary American humor.

The mountains, of course, are still there.

317